FOR LUCY

JEWEL E. ANN

PLAYLIST

"Start Again" — Isak Danielson
"Believe" — Mumford & Sons
"Breathe" — Forest Blakk
"Sinking In" — Katelyn Tarver, Jake Scott
"Fix It to Break It" — Clinton Kane
"Next to You" — Of Rust & Bone
"Easy to Lie" — Forest Blakk
"Broken" — Jamie Grey
"Arms Around You" — Jamie Grey
"If Walls Could Talk" — Emily James

For my husband, my "Emmett"

"No matter how undeserving one might feel of forgiveness, no one is unworthy of it."
—Emmett Riley

CHAPTER ONE

The lawn used to be mine—minus the dandelions, Creeping Charlie, and grub infestation. I took care of what mattered to me, like my wife. That's why I painted that fence at least a dozen times.

White.

She thought it symbolized our perfect life.

The only thing truly perfect about our life was the way I stole her. A brilliant move on my part. We joked about it for years. Tatum would blow her tawny and most unruly bangs out of her eyes, smirking and winking at the same time before saying, *"Emmett the Thief."*

I'm no longer a thief. I'm a martyr—only I'm still alive. Six out of seven days of the week, being alive sucks. Today is day seven. It doesn't suck, but staring at the weeds ... that's its own kind of torture.

Weeds were nonexistent when it was *my* yard. I deposited spores to keep the grubs at bay and pulled a striper behind my red Toro mower. I come from a long line of men who aspire to have the best yard. Under my watch, the basketball net came down in the winter. Now it hangs by a few weathered threads like a flag on the front line, tattered and worn after the last battle.

Come on, Lucy ...

I swear she keeps me waiting on purpose. She thinks I'll give in and fix all the things that are broken if I'm forced to stare at them long enough. Some things can never be repaired—like my marriage. I tried. Really, I did. For weeks, Lucy and her mom stood inside the house with their lifeless gazes lazily following me around the yard as I mowed, wrestled the weeds, replaced the mulch, painted the fence, and filled in the hole that used to be a swimming pool—replacing it with a firepit, a pergola that I constructed myself, and raised flowerbeds framing the new gathering spot.

Only ... no one ever gathered there. Sometimes I'd lounge by myself, the lone spectator gazing at the fire, wondering why fate decided to blow up my world.

When Tatum and I exchanged vows seventeen years ago, we said *'til death do us part.*

Done.

We didn't break those vows. Our marriage held on nearly six months past death. A death no one saw coming. The violent ripping away of a soul that made no sense.

It all started with a delivery room promise. Twelve hours into labor with Lucy, my wife made me promise to love our daughter more than her. She said parents were supposed to love their children more than each other—some sappy sentiment about our daughter being the best of us. With her hand gripping mine at the start of the next contraction, and the midwife giving me the just-say-it look, I returned several tiny nods.

"Of course, honey. Anything you want."

I had no true intention of loving our daughter more than

Tatum. It was only *because* I loved Tatum so much that we were at the hospital waiting for the fruit of our love to come into the world. Maybe I didn't feel the same shift in favoritism because I hadn't carried Lucy in my body for nine months. I'm not a stupid man claiming to understand a mother's love. And after witnessing Tatum's ability to function with only a few hours of sleep each night for the first six months of Lucy's life, I conceded that nothing could compare to a mother's love.

In fact, Tatum's love and twenty-four-hour devotion to our daughter only intensified my love for her.

I loved Lucy with ninety-nine percent of my heart, but I loved her mother with *all* of it.

Until ... death came. And we parted.

There is bad.

And awful.

Then there is the unimaginable.

No vow can prepare you for the unimaginable. The unimaginable breaks the strongest bonds, voids promises, and leaves irreparable wreckage.

"You know, you *can* come to the door. I didn't even know you were here." Lucy hops into my pickup truck and shoots me a grin, sun-kissed cheeks and hair, unruly like her mom's but a few shades darker, pulled into a ponytail.

I return a somber smile, wondering what happened to my little girl. When did she get boobs? And why must she wear tiny shorts that expose her long legs that I *know* punk-ass boys gawk at all the damn time? The pink-painted nails and makeup covered face—really? Where did my little girl go? "I wasn't in a hurry. I knew you'd eventually come out."

She rolls her eyes, lashes heavy with mascara. Why? Why must she try to look twenty? What happened to pigtails, ribbons, and cherry Chapstick?

"Is that ..." Before I put the truck in reverse, my chin juts in her direction and my eyes narrow to inspect her. "Is that a nose piercing?"

She wrinkles her nose and shifts her head to the right, hiding the shiny embellishment. "Don't." She sighs.

"Don't what?" I hook her chin with my finger and force her to look at me.

Lucy has the poutiest frown. Full lips. Mischief-filled eyes that blink with perfect timing. It's impossible to stay angry with this girl.

"Don't be such a dad."

Releasing her chin, I bark a laugh and back out of the driveway riddled with cracks and mounds of sand from an infestation of pavement ants. "But I'm so good at it. Wait until you start dating. I have all kinds of dad tricks up my sleeve to scare off any boys I don't find worthy of my little girl."

She snorts, head bowed to worship her phone. "Pfft ... sorry to break the news to you, but I'm already dating."

"Excuse me?" My head whips to the side as we pull up to a four-way stop three blocks down the street. Lined with drooping branches of oak trees, it's one of the last few charming streets in our little town of Redington, Missouri. A few years ago, an F5 tornado, manifesting without any warning, ravaged Redington. Miraculously, Quail Street and its historic tunnel of oak trees somehow managed to emerge unscathed.

I was out of town when it happened, but I remember my heart crashing against my ribs when I heard the news. Our family had already experienced the unimaginable. The close call of losing Tatum and Lucy nearly stole my last breath.

"There you go again," Lucy says ending in a sigh.

"There I go again, what?"

"Being overprotective." Her words hit hard. Maybe it's not her intention, but I read into it.

She can roll her eyes until they fall out of her head. Her sighs can shoot past her nostrils like the pulsing of a hot air balloon floating into the clouds. She can accuse me of being too much of a dad and overprotective, but I regret nothing.

I love Lucy more. That's what Tatum asked me to do. And that's what I did nearly five years ago. And that's what I'm still doing.

"I love you." She keeps her gaze forward, a tiny smirk playing with the corners of her mouth.

My grin swells to unnatural proportions. "I love you too."

We share an unspoken bond. A secret.

Sometimes I see it in her eyes, and I have to believe she occasionally sees it in mine. There's really nothing to say. That was the pact we made. *"We never speak about this again."*

"How's your mom?" I ask as we sip our milkshakes and wait for our burgers and fries in the diner a block from my office. When I clear my throat, she gives me a sheepish grin and clicks off the screen to her phone.

I don't have to say it. She already knows I refuse to compete with her twenty-four-hour instant access to the rest of the world. In the divorce settlement, Tatum wanted full custody of Lucy, claiming I wasn't fit to be a father. That hurt so fucking much. But I just sat there on the opposite side of the table as our attorneys disassembled our life and awarded pieces to the one of us they felt most deserving.

Nearly everything went to Tatum, and I didn't fight her for any of it, except Lucy. That part required a judge. After my attorney pleaded my case, I managed to get one day a week with Lucy.

One.

Measly.

Day.

Not even a night. Ten hours to be exact.

On Saturdays, I get Lucy, except when she has plans with friends, which seems to happen more and more. Sometimes she gets invited to go to the lake and she cancels our whole day together. And sometimes it's cut short by a few hours to accommodate sleeping in after a Friday night sleepover or skipping out early to go hang with her friends because … Saturday night.

I take what I can get. It's how I love her.

"How's Mom?" She manages to repeat my question. I'll give her credit; she can rapid-fire off texts to her friends *and* listen to me. "She's good."

"How's what's his name? Josh?"

She shrugs, lips twisted as if she's searching for the best answer.

The best answer is *"Josh is great. He adores Mom."* I love Tatum. I love her now as much as I did the day I married her, so her happiness matters as much to me now as it did the day I married her. It's just no longer *me* that makes her happy.

"He's … cleanly."

I laugh. "Cleanly? And that's a bad thing?"

Lucy's head bobs, contemplating her reply like a magic eight ball. "Not bad. Just … OCD. He's *always* washing his hands. It's like … Dude! You're not going to have any skin left. I mean ... sterile environments aren't exactly good for building your immune system."

As the waitress sets our plates in front of us, I smile and thank her. "He *is* a surgeon. Right? That's what you said he does, right?"

She nods.

"Well, I think hand washing and sterile environments are kind of his thing. And if you were the one on his operating table, you'd be thankful for his OCD."

"I suppose." She lifts the burger bun and discards the tomato and red onion.

"But you like him. Right?"

"I suppose. It's not like I see him that often. He's usually working. Or sleeping. Mom said he always falls asleep when they watch a movie together."

"Is your mom still teaching dance?" When I met Tatum, she competed in ballroom dancing competitions while selling real estate to make rent. After we got married, she rented space in Kansas City to teach classes three nights a week. I could barely snap my fingers to a simple beat. Yet we fit, and it was as perfect as that meticulously painted white fence for twelve years.

"Yes. Still teaching three nights a week. You know..." Lucy smirks, stirring her milkshake "...if you want to know how Mom's doing or what she's doing, you could ask her yourself."

My gaze relocates to my plate as I grab my burger and shrug. "Just making small talk."

"How's *your* dating life?" Lucy prods.

Shoving the greasy burger into my mouth, I buy a few more seconds to formulate a good answer to her question. I don't make the mistake of looking at her because I know she's judging me. It's hard to *still* love Tatum to the point that I don't have interest in anyone else yet reassure Lucy that I'm good.

Lucy won't believe I'm good until she sees me move on and find something resembling happiness again. Maybe I should make up a story. What's another lie at this point?

"It's going," I say, giving her a sweeping glance before redirecting my attention to the heat rising from the newly blacktopped parking lot out the window to my right.

"You're not seeing anyone … are you?"

"Well …" I wipe my mouth with the thin paper napkin. "I had a drink with my new neighbor last week."

"A woman?" Lucy's eyes widen with the same enthusiasm as her voice jumping an octave.

"Yes." I chuckle. "A woman."

"I didn't know anyone had moved into that house. So … what's her name? What does she do? Is she divorced? Widowed? Never been married? Does she have kids? What does she look like? Do you like her?"

She wants this so much. I feel like my response will completely make or break her.

"Her name is Nina. She's a nurse. Divorced. Two kids."

"How old?"

"I'm not sure." I take another bite of my burger and buy more time.

"Have you met her kids?"

My head shakes.

"Are you going to ask her out on a date?"

After I finish chewing, I take a drink of my root beer. Lucy has barely touched her sandwich. My ravenous daughter, who used to eat half a large pizza, now eats like a bird. I think she's had four slurps of her milkshake and two fries.

"She's my new neighbor. I'm not sure rushing into

dating her is a good idea. Things could get awkward if it doesn't work out." I nod toward Lucy's plate. "Are you not hungry?"

"It's a lot of carbs." With her fork wielded like a weapon, she fishes out the burger from the rubble of toppings.

"You could have ordered a salad." I stab my fork into the bun, cheese, and pickles she discards. No sense in wasting food.

"I don't really like salads," she says with a sour face.

"Then what is on your list of things to eat? Meat and ...?"

"Eggs. Cauliflower rice. Almonds. Yogurt. And you're changing the subject. I need to know that you're looking for someone."

This girl.

She *needs* this.

If I don't give her some illusion of happiness, she will drown in guilt because the secret we share is the kind that ruins lives—and marriages.

"I'm looking for someone, but she has to be *the one*. I won't settle."

Lucy points her fork at me. "You need to be looking online. You can't find *the one* in Redington. You need to get a profile. Ashton's mom is online, and she's had a half dozen dates in under a month."

"Who's Ashton?" I point my fork at her, mirroring her fork pointed at me.

She smiles, proving to be my constant sunshine, and taps my fork with hers like a sword. "He's a *friend*." Her cheeks tell the truth in spite of her best effort to downplay this Ashton kid. "And I may or may not be going out with him tonight after you drop me off at home."

Leaning back, I toss my napkin onto the table and cross my arms over my chest. "Then I will stay to meet him."

"You don't need to—" She uses her fork like a laser pointer again. "*Stay* as in come into the house and wait ... with Mom?"

"I can wait in my truck. I have some work I can do on my computer."

"Dad, you can't avoid her forever. It's been years. She's moved on. You've moved on. Things are good. Right? I mean ..." Her expression deflates into a sad state. "Life's not perfect, but it's good. Considering ..." As she trails off into dangerous territory, I lean forward and rest my hand on hers.

"If your mom is good with me coming inside, then I'll come inside to wait."

Her sad eyes shift, staring at our hands for a few breaths before her gaze lifts to meet mine. "A few days ago, she was going through some old shoeboxes in her closet. There were pictures of you and her. Before you were married. Before me."

The thick scars on my heart stretch, sending a dull ache across my chest. "Oh yeah? I'm sure you got a kick out of her big hair and my obsession with flannel and huge belt buckles."

Lucy giggles, a perfect salve for what ails my crippled heart. In so many ways, her giggle sounds the same as it did when I used to toss her in the air, stealing her breath for two seconds before I'd catch her. She'd explode into giggles as Tatum smiled in adoration at her little girl, showing complete trust in me.

I lost her trust.

I lost her.

I almost lost Lucy.

I'm pretty sure that would have killed me.

It only takes *one* good reason to keep going. To live. To feel necessary.

Lucy is my one. I just can't let her see that. It would kill her to know she is my entire reason for waking every morning. I endure the other one hundred and fifty-eight hours in a week just to have ten with her.

"What were we doing in the pictures?" I ask.

"Everything. She had photos from the Grand Canyon. You were pretending to fall over the edge. Mount Rushmore pictures from the Fourth of July. Pictures of you two skiing in Tahoe. Combing the beach for shells in South Carolina. Just … everything. I had no idea you guys traveled so much before you got married." She offers a polite smile to the waitress and nods when asked if she's done with her plate.

I see so much of Tatum in her. It's equal parts torment and salvation.

"What?" Lucy eyes me as she adjusts her ponytail.

"Nothing. I guess I didn't realize we hadn't shared that part of our past with you. We loved traveling. We basically lived to travel for eight crazy and amazing months—in an RV. And we towed your mom's car behind it. It was so impulsive. And I regret nothing."

My daughter's brown eyes fill with excitement and wonder. I like this version of Lucy. I *live* to see this version of her. "Mom said the same thing. She said it was reckless." She grins. "Then she got this look on her face. I think it was a smile. And she said those exact words. *I regret nothing.*"

Reckless.

I wonder what exactly Tatum was referring to? We were reckless in so many ways. The ones that stick in my mind involve her giving me head while I sped down highways and interstates at seventy miles per hour. Or sex in public restrooms *while* people occupied stalls beside ours. Something tells me she didn't share that information with our seventeen-year-old daughter.

"We sometimes drove too fast and didn't tip well at restaurants. So ... you should learn from our mistakes." No way am I telling her we had way too much unprotected sex. Nor am I telling her we dabbled in shoplifting stupid things like packs of gum and other cheap items just to say we lived on the edge—as if anyone was going to serve hard time for pocketing a pack of Big Red. I can't give her ammunition to make excuses for any questionable behavior she might have in the future.

God, I hope she behaves. I won't be able to handle having a rebellious teenager that I only get to see one day a week. Our time together is supposed to be fun, not a day of parental lecturing. Tatum has her for those other one hundred and fifty-eight hours every week. She can be the bad cop.

"Mom said you did more than drive a little too fast."

My cheek twitches, fighting the knowing grin that wants to form on my face along with the rush of warmth in my chest from the thought of Tatum reminiscing with Lucy about the love story we shared ... the one with an end neither one of us could have ever imagined.

But the beginning of our story ... it was The. Best.

CHAPTER TWO

THEN

My older brother, Will, married his first sexual conquest. A sticky situation that involved his seventeen-year-old girlfriend and unprotected sex. Worth mentioning ... his girlfriend happened to be his boss's daughter.

Will was nineteen.

He had two choices: marriage and job security or unemployment and castration.

So, Will married Andi a week after she graduated high school and two months before my nephew was born. Will moved into her parents' basement to help change diapers, and he rode to work every morning with his boss/father-in-law, Kenneth Coleman—owner of Coleman Inc., an environmental construction company. They handled everything from tree clearing and mulching to composting and chemical spills. Ken took over the company after his father died. He had hoped to pass the business on to his son, but he ended up with a daughter, a wife who had to have an emergency hysterectomy, and years later a hardworking nineteen-year-old who could run any piece of equipment better than guys twice his age but couldn't manage to roll on a condom before defiling the boss's daughter.

After Andi and Will had been married five years and added a second child, Kenneth Coleman died from a stroke at only fifty-five. Will took over running the family business (an incredibly young CEO) and offered me a job. There was no ladder to climb in the bartending profession, and at twenty-two I still hadn't figured out what to do with my life, so I let Will train me to bid jobs and operate excavators and tree grinders.

I'd been working for Coleman a little over six months when I found myself at a sports bar around seven on a Sunday night, watching the Chiefs get slaughtered by the Packers. Will stood me up at the last minute when Andi called for backup after both kids started to run a fever.

"Cody?" A woman's voice chimed from behind as I waited for my nachos with a half-empty glass of root beer sweating in my right hand.

A wavy-haired brunette with shimmering lips and rosy cheeks lifted her eyebrows in question as her smile swelled with caution. She didn't look familiar, but she did give off the vibe of someone I wished I knew. A stunning woman with delicate features and that hair. So much long wavy hair for such a petite figure.

The irony ... the song playing in the bar at that exact moment happened to be Rick Springfield's "Jessie's Girl." I had no idea who Cody was, but I wished I had his girl.

Those eyes.

That body.

"Red hair. Gray shirt." She nodded at my hair and shirt. "Alice said you'd be easy to spot." She slid off her navy wool coat and set her small black purse on the bar, climbing onto the stool next to mine.

I stole another few seconds to admire her baby blue V-neck sweater that looked soft like cashmere and those jeans perfectly molded to her tiny waist and toned legs. There was no doubt I wanted Cody's girl even if I remained clue-less to Cody's identity and Alice's too.

However, if she thought I was Cody, that meant she hadn't met Cody. One thing flashed through my mind. *Cody, you poor bastard. I'm going to steal your girl.* Rick Springfield would have been proud.

"Cat got your tongue?" Her smile was a little crooked, an irresistible imperfection.

Shaking my head a few times, I turned on the charm and initiated Project Steal Cody's Girl. "Sorry. I wasn't expecting you to be so beautiful." Reaching my hand toward her, I offered it to her in a rather sly move. "Let's start over. I'm Cody."

Giving my hand a slight inspection, she giggled and fit her hand in mine. "Well, thank you. I'm Tatum."

And just like that, I had her name. I could have been a successful stalker or serial killer.

"Tatum." I grinned, giving her hand a firm shake before releasing it. "It's a true pleasure to meet you."

The door to the bar opened. A guy with red hair entered, eyes squinted as he surveyed the area. Cody was about to learn some basic life lessons.

You snooze, you lose.

Finders keepers.

The early bird gets the worm.

And the most basic one of all: punctuality matters.

"How do you feel about something a little nicer than bar

food?" I pulled a twenty out of my wallet and tossed it on the counter.

"Oh ... well ... Alice said it would just be drinks. One drink actually. I'm a light weight, and I'm driving." Her nose wrinkled, and I knew there was no way I would let her get away, even if the thought sounded a little creepy in my head.

I grabbed my root beer and took a quick swig. "I'm driving too. So..." I jerked my head toward the door "... there's a cafe across the street. They put whipped cream on their hot chocolate. That's a drink. Right?" My gaze flitted over her shoulder to Cody taking a seat two stools down from her. His eyes continually scanning the bar.

Tatum rubbed her lips together, mulling over my offer. "Just across the street?"

I stood, keeping a close eye on Curious Cody. "Yeah. Across the well-lit street."

Sliding off the stool, she donned her coat and grabbed her purse. "Hot chocolate sounds perfect."

She was perfect.

Perfectly not mine.

"Your nachos?" the bartender said as he plucked the twenty from the counter.

I fished another five dollars out of my wallet and handed it to him. "Give my nachos and a beer to the guy at the end of the bar," I murmured with my back to Tatum.

"Okay." The bartender nodded.

"Ready?" I grabbed my jacket and followed her to the door, opening it before she had the chance to do it.

"So what do you do, Cody?" She strode beside me after looking both ways at the intersection.

"Alice didn't tell you?" It was less than convenient that I didn't know Alice.

"No. She just said that you play softball with Derek and you're a really nice guy. My standards are a little low because clearly I said yes to a blind date based on that alone." Tatum laughed and it became my favorite sound.

Things were looking up for me. I could play any sport, so softball with Derek worked for me. Whoever Derek was. Alice's husband or boyfriend, I assumed.

"That's interesting..." I opened the door to the cafe and Tatum stepped inside "...because I heard you were a little skittish because you've been a recluse with seven cats in your dinky apartment for the past three years."

She whipped around just before taking a seat in the booth at the far end of the diner. "Oh my gosh! Did she seriously say that? I'm allergic to cats. And I'm never home, so basically the opposite of a recluse. I'm going to kill her."

I grinned. Things were going quite well for what was truly a blind date for me. More like blindsided date. The date I didn't know I needed that night. What were the chances of my joke being so spot-on?

We sat in the booth and ordered two hot chocolates followed by a few awkward seconds of silence.

"I'm in construction of sorts. I work for Coleman. We do tree removal, environmental clean-ups, stuff like that. My brother and his wife own the company."

"I'm familiar with Coleman. I actually sold their house after Kenneth died. It was my first big sale."

"You're a realtor?"

"Yes. And I'm a competitive ballroom dancer. Do you need a house? Or do you need to learn how to waltz?"

By that time, I was ready to buy literally anything she wanted to sell me. But there was no way she would teach me to dance. "I'm going to ignore your love of dancing because I can't sway and snap my fingers at the same time. As for the house, I'm sure someday I'll need one. Do you own your own house? Have you scooped up a good deal? A banker friend give you first chance at a fore-closure?"

"No." She laughed just as the waitress delivered our hot chocolates. Fishing a spoon out of the silverware wrapped in a white paper napkin, she dipped it in the whipped cream and licked it.

I kinda died when she did that. It was a guy thing.

"I have an apartment with two roommates who recently decided to be more than roommates. It's now a little weird. I'm such a third wheel. How about you? Do you have roommates?"

Taking an extended sip of my hot chocolate, I licked my whipped cream mustache and nodded slowly. "I have three actually."

"Wow. In an apartment? Or are you renting a house?"

There was a reason guys like me were single, and Tatum teetered on the edge of finding out.

"Two of my roommates own the house."

"Married friends?" She continued to unknowingly prod.

Cody probably owned his own place. I had a knack for playing out of my league.

"Yes. They're married."

"What about your other roommate? Girl or guy?"

"Guy." I kept my answers surgically precise.

"How old is he?" She scooped more whipped cream from the top of her hot chocolate.

I found everything she did quite mesmerizing. "Uh ... he's younger than me."

"In college?"

If I didn't jump in and change the subject, things were

going to get bad quickly. "No. Are you originally from Redington?"

"Kansas City. And that's where our real estate office is located, but rent is cheaper in Redington. And so I've been given most of the listings for here."

"That's nice. Especially since you live in Redington. But the real question is ... are you a sports fan?"

Tatum lit up, eyes wide. "Total sports fan. My room-mates get Royals season tickets, and I get dibs whenever they don't go. And my boss has season tickets to the Chiefs, and he likes me a lot, so I get first offer at his tickets when he can't go, which lately has been quite often. And ... his seats are right on the fifty-yard line."

I robbed the bank. Lifted the biggest diamond from the museum. With Cody eating my nachos across the street, I couldn't call it fate or any sort of serendipity, but it was *something* for sure.

"So ... tickets as in plural? As in you need someone to go to these Chiefs games with you?"

Cupping her hot chocolate mug, she brought it close to her lips and grinned. "I showed my hand too soon. Now I'll never know if you like me for me or for my access to fifty-yard-line tickets."

"I liked you from the second I laid eyes on you. But I'm going to marry you because you have access to Chiefs tick-ets," I replied with a subtle grin.

Giggles erupted for several seconds before she sipped her drink, swirly brown eyes alight with amusement. "You're going to have to give me more than a proposal. I'm here because you're supposedly a nice guy. I only take charming, smart guys with me to games."

My fingers drummed on the table as I studied her. "You already know I think you're beautiful. I could have tried to get you drunk tonight, but we're here instead, getting a sugar high from chocolate and whipped cream. *That* tells you I'm charming. As for my intelligence … what do you want to know? Do you want to know that light travels eighteen million times faster than rain? The *Mona Lisa* was stolen from the Louvre in 1911—and one of the suspects was Picasso? There's a village in Tarsdor, Austria called Fucking, and its residents are called Fuckingers? Originally, heroin was marketed as cough medicine? Or … do you want to know that apodysophilia is a term (although rarely used) for a desire to remove one's clothes in public? I don't have it, but I think I've come across a few people who do."

By the time I finished my impressive and rather random spiel, Tatum's jaw hung wide open.

"Is it because I said the F-word?"

She laughed, inching her head side to side. "You don't look like a nerd." Her jaw clamped shut, replaced with a smirk.

True. I didn't look like a nerd. Football player? Hockey player? Sure. Six feet four inches and a passion for weightlifting wasn't a nerd look.

"Looks can be deceiving." I shrugged.

"Indeed. Cody. Indeed."

Cody.

"Are we good? Am I officially charming and smart? Am I invited to a game with you?"

She shrugged. "I'll have to talk to Alice and Derek. They said you weren't really interested in getting into a relationship at the moment, which I'm cool with, but I also don't want to feel used for my assets."

My head eased back. "Let me get this straight. You're fine with the no relationship part, but you're still here … which leads me to believe you're looking for something

20

casual ... which I believe implies sharing certain *assets*. And *that* you're okay with, but sharing season tickets is somehow more personal?"

Her cheeks pinked a smidge, which meant she wasn't someone who had a ton of casual sex. Tatum was confident, but not that confident. "Casual sharing of *assets* is a mutual give and take." She frowned. "At least it should be. But what do I get out of sharing tickets with you?"

"More of my charm and unmatched intelligence of course."

Her neutral expression held strong for a few seconds. Then she grinned. "I paint my face ... for games. Are you *that* kind of diehard fan?"

"I don't wear a shirt to games because I paint my chest."

A lie.

That lie led to another hour of conversation, two more hot chocolates, a shared order of Belgian waffles, and so much laughter my stomach hurt almost as much as the seventeen muscles in my face it took to smile. I stole someone's blind date.

Best. Bad. Decision. Ever.

With her own grin permanently frozen in place, she emptied the last few drops of her hot chocolate onto the tip of her tongue and scooted toward the edge of the booth. "I should go. So much for a 'quick' drink. Thanks for the hot chocolate and waffles. It's been ..."

"Perfect," I said before she could taint it with anything less.

Tatum bobbed her head a few times, letting my word roll around in that beautiful head of hers. "I concur."

Yes!

"We could catch a movie or something." I wasn't ready to say goodbye.

She stood. "I'll call you." The wink that punctuated her sentence would have felt promising had I been Cody.

"Wait. You don't have my number." I followed her toward the door.

"I'll get it from Derek and Alice."

Before she crossed the street, I had to say something. I'd gone through too much work to let her walk away. "They don't have my number."

She pressed the button at the intersection and waited for the light to change. "Then how did they contact you about our date?"

"They didn't."

The light turned green, and she waltzed across the busy street as only a dancer could do, tossing me a funny look over her shoulder as if I were playing games like I did about her being a recluse with seven cats. I jogged behind her. "I work at Coleman. I love the Chiefs. And I'd love a real date with you because your face is branded into my brain, and that's just not fair for all other women who could come after you should you choose to never see me again."

Tatum whipped around just before opening the door to her white Toyota Corolla. "Cody. I like you." Her teeth snagged her lower lip. "A lot. So I highly doubt this will be the last time you see me."

I patted my hands over my pockets, searching for anything to write on, half-tempted to use my car key to etch my phone number into the side of her car, but I quickly discarded that idea into the growing pile of impulsive things I'd done in my life.

"Goodnight, Cody."

"I'm not Cody," I replied just above a whisper, my confession carrying a backpack of guilt.

Her smile all but vanished, leaving a tiny curl to her lips

on one side as she eyed me, head tilted. "No? Then who are you?" She laughed.

Of course she laughed. Stealing someone else's date was crazy. *I* was laughable that night. But also …

Spontaneous.

Courageous.

And I hoped one day we'd look back to find my bold actions romantic and admirable as well because I lassoed my gut feeling and chased what felt like fate. Or insanity. The two often blurred as they mingled next to the same line.

The truth contorted my face into an ugly cringe. "A redhead who happened to be in the right place at the right time … depending on your perspective."

"I'm not following. It's like you're talking in secret code." She deserved credit for laughing everything off as if she couldn't get enough of my humor, but by that point her amusement lost momentum.

"I'm not Cody." I shoved my hands into the front pockets of my jeans, lifting my shoulders into a preemptive apologetic shrug—an *"oops … no harm, no foul."*

There it went … her smile succumbed to my confession.

"You thought I was this Cody guy. And I thought he would never be able to appreciate that smile of yours like I could, so …"

Her eyes flared as did her nostrils while she drew in a slow breath. "You lied? You … you're … oh my god! What is wrong with you?"

I realized that was often a rhetorical question, but I still felt the need to explain why my actions were far more right than wrong. "Give me a chance to—"

Shaking her head, she backed away from me and her car. "I gave you, a complete stranger, nearly two hours of my night while my real date ..." Her gaze drifted to the bar where we met. "Crap. Alice is going to be so mad. And Cody ..." Taking long strides, she made her way back to the bar.

"There's a new Bond movie out if next Friday works for you," I called as she ditched me along the side of the road like the rotten apple core I was at the moment.

I didn't receive so much as a brief glance backward. I did, however, get the middle finger just before she disappeared into the bar.

CHAPTER THREE

NOW

"Please tell me you were kidding about staying in your truck." Lucy pauses, door ajar and one leg reaching for the ground as I drop her off after a great day of biking followed by a painful trip to the mall for "a few things" that assaulted my checking account.

"When is this kid picking you up?"

"His name is *Ashton*. And not for an hour. I need to shower and get ready."

"Perfect. I have about an hour's worth of work to do on my computer."

She gives me that pouty face again. "You're not *fine* if you sit in your stupid truck and pretend to work just to avoid Mom. And if you're not fine, then I'm not fine."

When you share a life-changing secret with your child, it opens you up to nonstop blackmail. The truth? I don't really know what Lucy thinks about our secret or if she even knows it's a secret and not just the truth, which it's not.

"Then I'll come inside and wait. Or wait out back. Is my firepit still there?"

"It is. Mom sits out there all the time."

This revelation gives me pause. Does she sit out back to enjoy the space I created for our family—when we still resembled a family? A badly damaged family, but still a family. Or does she feel *him* there? Does she replay that day in her mind like I do? We can't rewind. I would change the tragedy if I held some kind of otherworldly power, but I don't. As often as I replay my knee-jerk reaction to limit that day's tragedy to one instead of two, I have never regretted my decision. I think I knew, at the very moment I made the decision, that my marriage was over.

We were perfect ... until we weren't.

"You're okay. Right?"

I blink slowly.

Lucy comes first ...

"Right," I lie.

Since the divorce, my communications with Tatum have involved the occasional phone call when Lucy's sick and we need to cancel her day with me. Our face-to-face encounters comprise of school events and dance recitals where we keep a safe distance but occasionally find ourselves brought within feet of each other connected by Lucy for a photo or sometimes sitting next to each other at parent-teacher conferences.

I haven't been inside the house since the day I hauled away my last box of personal belongings, driving away from that damn perfectly painted white fence.

"What if your mom's not okay with me waiting inside?" God ... do I sound as insecure as I feel?

"It's fine. She's probably busy on her computer and

won't pay much attention to you anyway." Lucy opens the front door.

I'd forgotten how our house always smelled of lavender —Tatum's favorite scent for everything from candles to cleaning supplies and fabric softener.

"Hey, Mom. I'm going to jump in the shower before Ashton gets here."

I attempt to hide my heart sprinting out of control when Tatum glances up from her computer at the kitchen table— that unruly hair (now a few shades lighter) in a messy bun, royal blue framed reading glasses sitting low on her nose. She uses the back of her hand to push them into place as her lips pull into a tight line that she tries to pass as a smile.

It seems like a lifetime ago—at the same time I remember it like yesterday. Her smile engulfed her face without any sort of control just from my walking into the room. There's nothing more magical than your mere exis- tence bringing complete joy to another human. And there's nothing more soul crushing than that same existence inflicting an eternity of pain.

I'd kissed those lips so many times it felt like they were made for that very reason. Did they miss me even a little? Were there tiny pauses in Tatum's life that allowed her to forget how we got here? All the moments that led to purchasing this fixer-upper and filling it with a life?

When the bathroom door upstairs slams shut, I clear my throat, feeling as nervous as I did the night I told her I wasn't her blind date, Cody. "Hi. Uh ... Lucy said I could meet her date. I offered to stay in my truck. I have work to do as well, but she was pretty adamant about me coming inside."

Tatum studies me for several seconds with an unreadable expression. "I'm selling the house," she says as if the words won't completely fit through her throat.

What I hear is *In case the divorce wasn't enough, I'm separating from you even further.* I nod slowly. When we divorced, I didn't ask for anything except Lucy, but there was a condition for selling the house: either we would split the profit from it or I would buy her out. We moved into this house just months before having Lucy. We gutted it and renovated it one room at a time as we could afford it. This house bore witness to every important moment in our life together.

Birthday parties.

Over a decade of Christmases.

Pictures on the front porch swing the first day of school.

We took this house and made it our home.

"Can I ask why?"

Her flinch is slight, but I catch it. "Do you really have to?"

"Where are you going?"

"There's a foreclosure on Edmond Street."

"Edmond Street?" My brow furrows. "You're selling our house to move two blocks north? Does Lucy know?"

Tatum shifts her gaze out the window to the backyard. "Of course she knows."

"And she's okay with it?"

Her attention returns to me, and she nods several times while blowing out a long breath like she's been dying to get this off her chest. "I actually have an interested buyer, and—"

"No." My voice snaps with irritation. "I'll buy you out."

She scoffs. "You can't be serious. Why would you want it?"

Because I refuse to erase all the good because something

bad happened here. Maybe she can no longer see the memories that brought us joy, but I can. This house has a pulse. It's seen everything. It will always hold the memories that I need to remember.

"Whatever, Emmett." She glances at her phone and types something into it, her lips twisted to the side for several seconds as she nibbles the inside of her cheek. I know all her looks. And I know what they mean. I can see her without opening my eyes. Maybe I never got that college degree, but I have a PhD in my wife—ex-wife.

"Go."

She glances up.

"I know that look. You have plans. But now I'm here. Clearly you've met this Ashton kid before. No need to stick around. I know how to lock the door behind me."

"It's nothing. And you don't know my looks." She bristles, pushing her chair back and taking her water glass to the sink.

I'm not sure if she truly hates me or if she hates the fact that she should hate me and it's not easy to do. It's not a cliché—there is a thin line between love and hate. Investment breeds emotions, and we were nothing if not fully invested in each other.

"My apologies. I don't know your looks," I say, but … I absolutely know her looks. "Just a guess." I plop down into the paisley armchair next to the velvet eggplant sofa. Not only is lavender her favorite scent, purple is her favorite color. And our house is professionally decorated in shades of purple and cream with tiny splashes of gold or something I think she calls lemon tart. The built-in bookshelves are filled with books and trinkets, candlesticks and air plants.

I wanted to fill those shelves with albums we used to listen to on the turntable I inherited from my grandfather.

And I had books too—but she rolled her eyes at their worn spines, curled corners, and stained rings on the covers from where I'd leave a can of A&W Root Beer for too long.

It's hard not being her husband. I did it well until the very end. And maybe she'll never know that my last act was exactly what she asked me to do, but *I* know it. Still ... it's like doing the same thing for so long you don't know—or can't imagine—doing anything else. I never could imagine being anything but her husband.

Here I am.

Not being her husband.

And five years later, it's still unimaginable.

She exhales, letting her shoulders release the tension my presence has caused. "How are you?" she whispers as her gaze makes a slow climb to meet mine. There is so much packed into those three words I find it hard to take my next breath.

Five years.

It's taken her five years to ask me that.

Does she want my honest answer? I can't imagine she does.

Not wanting to lie, I search for facts. I tell her what I know because it doesn't give away how I feel. Besides, there are no words for how I feel. "I'm working a lot. Next month, I'll be out of town for several days at an auction. We're looking to buy another grinder."

Her delicate fingers fold in front of her as she leans against the counter. She's the complete opposite of me—graceful in her moves, petite in stature, and every inch of her skin is soft and flawless. I'm a pile of big bones wrapped in thick layers of muscle. My hands are large and calloused. A harsh terrain of bristly whiskers in dark red and a few patches of gray cover my face. Her eyes are rich shades of brown with flecks of gold that illuminate in certain lighting. I have eyes in a standard blue color. Nothing deep. Nothing icy and mesmerizing. Just … run-of-the-mill blue eyes.

"Lucy said your dad's closing up shop."

I nod, feeling the twinge of a smile pulling at my lips. My dad has always been the ultimate litmus test for every relationship I've ever had. Hal Barnes, my best friend from high school, thought it was hard to find friends, especially girlfriends, because his parents owned a funeral home. His grandfather had been an undertaker as well. Hal's mom excelled at making dead people look alive again. However, Hal preferred to say she was a cosmetologist—which she was—but she chose to be a mortuary makeup artist after she married his dad.

I managed to make Hal and his family look completely normal. Funeral home directors and mortuary makeup artists are necessary jobs. People die and someone has to get them ready for their funeral and burial.

My family, on the other hand, took death and preservation to a whole new level—one a little less necessary—but there is … or was a demand, a disturbing demand, for what they did.

CHAPTER FOUR

THEN

I DIDN'T KNOW Tatum's last name, so I couldn't look her up. Lucky for me, Redington was a small town with only one realtor named Tatum. *Tatum Bradshaw* the sign said when I parked my truck on the street to attend the open house at a home I couldn't afford. My living situation was complicated—some might have even said flat out lazy.

Straightening my tucked-in button-down and running my hands through my shaggy red hair, I clomped my "nicer" work boots across the street to the two-story house with a paneled wood door stained deep brown. As I contemplated knocking or just walking into the house—after all, it was my first open house—the door opened and a young couple holding a brochure passed me.

Tatum's wide smile vanished when her focus shifted to me. I half expected her to slam the door in my face.

"Sorry, you can't afford this house," she said with big attitude and narrowed eyes.

"That's a little presumptuous of you." I smirked, taking

in her fitted black dress pants, floral sleeveless blouse, and high heels. Her wayward hair spilled over her shoulders and down her back. When she moved one hand to her hip, her gold bracelets clinked against her watch. I devoured all five feet, six inches of her attitude and silently begged for more.

"I'd hardly call it presumptuous given the fact that you live at home ... with your parents."

It should have been a little embarrassing—being called out like that. But I saw the bigger picture. She looked me up. After she stormed off and gave me the bird, she looked me up.

"By choice. Not necessity," I said with the biggest grin on my face. My three roommates were my parents and my younger brother—not exactly things to share on a first date to impress a woman when you're twenty-two with a full-time job.

Tatum didn't give me an inch. She held her scowl firmly in place. Earning every ounce of her affection gave me a lot of gratification. I would have been disappointed had she conceded her interest in me too quickly.

Her head tipped to the side like my—well, my parents'—dog. In hindsight, all the uneasy feelings she gave me in that moment were the start of something I would later recognize as love.

Fluid.

Ever changing.

A shifting pendulum of intensity.

"Is that why you tried to steal me? By choice, not necessity?"

Steal her ...

I grinned. "No. I'm certain that was out of necessity."

Tatum didn't want to grin, which made the hint of a smile ghosting along her face that much more spectacular.

"You're such a player. And a cheater. A thief. You were ..." Her pink glossed lips rubbed together as she contemplated her next words.

I stepped inside, taking a glance around the two-story foyer. "I was enamored. Hanging on your every word. Dumbfounded by that smile." My attention refocused on her face, which was far more appealing than the over-priced house she was trying to sell. "And you left me wounded on the sidewalk. Shot down with your middle finger." I toed off my boots and made my way to the living room, through the library, and around to the kitchen overlooking a manicured backyard with a fenced-in garden at the far corner.

"You're a liar and a thief," she said, her heels clicking behind me.

I turned and she came to an abrupt halt, chin tipped up to me. After studying her for a few seconds, I shrugged. "I've never stolen anything in my life, but I'd steal you if I could, and that's the truth. So now I'm just a thief, not a liar."

"You live with your parents." She chuckled, taking a step back, peeling her gaze from mine.

"So we're past the part where I lied to you and tried to steal you." I nodded several times. "That's good. That's really good. I can deal with your apprehension to fall for a guy who still lives with his parents."

"Whoa ... fall for you?" Her attention snapped back to me.

"Was Cody still in the bar?" I asked.

"No." She crossed her perfectly defined arms over her chest, making those bracelets clink again.

"Did you have your friends reschedule your blind date?"

Blinking several times, she remained quiet.

"I'll take that as a no." I winked.

She shook her head, rolling her eyes to the ceiling. I could smell something floral. Lavender. God ... she smelled amazing and so out of my league.

"Because you were too busy doing recon on me? Finding out that I live with my parents, which means you figured out my real name. How did you do that? Did you wait for me to finish work and follow me home? Did you have a friend tail me? I'm flattered. Really."

"You're arrogant."

I chuckled, sliding my fingers into my back pockets. "I'm feigning confidence because you make me nervous."

Something in her expression changed. A subtle shift. It felt ... real. A glimpse of what was to come for us. It stole my breath.

"Tell me those two hours at the cafe with me weren't the best two hours you've experienced in a long time. Tell me you stayed for me, not just another cup of hot chocolate. Tell me over the past ten days you've secretly hoped we'd run into each other, and that's the reason you haven't asked for a redo with Toby."

Pinching the bridge of her nose, she blew out a quick breath while her lips made a reluctant bend into a smile that showed her teeth. "Cody. His name is Cody."

"Toby. Cody. Dopey. Doesn't matter. He's an idiot for not being on time to your blind date. My name is Emmett Riley, but you know that. And I'm punctual."

The more she laughed, the more nervous it made me. I liked her so much it became increasingly difficult to imagine her not giving me a second chance. "You weren't punctual that night. You were just there."

"Timing, accidental or not, is everything. Seconds matter."

Lips pressed together, she gave me nothing more than an undecipherable glare. "Jobs matter too. And you're not seriously interested in this house, so you should go."

"I'm interested in you."

"I'm not for sale." She curled her hair behind her right ear, revealing a gold hoop earring.

"That Bond movie is still playing." I ignored her comment and stayed focused on my goal. "I think there's a seven o'clock showing tonight. The drive-in theater is still open."

"Thanks for the information. Do you need me to see you out?"

"No. I can find my way out. Then you can watch me leave. I've been assured I have a nice backside."

Her mouth trembled as if it was killing her to keep from relinquishing another smile. "You should get better friends. Honest friends."

"Ouch." I gave her five more seconds to change her mind, but she held strong, so I turned and retraced my steps to the front door.

Tatum kept a good distance behind me, staying silent as I slipped on my boots and opened the front door. I played it cool like it wasn't a big deal, all the while feeling disappointed that I'd gotten it wrong. Those two hours at the cafe weren't just any two hours. They really were unforgettable —apparently just to me.

"Chiefs are at home this Sunday," she said.

Without turning back to her, I paused, waiting for her to elaborate while my gullible heart skipped a few beats.

"Not a date. Just two people who like football sharing free tickets."

My grin nearly broke my face.

"I'll put your ticket in your ... uh, your parents' mailbox after my class tonight."

I didn't look back. Not once. I exuded complete confidence in spite of sweat dripping down my back all the way to my truck, and it wasn't hot outside.

"A DATE, HUH?" Andi said as she and my mom filled the dining room table with food for my brother's birthday party, the Saturday before the Chiefs game. "You should have invited her to the party. We'd love to meet her."

I helped my niece into her high chair. "Not a date. She was clear about that."

Andi clucked her tongue several times as my parents and brother laughed a little at my predicament. "Nonsense. She's just playing hard to get because you lied to her. I suggest you play hard to get as well. Play her game. It will drive her crazy."

"I don't want to play her game. I just want ..."

My mom perked up, eyeing me with her usual knowing look. "You just want *her*. Oh, my boy is quite taken with a girl. I'm not sure I've ever seen you like this."

"I'm not taken. I'm just *interested*. That's all."

"Well, she offered you a ticket on the fifty-yard line. I'd say she's interested too." Will added his two cents to the conversation as I wrangled Miss Squirms A Lot into her bib.

I knew she was interested, or at least curious, in spite of my living situation. "I need to get my own place. It's time."

"Ya think?" Will razzed me like only he could do.

"You have the entire basement to yourself, including a minibar with a microwave and fridge. Rent is such a waste of money, Emmett." Mom had no desire to lose another baby to the big bad world.

Dad stayed quiet because he understood me, but he also didn't want to get smacked upside the head by going against Mom.

"I agree. You need to move out." Andi nodded, retying the bib after I managed to do it incorrectly. "No woman wants to be intimate with a guy at his parents' house." Her nose scrunched as she eyed my mom. "No offense."

"They just met," Mom said. "I think intimacy is at least a few months out *if* they make it that long."

"Bec, I don't think this generation waits a few months to have sex."

Mom scowled at Dad, jabbing her head toward my niece as if a toddler knew what sex meant.

"I have quite a bit of money saved up. Buying something small, maybe a duplex where I can rent out the other side, wouldn't be a bad idea."

"Oh, I like that idea." Andi ruffled my hair.

"We're putting the cart before the horse. He hasn't even had a real date with her yet." Mom knew how to keep it real.

"So I should play hard to get?" I shifted the subject back to my current situation instead of hypotheticals.

THE FOLLOWING DAY, I painted my chest for the first time, dug out my favorite Chiefs hat, and headed to the stadium for my "not date" with Tatum. A few rows from my seat, I stopped to admire her before she knew I was there. Maybe it was just the back side of her head—hair down and straightened under her red hat—but I still felt my chest constrict thinking about all the possibilities.

As if she sensed my proximity, she glanced over her shoulder and smiled through her red and yellow painted face, giving me a little wave with her mitten-covered hand.

Keep cool. Play hard to get.

I smiled in return and sidestepped my way to her.

"Thought you painted your whole chest. Or was that just another lie?" She wasted no time busting my balls.

After plunking into the seat next to her, I unzipped my jacket, exposing my painted chest. Complete satisfaction lit up her face all the way to her eyes. "I see you even painted on abs. Nice touch."

"They're the real deal. Since we're *friends*, you can feel them, but since this isn't a date, I'll need you to keep it brief so other available women in the vicinity don't think you've laid claim to me."

Her lips parted for a second before she swallowed. "You're using my generosity as an opportunity to pick up women?"

I shrugged, forcing my gaze to the field, basically anywhere but directed toward Tatum. Just me ... playing it cool. Playing hard to get.

"Well," she scoffed. "Looks like I know who *not* to ask the next time I get tickets."

"So ... let me get this straight. You invited me, but not as your date. Yet I'm not allowed to look around?"

"You're supposed to be watching the game."

"The game hasn't started."

"But..." she extended her arm out, gesturing to the field "...the players are warming up, and that's part of the experience of being here!"

She liked me. A lot. Of course she was too stubborn to

admit it. And I bore part of the blame. Her ego refused to let her completely ignore the lie, the stolen date.

We watched the game. Cheered and yelled until we had hoarse voices. I bought us hot chocolate, popcorn, and nachos. She bought us foam fingers. Every time the Chiefs scored, she jumped up and down before throwing herself into my arms for a celebratory hug that left me with a full-on erection by the end of the game. The day ended with an adrenaline high as we spilled out into the parking lot with the rest of the spectators. It wasn't until I hit the point of veering off into the lot where my truck was parked that I focused on the fact that Tatum had my arm hugged to her chest to keep us from getting separated in the crowd.

"I'm parked this way." I nodded to my lot.

"I'm this way." Tatum nodded in the opposite direction as she slowly released her hold on my arm.

"Well, thanks for the ticket. I had a blast."

Her smile deflated a bit. "Yeah. Sure. You're welcome."

I didn't want to play hard to get. I wanted to ask her to a bar or that same cafe again because I liked being with her. And I was perfectly fine with it being easy. Life was hard enough. Why couldn't something so nostalgic as love and attraction be easy? Did it have to be a game with winners and losers?

"I should walk you to your car."

She shook her head. "No. Don't be ridiculous. It will take you forever to get back to your truck. Totally unnecessary. Oof!" Her body landed against my chest as a group of drunk fans rammed into her.

I hugged her to me and pivoted to put myself between her and the slow-moving group. "You okay?" I peered down at her as she gazed up at me, her arms wrapped around my waist.

Just as I thought about kissing her—as I had already done a gazillion times that day—we were shoved again.

"Sorry, but I have to insist on being ridiculous and walking you to your car."

Tatum didn't argue. In fact, she grinned and nodded several times. When we made it to her Corolla, she pulled off her mittens to unlock her door. "Brr ... It's so cold." She opened the door and turned toward me.

And ...

I kissed her.

It was inevitable. It was the opposite of playing hard to get.

It was perfect.

I didn't really plan it, but once my lips pressed to hers, I knew I would have to make it quick before I lost all sense of control—all sense of pride. But when I went to release her mouth, her hands slid around my neck, pulling me back to her.

Play it cool!

When a woman you are attracted to so very, very much flicks her hot tongue against your lips, asking for permission to taste the inside of your greedy mouth, it's nearly impossible to deny her.

Nearly.

Unless you're an idiot like me who wanted said woman so much you were afraid of looking too desperate and easy and therefore somehow less manly. So I manned up and denied her, pulling us apart.

"Drive home safely."

Bonehead of the Year Award.

I was twenty-two. TWENTY-TWO!

Twenty-two-year-olds didn't say, "Drive home safely." We said, "Your place or mine?" We recklessly drove to a secluded spot, fondling each other the whole way, before screwing like rabbits with our clothes half on half off. I had my whole life ahead of me to be chivalrous and old as fuck saying things like, "Drive home safely."

At twenty-two, a condom should have been the extent of my precautionary concerns.

Tatum rubbed her lips together.

I was *so* close to saying "just kidding" and tossing her in the backseat to be reckless and twenty-two with her right there in the parking lot. But ... I choked.

I choked by holding to my sage advice for her to drive home safely.

"I wouldn't completely be opposed to getting a drink," she said, batting her eyelashes at me, the paint on her face smeared from my hands holding her face to kiss her.

As only purebred boneheads did, I continued to play hard to get or maybe it was just plain old stupid by that point. "I have to work in the morning."

And take my laxative and soak my dentures.

STUPID!

Did I mention it was not even four o'clock?

"O ... kay." Tatum bit her lips together and returned a sharp nod.

"Well, thanks again. See ya around." And I turned and weaved my way back to my truck before I had the chance to say one more stupid word. "What. Is. Wrong. With. YOU?" I hammered my head against the headrest as I gripped my steering wheel.

At the end of our "not date," I still didn't have her phone number or her address. If I wanted to see her again, I'd have to stalk her at open houses.

Good job, Emmett. You're real smooth.

God bless fate.

She was a beautiful angel who looked out for me because five days later, as I headed toward my truck after clocking out on Friday afternoon, I noticed a figure sitting on my tailgate. That figure came into focus the closer I got, and my lucky-as-shit grin painted itself to my face again. Only ... she wasn't grinning as she sat there with her gloved hands gripping the edge of the tailgate, legs swinging back and forth.

"You're an asshole. You know that, right?" I didn't see that greeting coming.

My smile wavered a bit. "Uh ..." I slowed my stride, trudging through the thick mud of her question or maybe accusation. "Did I miss something?"

When I reached five feet from my truck, she hopped off the tailgate and parked her hands on her hips. "Wow! I don't know, Emmett. Did you miss something? Or am I the one missing the fact that I was nothing more than a game to you? A toy for you to play with? Gullible Tatum invites you to a game, so you have your fun and kiss me like you liked me when it was clearly just a kiss off. A fuck off."

Other than her physical features, I wasn't at all sure I knew the little spitfire standing in front of me. The girl I stole from Toby ... Cody ... Dopey was confident and cool. I had no real clue if she was interested in me until she kissed me back after the game. And honestly, I thought I blew it.

On a slight grimace, I scratched my scruffy jaw. "I didn't have your number or address or I would have called."

"Bullshit. You didn't want to call me. You had every chance to ask for my number, and you didn't ask."

I had a holy-crap moment that resurrected my grin

which, from the menacing expression on Tatum's face, didn't seem to sit well with her.

She liked me.

Truly.

Madly.

Maybe even a little angrily liked me.

And she was pissed off that I hadn't made an effort to contact her.

"I like you too." I brushed past her, tossed my backpack into the bed of my truck, and closed the tailgate.

"You don't. And I'm not here to beg you to like me. I just wasn't okay with you playing me like that without giving me the opportunity to have the final word. So listen up, asshole. You're a total—"

I shut her up with my mouth on hers, with my hands fisting her hair, and with my body shoving her against the side of my dirty truck.

I shut her up with my tongue prying open her mouth in spite of her weak resistance.

God ... I loved shutting her up almost as much as I loved listening to her go off about my asshole status. I really wasn't playing hard to get that week. In all honesty, I felt like a fool. It really never occurred to me that she still wanted me to pursue her. Had I known, I would've been booking appointments to see houses that were out of my price range. I would have followed her home and climbed the fire escape after her roommates were asleep, just to kiss her one more time.

When she pushed against my chest, I released her. For a moment, I half expected to feel the palm of her hand slap my face. She looked a little feral, but that might have been because I thoroughly messed up her hair during that epic kiss.

"I sold a house today. A big one." Excitement grew in her voice. "I think my fake blind date should take me for a celebratory drink. Unless ..." she slid her sleeve up an inch and glanced at her watch "...it's too close to your bedtime?"

I opened my mouth to defend my actions, but they really were indefensible. "I have to shower, but I think I can stay awake a few more hours."

"Great! I'll follow you to your house and hang out with your parents while you shower."

My head shook several times. "That's not a good idea. How about we meet at a bar?"

"Why? Do your parents assume it's serious if you bring a girl home?"

"No."

"Then what?"

Removing my baseball hat, I scratched the back of my head. She made me nervous ... and itchy. "Then nothing. Fine. Whatever. You can follow me home and chat it up with my parents if that's what you want."

"Perfect. Thanks for the invite. And I promise I won't tell them that you tried to steal me from another man."

I unlocked my truck and opened the door. "They already know."

"They do? So ... you've told them about me? Which means you like me."

When I turned back toward her, she greeted me with a crooked flirty grin. My focus went straight to her mouth, a mouth that tasted like peppermint Tic Tacs. "You're okay, I suppose. And you came up in conversation when I said I'd already eaten that night we went to the cafe. It was just a brief mention. No big deal."

I changed my mind. Once I knew she was fully on

board with Emmett Lives at Home, playing hard to get felt like a game that I liked after all.

"No big deal, huh?" She did that doglike head tilt again. "So that's how it's going to be?"

"No. That's just how it is."

Something in her eyes shifted. Hell … something in her everything shifted from the moment I walked up and saw her sitting on my tailgate. I got this "all in" vibe that felt exhilarating.

She liked the chase.

She liked the game.

But most importantly, she liked me.

And while we had only been around each other twice before she showed up at my work, I'd thought about her pretty much nonstop for those two weeks, which felt like being with her every day for two weeks. That was the shift in her eyes—that silent admission that she, too, had been thinking about me nonstop for two weeks.

Tatum held her response, biting her lips together. I hopped into my truck and sped off toward home. Ten minutes later, she pulled off the road and followed me down our long dirt lane just outside of city limits where a few farmers still had land. We didn't farm, but my dad liked to hunt. And his business required some extra space and a building separate from the house.

My time had come—sink or swim. We were about to find out just how much Tatum liked me. I thought of Hal and that moment when a girl discovered the family business involved working with the dead.

"Are there animals in the barn?" Tatum asked as we emerged from our vehicles. She brushed her hair away from her face as the wind tangled it.

"Sort of. And it's not really a barn." I gave her a tight

grin and wide eyes as I gestured for her to follow me into the house. The truth sounded better coming from my dad. He had a spiel that made it sound a little less crazy.

"If your parents ever decide to sell this property, they should list it with me."

Just before opening the front door, I glanced back at her. "Duly noted."

Tatum rolled her eyes at my monotone response.

After removing my boots, I headed toward the living room. "Hey, Mom," I said as she glanced up from the sofa with a bowl of apples and peelings on her lap. "This is Tatum. Tatum, this is my mom, Rebecca."

"Nice to meet you, Mrs. Riley." Tatum smiled. "You making a pie?"

"Nice to meet you too. And quite the surprise." My mom gave me a sly grin for a second. "And yes, I'm making apple pies for Charlie's bake sale fundraiser for basketball. Charlie is my youngest, in case Emmett failed to mention he has a younger brother. He had a hard time not being the baby anymore, and he still hasn't gotten over it."

"I forgot to mention my mom is delusional."

Tatum giggled, her animated gaze ping-ponging between my mom and me.

"Where is the twerp?" I shrugged off my Carhartt jacket, tossing it onto the banister to the basement before peeling off my tee shirt.

Tatum's eyes flared, but I pretended not to notice. Mom ignored me because it wasn't unusual for me to be half naked before making my way to the basement to shower.

When Tatum's gaze remained affixed to my chest, I pointed to my abs. "See. They're real. Not painted-on."

Her cheeks turned red as she averted her gaze to the

windows as if she were watching a bird instead of counting my abs.

"Yes. My boy became a man overnight. The growth spurts of all growth spurts. His older brother still looks like a twelve-year-old compared to Emmett. And when Emmett grows out his full beard, it's much thicker than his dad's. I can't for the life of me figure out what I ate differently during my pregnancy with Emmett." Mom chuckles.

"I'm going to shower. Tatum sold a house today, so we're going to celebrate."

"She can help me peel the rest of these apples."

Tatum didn't hesitate. She slipped off her wool coat and pushed up her sleeves. "Let me just wash my hands."

Grinning to myself, I headed downstairs to shower. By the time I finished getting ready, I heard my dad's deep voice from the kitchen. While buttoning my flannel shirt, I poked my head up the stairs just enough to hear them more clearly.

"So you're a realtor?" Dad asked Tatum.

"Yes. I'm not sure it's what I'll do forever, but I like my boss. The money is good. And I've been told I have a knack for selling houses. How about you? What do you do?"

Here we go ...

"I'm a taxidermist. But last year I started offering freeze-drying services, and it's really taken off."

A pause followed. I cringed. Hal's parents prepared dead bodies for funerals and burials ... my dad preserved animals. It started out as a service to hunters and a few of the big sporting goods stores in Kansas City. But then he purchased freeze-drying chambers and started offering that service to pet owners. Who would want to freeze-dry their family dog?

Apparently, a lot of people in Missouri and other states in the Midwest.

"Oh ... freeze-drying?" Tatum asked after clearing her throat.

"You betcha. It's a much better final product. We freeze them first. Then we can thaw them just enough to pose into the desired position ... then it gets put into the top chamber of the freeze-dryer at zero degrees. After that, it gets put in the lower chamber which is a condenser chamber. That's set somewhere between negative fifty-five to negative seventy degrees Fahrenheit. That low pressure draws out the moisture quickly from the ice state to the vapor state. It keeps it from deteriorating and prevents the tissues from shrinking. All the organs, bones, skin ... it all remains intact. It's really quite amazing."

Another pregnant pause.

It wasn't my MO to spring the freeze-drying on my dates so early in a relationship, but Tatum insisted on coming to my house. And honestly, I hadn't had actual relationships beyond a single date and casual sex.

"It's ... fascinating. And ... people ... like pet owners really freeze-dry their pets? And keep them in their house? Uh ... dead?" She asked all the usual questions.

"Absolutely," Dad replied with enthusiasm.

I climbed the stairs to rescue her or maybe to get the quick brush-off as she ran out the door. "Hey. Ready to go?" I grabbed my leather jacket off the back of the dining room chair.

Tatum wore a cautious smile as she finished peeling the last apple in the bowl my mom gave her. "Yeah. Just let me wash my hands and put on my jacket."

"Thanks for your help, Tatum. I hope we get to see you again." Mom's code for "if my son doesn't blow it."

"Anytime. It was nice meeting both of you." She dried her hands, and I helped her put on her jacket, which earned me an approving smile from my mom.

"I'll drive since you'll be the one celebrating." I opened the passenger's door to my truck.

Tatum inspected the mud caked on the running board of my truck before grabbing the handle and landing in the seat—a graceful deer hopping over a fence—without touching the running board. "And why aren't you celebrating with me?" She fastened her seat belt.

I shrugged. "Not much of a drinker." Before she could respond, I shut the door.

We made it several miles down the road with my country music station on the radio before Tatum broached the topic, the elephant in the truck. "So ... your dad freeze-dries animals. That was unexpected."

My mouth twitched on one side, but my gaze remained on the road before us.

"My dad drives a truck for Waste Management. He has for over thirty years. And my mom teaches music lessons out of their home. Mainly flute and piano. She's also a crossing guard on Walnut Street, north of the elementary school. Someone has to pick up the trash. Right? And help kids cross the street?"

It was like she forgot who she was talking to—the guy who graduated with straight A's but didn't go to college. I worked for my brother, running heavy equipment because ... someone had to clean up chemical spills and remove trees after storms. Right?

"My best friend's parents work at Clayburn's Funeral Home. He's the director, and she puts makeup on dead bodies. If everyone wanted or had the same job, the world wouldn't function. Can you imagine your dog dying and having to have it cremated or burying it in the backyard instead of being able to freeze it and set it by your front door to scare the crap out of everyone who came to visit?"

After a long pause, Tatum giggled, pressing her hand to her mouth to hide her grin.

"I'm going to freeze-dry my parents when they die. Prop their old asses on a love seat so it doesn't feel like they're dead," I said without missing a beat.

Tatum's giggle exploded into a full-on laugh. "Oh my god! That's terrible."

"It would save me and my brothers time. We wouldn't have to visit them at the cemetery. Spend money on flowers. They could sit in the front row at their own funerals. We could wrap lights around them for Christmas. Hide Easter eggs around them. Of course we'd have to keep the love seat away from the window and direct sunlight. And moisture … and bugs. Nothing a little Borax sprinkled around them won't remedy."

"Stop!" Tatum leaned forward, holding her stomach as she fought to catch her breath. She blotted the corners of her eyes. I'd brought her to tears from laughter, and that made my chest fill with pride.

I liked her laughter and her smile.

I liked how right my world felt in her presence.

"You're so morbid."

"It's an inherited trait," I replied.

"Oh …" She hummed on a long sigh. "I can't remember the last time I laughed that much."

I couldn't remember the last time another human being made me feel so enraptured.

And that feeling? It never faded.

CHAPTER FIVE

NOW

"Emmett?"

I glance up at Tatum. "Um ... yeah. My dad's officially retiring. I'm sure he'll keep the equipment so we can freeze-dry him and Mom."

Tatum doesn't wince. Not even a blink. She knows why I said it, but it no longer makes her laugh. I no longer make her smile. That feels like its own death I would grieve for eternity. Her dad still drives for Waste Management. He'll drive for them until he can no longer physically drive. And her mom still teaches piano and flute lessons in spite of her arthritis. But they did take off the entire month of February to stay with Tatum's sister in Florida. That was her dad's idea of partially retiring—saving his vacation to use all at once each year.

I know everything about her family because I bled Lucy for every detail. And I like to believe she asks our daughter for details about my family—and maybe even me.

Pretending Tatum still loves me in some small way makes my life a little less awful.

"So are you serious? About wanting the house?" She pushes off the kitchen counter and makes her way into the living room, taking a seat on the cotton side chair that was not made for normal sized people or giants like myself. But my wife (she will always be my wife to me) is still a tiny dancer.

"Of course." I lean forward on the sofa, resting my forearms on my knees.

"Do you want to discuss it with Lucy first?"

"Why? Is it her idea to sell it or yours?"

"Both. We've discussed it, and we agree it might help."

"I'm confused. Help? Who? Does she need help?"

Tatum picks at nonexistent lint on the arm of the chair. "That's the thing ... I think she should be done with therapy by now. And I can't help but wonder if living in this house is the last thing holding her back from completely moving on."

I clear my throat. "Did she say that?"

"No."

"Did her therapist say that?"

Tatum rolls her eyes. "Dr. Kane never says anything to me. Why would she? I think she likes all the money she's getting just to chat with Lucy. I don't think there's much actual therapy taking place anymore. But Lucy feels she's not ready, and she won't say why exactly, so the only thing that makes sense is the house."

"I'll talk with her."

"Fine, Emmett. You talk with her. I don't know what you say to her every time you two have your little *talks*, but clearly you have more influence over her than I do." Tatum's voice holds a world of resentment. She got custody of Lucy. They spend so much time together, but Tatum doesn't have the same bond that I have with Lucy. And she doesn't understand that it's not a bond that she should envy.

"I think the influence is time." I give her a sad smile. "I don't get to see her that often, which means I don't have as many opportunities to butt heads with her. I get to be her friend more than her dad. You have to balance the friend role with the mom, disciplinarian, role."

Tatum slides her gaze to the front window, dragging her teeth over her lower lip a few times. "You know … she's seventeen now. She's driving. She's becoming a responsible young woman. I think she should start making some of her own choices when it comes to you." When her gaze returns to me, it's softer.

"What do you mean?"

"I mean … if she wants to see you more often, then I think she's old enough to make that decision. It's not like she needs a babysitter anymore. I don't have to worry as much about …" Her forehead tenses.

I feel a chill in the room from her words—specifically the words she stops short of saying. Then I glance up to one of the bookshelves and see a silver framed photo of a little boy with a big cookie in his hand and chocolate smeared on his exuberant grin. Blue eyes like mine that will never shine for me again. Full lips like hers that will never offer me fish kisses.

The big hugs.

The shrill of excitement in his voice.

The tickle in my tummy from his contagious giggles.

The perfect fit of his tiny hand in mine.

"You know," I say as if the wind just got knocked out of me, "I can meet Lucy's boyfriend another time." Standing on heavy legs, I turn to leave.

"I think it's time for you too."

I glance over my shoulder as Tatum stands, making a quick glance at the photo before letting her attention refocus on me.

"Time for me?" I don't know what she means because my mind has opened that door again, and now my chest hurts which makes it hard to breathe.

"Time to forgive yourself," she says just above a whisper.

Her suggestion doesn't sit well with me. I don't have to forgive myself. I have no regrets—at least not for the things I said. I did what *she* wanted me to do.

"Do you? Do you forgive me?" I ask. I've never asked for her forgiveness, but now I'm curious.

In a blink, her jaw tightens and emotion floods her eyes, turning them red and watery. The rest of her body follows ... going rigid. Her cheeks bloom in shades of pink, but not like the blush she used to get when I made her fall in love with me. No. This is anger and pain.

This is what it looks like when the love has died and been replaced with a toxic pain that will linger forever like a slow poisoning of one's soul.

I did that to her ... but she asked me to do it.

"Tell Lucy I'll meet him next time," I murmur on my way to the front door.

"You never asked," Tatum says, her words cracking on their way out of her mouth.

I keep my back to her to avoid looking into her eyes and seeing the hollow place where the love used to reside. "Never asked what?"

"You never asked me to forgive you. Never ... not once have you uttered the words."

"Because it's not for me. It's for you." I shut the door

behind me and bolt to my truck before I lose my shit in front of her or even worse ... in front of Lucy.

***

THEN

WE GOT THAT CELEBRATORY DRINK.

I discovered that Tatum drank wine to fit in, but her alcoholic beverage of choice was wine coolers. She discovered that my favorite beer was root beer. Specifically A&W, but I could do an off-brand in a pinch.

I drove her slightly inebriated self to her apartment later that night. In return, I got a kiss. The next day, my dad followed me to her place to drop off her car. That night, she was waiting by my truck again when I clocked out.

Another kiss.

I wanted all the kisses.

All the dates.

I wasn't sure what it was like to have an actual girlfriend since I'd never had one, but I felt certain it involved a different set of rules or standards. The one-night-stand part was easy. There seemed to be this unspoken look that happened before clothes were discarded and condoms were pulled from purses or wallets. If you both mutually needed sex, there was nothing wrong with scratching an itch and moving on.

Tatum evoked new feelings. Sure, I wanted to have sex with her, but then what? So while I worked out the "then what" question in my mind, I spent weeks ending our dates by midnight and finding every excuse in the book to not go up to her apartment or invite her into my house—well, my parents' basement. It wasn't that I needed to wait until marriage to have sex with her, but I wanted her to know it meant something, and I felt the best way to show her that was to wait for sex.

Said no twenty-two-year-old man ever!

"My roommates are gone this weekend," she casually said as we talked on the phone late on a Thursday night.

"Yeah? Where are they going?"

"Does it matter?" She laughed.

"Just making conversation," I said, staring at my bedroom ceiling as I twisted the phone cord around my finger. I had the only corded phone in the house.

"I know, Emmett. You're a great conversationalist."

"Sounds like sarcasm?"

She laughed. "I'm not trying to be sarcastic. I'm just ..."

"Just ... what?"

"Can I ask you something? And I don't care what the answer is. Really. I won't tell anyone. And it doesn't affect the way I feel about you."

"Sounds serious." I paused my fiddling with the phone cord and rolled onto my side with my head propped on my arm.

"It's not really serious, just awkward. Like I'm afraid you're going to feel embarrassed that I'm asking you this."

"Jeez, Tatum. Just ask me. Why would I get upset?"

"Fine ... are you ..."

"Am I?"

"Are you a virgin?" she asked just above a whisper, which made me wonder if she was in the same room as her roommates who were *not* out of town yet.

"What?" I held the phone away from my ear and stared at it as if I hadn't heard her correctly, or it got messed up through the phone like a bad game of Telephone.

"It's fine if you are."

"I'm not!" That came out a little harsher than I intended.

"Okay. But it's okay if you are."

"But. I'm. Not!"

"Okay. Okay. I just had to ask."

"Do I look like a virgin?" I sat up in bed, propelled by adrenaline.

"Well…" she chuckled "…I don't think virgins have a look. But you said last week that you've never had a girl-friend. And you read a lot of non-fiction books. And you live with your parents. So if one *were* to stereotype a virgin, you'd kinda fit."

"Jesus, Tatum. Thanks a lot."

"See. I knew you'd get upset."

"I'm not upset. I'm …"

I wasn't sure what I was at the moment.

Offended?

Shocked?

Emasculated?

Definitely confused.

"Emmett … it's also because you haven't … well … you know."

"No. I don't know."

She blew out a long sigh. "You end our dates with a kiss. And it's been a month. And I know that everyone has a different timeline for things like sex, but I thought you were really attracted to me. But every date is a kiss goodnight. Every time I invite you to my apartment, you turn me down. So I'm sorry, but it's starting to feel like maybe you're saving yourself for marriage, and you just don't have the nerve to tell me yet. And again … if that's the case, I don't care. I just want to know so I don't come across as some hussy begging for sex with my boyfriend. I mean … if you're

... you know ... if you are in fact my boyfriend. Cause it feels like you are."

I couldn't have felt more blindsided had she literally ran me over with her car. God ... the embarrassment. Where did I go wrong? How did I misread her cues?

Click.

I hung up the phone. It wasn't a great move, but I had nothing to say, so what other choice did I have? Things were really messed-up. I needed to fix them. Pacing the old shag carpet in our basement for the better part of the night, I waited for her to call back in case she had more to say.

She did not.

The next morning, I called in sick to work, a risky move given the fact that my boss was my brother, and he would likely follow up with Mom on my condition. What was I supposed to say? I couldn't work because I had a bad case of Mistaken Virginity? My parents were none the wiser since I packed a lunch as if I were going to work, donned my usual work clothes—old jeans and a Carhartt sweatshirt—and headed off to work on time.

Instead of work, I grabbed breakfast at the café then drove around town before settling on a new construction house with Tatum's name on the real estate sign and called the number.

"Hi. Is there any way I can get a tour of the house for sale at 219 SW 3rd Street?" I asked some woman named Susan who answered the phone at the real estate office. If I'd have called Tatum, there was a chance she would not have answered me.

Thirty minutes later, she was at the house. I hopped out of my truck parked across the street and made my way to the door as she inspected me through narrowed eyes just as she got the key out of the lockbox. "Let me guess ... you're

Richard Head? No wonder my boss told me to proceed with caution and bring my pepper spray." She rolled her eyes as she unlocked the door. "So you're suddenly in the market for a new house? A three-hundred-and-fifty-thousand-dollar house?"

"No. I just didn't like the way our call ended last night." I followed her into the empty house. It smelled of new everything—a mix of paint and other odd chemical odors.

"Things ended with you acting really weird about your virginity then hanging up on me." She turned, slipping off her wool coat before leaning against a round white pillar at the entrance to the great room. "You *hung up on me.*" She crossed her arms over her chest which pulled down the V-neck to her cream sweater that looked incredibly sexy with her black mini skirt, opaque tights, and knee-high boots.

Red lipstick.

Tawny hair pulled into a low sophisticated ponytail.

Cheeks kissed pink from the cold wind outside that day.

"You implied I'm a nerd. A virgin nerd. What did you want me to do?"

"I *asked* if you're a virgin. I never said the word 'nerd,' and you could have just said no. Or yes. Because either way, I don't care. I'd be flattered to be your first."

I fisted my hands. "Well, you're not my first, so don't be so quick to feel flattered. And for that matter, you're not my second or third or—"

"Jeez! Okay. You're not a virgin. I get it. You have lots of sex with lots of women. Good for you. But how was I supposed to know that when I *haven't* been one of those women?"

"Maybe I just wanted to wait until you knew I didn't want you to just be another woman. Maybe I wanted to make sure you knew ..." I ran my hands through my hair, feeling stupid and nothing short of a train wreck of jumbled thoughts.

"Knew what, Emmett?" she whispered.

I lifted my gaze from the floor to meet hers as I dropped my hands from my head in defeat. "I wanted you to know that you matter. And that sex wasn't the goal ... wasn't my endgame with you."

A slow grin crept up her face. "Did you take off work today just to tell me this?"

I nodded even though I didn't exactly "take off" work—called in because I was a lovesick fool might have been a more accurate description.

Tatum pushed off the pillar and sauntered toward me, resting her hands on my chest, head angled back to look up at me. "Can we start over?"

My eyes narrowed.

She wet her lips. "Our conversation last night. It started with me telling you in the most suggestive way possible that my roommates will be out of town this weekend. In fact, they've already left. Maybe you can pack a bag and stay over this weekend?"

I liked the way she hit the reset button, but it didn't change the fact that I was still bothered by the virgin conversation. As much as I needed to let it go and forget that she ever asked me, I couldn't do it.

Taking a step back to remove her hands from my chest, I shrugged off my hoodie, leaving me in a white Nike tee.

"What are you doing?" she asked, eyeing me carefully.

With one swift move, I removed my T-shirt and tossed it onto the wood floor next to my sweatshirt.

"Emmett ..." Tatum said with a nervous timbre to her voice.

I slid my hand along her jaw and cupped it while

stealing her breath with a hard kiss. Her hands grabbed my arms to steady herself.

Wanting her so completely in that very moment wasn't planned.

Like we weren't planned.

"Emmett ..." She pulled away just enough to make eye contact as we exchanged labored breaths from that kiss. The look on her face conveyed concern and a healthy respect for common sense. I returned the same look.

But ...

Our hands had other ideas as we kissed again.

As I pulled her sweater over her head and shoved her bra straps down her arms so I could see her breasts—so I could taste them.

As her fingers curled into my hair while her back arched.

As she kicked and wiggled out of her boots, and I removed her tights.

As she gathered her skirt in her hands, pulling it up to her waist, and I slid her panties down her legs.

"Emmett ..."

Emmett ... Emmett ... Emmett ...

She chanted my name, making me feel like a god, as I backed her into the shiny pillar.

"I'm not a virgin," I said as I slid my fingers between her legs, reveling in the way her eyelids moved in slow heavy blinks.

She tried to speak, but the only thing that fell from her lips were sharp breaths.

We kissed until we couldn't hold back any longer. I pushed inside of her, gripping the back of her legs. It wasn't slow and beautiful—maybe someday we'd try that.

It was hard and fast.

Desperate.

Uncontrolled.

It was the best sex—in my humble opinion.

"Don't ... stop ..." she begged.

Stopping wasn't my intention, but after a long month of *not* doing this with her made it impossible to slow down.

Then ...

I was done. Efficient Emmett. However, I tried to keep going for her. I didn't say the words, "Okay, but only because I love you and really want to worship you for eternity," but I thought them.

At twenty-two, I was still a bit of a novice at sex and definitely in the habit of looking out for myself in the pleasure department. Unfortunately, keeping pace at fifty-five miles per hour with a deflating tire wasn't the easiest thing, so I eased her to the floor on her wobbly legs, dropped to my knees, and did "really good" things to her.

Her words. "Emmett, what are you ... oh my god ... yes, yes, yes!"

Low moan ...

Her orgasm declaration. "Th-that's good ... *really good* ..."

The biggest grin captured my lips before I even removed said lips from between her legs.

From that moment on, we were inseparable.

And reckless.

We'd meet over my lunch breaks and have sex in my truck.

Sometimes I'd run to get fuel and take the long way via whatever house was on the market, vacant, and that Tatum had access to the lockbox. We christened many kitchen islands for new, unsuspecting homeowners. Tatum occasionally had rug burns on her back from large unfurnished rooms—basically we used the first surface we could get to before our clothes were completely off and my dick was inside of her.

Our living situations—me at home and her with room-mates—made our middle of the day sex dates not only exhil-arating but necessary.

I loved new love. New lust. New everything with Tatum.

I even loved the day it came to an end and sent us on a new path. Tatum ... she wasn't as fond of the way our routine ended that day.

"Skirt ..." I sucked at her neck while my hands fought with the belt to her pants. "It's so much easier to fuck you in a skirt. What's up with the stupid pants?"

She giggled pushing my tee over my head as we paused our frantic motions just long enough to allow her to get it over my head. That day we were taking a bigger risk. Tech-nically, the house was no longer on the market, but Tatum had access to let the movers in ... which she had done that morning. So we had a partially furnished house in which to fuck about, and the owners weren't scheduled to arrive until the following week.

By the time she kicked off her shoes and wiggled her way out of her pants, her underwear was partially ripped from my impatience. And we had a bed. No bedding, but we had a mattress and box springs that we were about to break in quite thoroughly.

Was it wrong to have sex on the clock? In a house that wasn't ours? In a bed that wasn't ours?

Probably.

Was there something to be said for the perks of being young and dumb?

Absolutely.

We wouldn't remember all the times we stopped at a red light, paid our bills on time, or followed the rules of society to a T. However, we would *forever* remember the time we got caught.

I wondered how long he watched us ... her boss.

CHAPTER SIX

NOW

Seeing Tatum again shook me. The memories. Her moving announcement. It's taken me a few days to find that breath again and resume the monotony that is now my life.

"We really must stop meeting like this," New Neighbor Nina the Nurse says to me as we reach our mailboxes at the same time.

I chuckle. "I'm not sure why I even check it. Maybe just to empty the junk from it. I pay all of my bills online now. I can't remember the last time I received an invitation to a wedding. And even Christmas cards seem to show up in my inbox instead of my mailbox." I hold up my pile of advertisements and credit card offers as if to say, "See what I mean?"

"Not me." Nina pulls an envelope out of her mailbox and opens it. "I've been expecting my swatches." She shows me the pieces of material. "I'm getting new furniture, but I'm ordering it online. What do you think?"

They're all too flowery for my taste, but instead of

saying that, I smile and shrug. "I think you shouldn't care what I think because I'm a guy with no sense of style."

"Fine. I guess I'll make the decision on my own. It's my retirement gift to myself."

I failed to tell Lucy that my new neighbor is sixty-eight and has had a knee and hip replacement. It's not that I'm against older women (even if she's only a few years younger than my mom) or joint replacements. After all, Tatum is older than me. It's just that I'm not interested in anyone who isn't my wife.

Yes, I realize I don't technically have a wife anymore.

"I'm envious of you. I hope I can retire before I'm seventy. Anyway … I'll see ya around."

"I'm going out for pasta," she says before I have a chance to take more than two steps.

I glance back at her.

"If you like pasta, I wouldn't mind the company. Not a date, of course. I'm clearly out of your league. I just think life's too short to eat alone all the time."

"I'm a big fan of pasta. Give me twenty minutes to shower?"

"I'll drive. I don't think I could get into that truck of yours."

"Fair enough. See you in a bit."

Nina proves to have excellent taste in restaurants. And expensive taste. I've only been here once before, on my tenth wedding anniversary with Tatum. We made it to twelve.

I thought we would make it to eternity.

"So how's that daughter of yours?" Nina asks as I pretend to like the wine she insisted on ordering for us.

"Lucy is good. She has a boyfriend. I'm not sure how I feel about that."

"You said she's seventeen?"

I nod, shoving bread down to erase the bitter taste of the wine.

"Then you can't be surprised. She's a young woman."

"She's my baby girl." I shake my head.

Nina chuckles. "And have you met this young man?"

"I have not." A familiar figure snags my attention over Nina's shoulder.

A couple is seated at the table behind her. It's Tatum and who I assume must be Josh. As he pushes in her chair, her gaze lifts and meets mine. The unexpectedness pauses her motions, forcing Josh to look in my direction as well before taking his seat behind Nina.

Nina twists around to follow my gaze. "Do you know them?" She returns her attention to me. Now it's just awkward.

"Hi," I say to Tatum, giving her date a stiff smile. Another man with my wife (yes, I know, I know ... she's not my wife), pushing her chair in and getting ready to eat at a fancy restaurant with her, is a unique kind of torture—so is the red blouse she's wearing with her tight gray skirt and red heels. Hair down. Makeup accenting her eyes, but not over-done. And I can smell lavender. I can smell her, and the familiarity stings. For twelve years I nestled my nose into her hair as I held her in our bed. I know how she sighs and slides her foot down my calf to run her toe along my instep. The ghost of her touch still molded to me.

"Hi." Tatum looks up at Josh. "Um ..." Her smile falters. "Josh this is Emmett. Emmett ... Josh."

I return a manly chin lift. "Josh."

"Nice to meet you, Emmett. Lucy talks about you all the time." He takes two steps to shake my hand, which forces me to stand.

"She's mentioned you as well." I return a firm handshake.

And your incessant hand washing.

"Oh ... this is Nina."

"Hi, Nina." Josh nods politely at her.

"And that's Tatum, my um ..."

Wife! She's my wife!

"Oh, Lucy's mom. It's nice to meet you. Wow, you look just like her. Emmett showed me a picture of her. She's a beautiful girl."

Neither one of the women stand. They share a greeting from their chairs—Tatum staring ahead at us and Nina twisted in her chair.

"Thank you. That's very kind of you to say." Tatum offers a reserved smile.

I see the question on her face. Am I on a date with this much older woman? Nina doesn't look sixty-eight. Maybe in her fifties. I'm pretty sure she colors her blond hair to keep it more blond than gray. She might have a new hip and knee, but she's in good shape. And she's in a pretty dress that doesn't look like a frock. Did I mention she drives a nice BMW?

"Enjoy your dinner. It was nice meeting both of you." Josh ends the idle chitchat and takes a seat with his back to us, leaving me with a clear view of Tatum.

Our food arrives and I focus on eating as quickly as possible. Spending the evening watching Tatum smile at Josh, laugh at things he says, and occasionally meeting my gaze only to have it erase all the joy from her face? No thank you.

"Did it end badly?" Nina asks in a hushed tone.

How do I answer that? I'm not sure badly is the right word. It's not exactly the wrong word either. Maybe just not the best word. I never talk about my divorce, the end of my marriage. Maybe it's my delusional mind waiting to wake up and discover that it's all been a bad dream.

Something about Nina's tone and the kindness in her light blue eyes makes me breathe the truth. "It ended tragically."

With concern etched into her forehead, Nina nods slowly. "I'm sorry to hear that. I sensed tension between the two of you, but it didn't feel like enemies. It felt different. That's why I asked. I hope I haven't upset you or dug up old feelings."

The feelings aren't old. They're constant and as fresh— as raw—as the day it happened. The "it" that I never speak about. And yet the words tumble from my mouth as soon as Tatum starts talking to the waitress.

"We had a son. He died."

Then we died.

Nina's hand flies to her mouth, pressing her napkin to it. Her eyes fill with tears.

I can't believe I just said that to her. In reality, I don't think I *did* say it to her. I said it to Tatum when I knew she wasn't looking at me, when I knew she was too distracted to overhear me.

We had a son, Tatum. He died. WE didn't have to die. I did what you asked me to do. Why can't you see that?

"Emmett ..."

I shake my head. "Don't feel bad. I didn't have to tell you. I'm not sure why I said it." I force a smile. "You're just easy to talk to, I guess."

"Have you talked to anyone about it? Like a therapist?"

"No. Lucy sees a therapist. Tatum did for a while too."

"But not you?"

I shake my head.

Nina gives me a motherly, disapproving frown.

"Do you want dessert?" I end the conversation with a swift subject change. Saying anything at all has been a tiny breakthrough for me, but that's as far as I can go tonight.

"I'm good, thanks." As soon as the waiter sets the check on the table, she grabs it just as I go to reach for it. "I invited you to dinner. I'm not letting you pay."

"Nina—"

"Don't 'Nina' me." She winks before glancing into her open handbag and retrieving two fifty-dollar bills.

When the waiter returns, she tells him to keep the change and pushes her chair back. I jump up and help her with her raincoat, not because it's a date, just because I do have a few gentlemanly qualities that my mom instilled in me.

"Oh, sorry." Josh pushes his chair back, nudging Nina. "Just need to use the men's room. I should have paid better attention to my surroundings."

"You're fine, dear," Nina assures him. "I need to use the ladies' room as well. Maybe you can show me the way?"

"Of course." Josh nods toward the back of the restaurant, leaving me alone with Tatum.

She sips her wine, eyeing me cautiously as I take a seat in Josh's chair.

"You look wonderful tonight."

A little pink stains her cheeks at my comment. Is she blushing? Is she angry that I'm here?

"Thank you. Nina seems ... nice." There it is again, that question she's dying to ask. Am I dating someone close to my mom's age?

"So does Josh."

"He's a doctor." Her comment feels like a slap in my face. I don't think she intends for it to come across that way, but it does. Josh is a doctor. Josh makes lots of money. Josh is responsible.

He's all the things she thinks I'm not. Well, she's right. I'm not a doctor. But I make okay money. And her perception of my level of responsibility is tainted by things she doesn't know.

"Yeah, Lucy told me he's a doctor. And clean. She said he washes his hands a lot. I told her that's good."

We haven't seen each other or talked beyond quick texts about Lucy in over nine months, yet here we are face-to-face for the second time in less than a week. I'd hoped seeing her would bring me closer to my own closure, but it only makes me miss what I had so much more. I still love this woman as much as I did the day I married her.

"He adores Lucy."

"He should," I reply in the most protective way.

Rubbing her lips together, she drums her fingers on the table while her other hand cups the stem of her wine glass. "Lucy was disappointed that you left before Ashton arrived last Saturday."

"I know. I called her Sunday to apologize."

"I felt like you left because of me. In fact, that's what she asked me. She wanted to know what I did or said to make you leave. I got this crazy lecture from her about being nicer to you. As if I've been anything but nice." Tatum holds an expression of shock and guiltless innocence. "So if you felt like I was running you off, then I'm sorry."

My tongue starts to swell from biting it so hard. She's sorry for running me off, but she's okay with divorcing me for doing exactly what she made me promise to do. Oh, the irony.

"I'm fine." I shrug it off.

"You're always fine." She bristles as if my being fine is a bad thing.

For the record, someone had to be fine or at least play the part. Tatum was not fine. Lucy was on the verge of being traumatized for life. I'm still not sure if she will ever be okay.

But if Tatum could see me the way she used to see me, if she would just open her eyes, she'd see that I'm not fine. I never was fine. She'd see that my date tonight is a neighbor, a friend, not a romantic interest. Not her replacement. She'd take one look at me and drown in the hollowness that is my fucking soul at the moment.

There's nothing more to say. We've hit this wall too many times to count. She baits me, and I want so badly to tell her everything. But I don't. I can't. It's the promise I will never break. It's the secret I will take to my grave.

I stand, knowing Josh and Nina will return soon. A smile finds its way to my lips. It's genuine. Everything I feel and have ever felt for this woman is real and unwavering. "I see the way you look at him and the way he looks at you. I remember what that felt like." I take a step forward and her body stiffens. Her lower lip quivers a bit, and she bites it. I know she's holding her breath, waiting for me to leave. I rest my finger under her chin, forcing her to look at me. "You were never really mine."

Her eyes gloss over with unshed emotion, but I walk away before she has the chance to blink. If she blinks, I will not be able to leave without catching every tear. I don't think Josh wants to emerge from the men's room seeing me touch the woman he seems to like. Maybe love. I don't know if he loves her. It's nearly impossible to not love her. But he can't love her like I do, and that sucks for him. And that sucks for her. She might make it her life's mission to hate me, but she'll fail because the only thing she hates is her love for me.

We made it twelve years. Every day I felt like a thief on the run. I stole the girl—her heart, her babies, her hand in marriage.

CHAPTER SEVEN

THEN

TATUM'S BOSS dropped by the house to let someone in to measure for window coverings. His subtle throat clearing stopped our motions.

Our naked-on-someone-else's-mattress motions.

When I glanced over my shoulder, he stared at me with a blank, almost bored expression, shoulder casually pressed against the doorframe like he'd been watching for quite some time.

"Shit! Ryan! Oh my god!" Tatum hugged her body to mine, using me as a shield so her boss didn't see her naked.

"I think it goes without saying, but I'll say it anyway. You no longer have a job. Now get dressed and see yourselves out right this minute."

We were over. I knew it. Fate landed its boot right in my ass, reminding me that I can't steal the girl and get away with it. I'd like to say I didn't think about losing access to fifty-yard-line Chiefs tickets, but I did. I couldn't help it.

When Ryan continued to stare at my naked backside

hiding Tatum, I narrowed my eyes. "You can fire her, but you sure as hell don't get to see her naked. So fuck off while we get dressed." It was as if I had to make sure she had no chance of salvaging her job (or the Chiefs tickets). If his knee-jerk reaction of firing her might have had a chance of being overturned, I obliterated it.

Ryan turned and sauntered down the hall toward the stairs. When I returned my attention to Tatum hidden under me, she shoved my chest and flew out of the bed, plucking her clothes off the floor and donning them in record time.

"Tatum ..."

She shook her head, chin tipped toward her chest, trembling fingers buttoning her blouse.

"I'm sorry."

She continued to shake her head. "Don't say anything unless you're going to make things right. Can you do that?" Her head snapped up. "Can you tell me what I'm supposed to do now? I have rent. Car insurance. I'm screwed."

"You could ..." I paused, not really knowing what I wanted to say to her.

"I could what, Emmett? Move in with you?" She grunted a laugh. "With your parents? With my parents? I'm sure they'll be super welcoming after they find out why I was fired. And even if they let me move back in with them, I don't want to do that. So now I have to find another job, and there's no way I'll find one that pays as much as I'm making now ... *was* making."

I buttoned and zipped my jeans. "I have money in savings. A lot actually. It's one of the perks of working full-time and living at home."

"I don't want your charity."

"That's not what I'm saying." I stepped toward her and helped her with her shirt.

She batted away my hands. I frowned. "The buttons are crooked."

On a heavy sigh that felt like the verge of a total emotional breakdown, she tugged at the buttons. I gently pushed her hands away and fixed her shirt.

"You said you wanted to travel. You said you've never been outside of the Midwest. My parents have an RV. They never use it. I say we just go. Take six months ... maybe longer ... and we drive. We see. We live. And we figure shit out later—when we're ready to come back home."

Her rich brown gaze shifted to me. "You can't be serious? You still have a job. And who just packs up and leaves without any plans for where they're going or what they're doing?"

I framed her face with my hands. "We do."

She blinked and blinked.

"Tell me to take a hike. Tell me you were never really mine. Or ... say yes."

I loved her. I loved being young and dumb with her. I loved that we had our whole lives ahead of us. And I loved that everything I felt about her and life with her in it started with those two words ... *I love*.

A few more blinks later, she whispered, "We drive."

I smiled. "We see."

She grinned. "We live."

I nodded. "And we figure shit out later."

Indecision, fear, and exhilaration played along her face.

"Say yes, Tatum. Just fucking say yes." I leaned forward until our noses touched.

As soon as I closed my eyes, she whispered, "Yes."

CHAPTER EIGHT

NOW

It's Saturday. My Lucy day.

Again, she's making me wait for her.

"Finally," I whisper as the front door opens, but it's not her.

Tatum shuffles her flip-flop clad feet toward my truck, a light breeze ruffling the skirt to her strapless sundress.

Slender shoulders with perfect posture.

Flawless skin bronzed by long summer days.

It's hard to believe she said yes to getting into an RV with me and taking off to destinations unknown. It's hard to believe the graceful dancer fell for the guy in dirty work boots who lived with his parents. It's even harder to believe I lost her.

I climb out of my truck and shut the door behind me. "Good morning."

Tatum works for a smile that looks amicable at best. "Morning." She fiddles with her watch. "What's your situation? Do you need to sell your house before you can buy me out of this one? Because I'd like to close on our house in two weeks." She presses her lips together for a beat. "Lucy's and my house."

Good thing she clarified that. I might have thought she was offering to take me back. The urge to roll my eyes at her nervous chattering nearly wins, but I control it.

"Unless you've changed your mind. I really think you should talk to Lucy about it first. And I do have a potential buyer if you don't want it."

When I don't answer, she clears her throat. I've been staring at her. All of her.

"Don't look at me like that," she whispers as her gaze cuts to her feet.

"Like what?"

"Like we're still married."

I laugh in spite of the pain in my chest. "Is that such a bad look?" Sidestepping her, I head toward the house to find Lucy. Her bedroom door is shut, and I knock twice.

"Come in," she says.

"What are you doing?"

Lucy turns away from her window. I know what she was doing ... watching me talk to Tatum.

"I've wondered where this was at." I pick up my book from her dresser. One of my amazing facts books. "This one has some of my favorites. A strawberry is not a berry, but an orange is. And speaking of oranges, Bobby Leach went over Niagara Falls in a barrel and survived, but he later slipped on an orange peel and died as a result."

"Mom said she was drawn to your nerdy side as much as your 'handsome side,' which I think she means sexy but doesn't want to say that to me. She said you're always the life of a party with your random facts."

My smile grows just knowing that Tatum talks to Lucy

about me in a positive way. I miss wooing my wife with randomness and vocabulary like *Lachanophobia*—fear of vegetables. I miss the way she'd smile at parties when I geeked out. I've always known she liked my nerdy side. And I always liked the way it made her giggle and shake her head. I used to convince myself that she was thinking, "How did I get so lucky?"

But ... maybe that was just my mantra for her.

"While my friends played video games, I read Encyclopedia Britannica. I asked for the whole set for Christmas when I was twelve."

"Oh my god." Lucy laughs like her mom used to laugh at me.

"Do you miss her?" Her humor fades.

My forehead tenses as I scratch the back of my neck. "Who?"

"Mom."

"Lucy, I miss our family. I miss your brother. I miss a lot of things. But it changes nothing. Life goes on. I'm good. Are you?"

She shrugs one shoulder. "I guess."

"Your mom thinks moving will help you. She thinks you've hit a roadblock, some final obstacle in therapy, and that moving out of this house will help."

"I know," Lucy murmurs from her window seat.

"I'm thinking of buying the house."

"I know."

"Are you okay with that?"

Another half shrug. "Why do you want to live here?"

"For all the reasons your mom doesn't want to live here. The memories."

She grunts. "Memories. Why would you want the memories of this house?"

"Because most of them are the best memories of my life."

Her gaze lifts to meet mine. "And the ones that aren't?"

"I need those too. I won't forget him. I don't want to forget him. He's here. And I know that's precisely the reason your mom needs to leave it all behind, but for me, it's why I can't let anyone else live here."

"He's not here. He's in a casket six feet under the ground two miles from here."

I nod slowly, fisting my hands and cracking my knuckles a few times. "That's just his body." I survey the room slowly. "His soul is still here. I feel it. I feel the memories, his little giggle, his high-pitched scream when I'd tickle his belly. It's very real to me, still. Always ..."

Her eyes fill with tears that she quickly blinks away. "Doesn't that hurt? Doesn't that keep you from moving forward?"

"Children are anchors no matter where you are in life. We have children to make memories. And we have to take the bad with the good. When you're married with a family of your own, I will still look at those stairs..." I nod out her doorway toward the stairs "...and remember the first time you understood the idea of Santa Claus and flew down them to see if he'd brought you gifts and taken the cookies and milk you left out for him. I will welcome every new day and love all the new memories we make, but I don't want to forget how we got here. Even if parts of the journey have been really painful."

Lucy remains silent for a few moments before standing and grabbing her purse. "Do you think Mom wants to forget him?"

I flinch. "No. I think she just wants to forget why he's not here the way he used to be here. I think she can no longer see those Christmas morning memories the way I do. And that's okay. Everyone handles loss differently. But if my living here is going to be a roadblock for you, then I'll let her sell it."

Stopping at the doorway, she glances up at me. "My roadblock isn't this house."

With a single nod, I let her know she doesn't need to say anymore.

"You should have the house," she says, leading the way down the stairs where Tatum's waiting at the bottom.

"Have a fun day." Tatum runs her hand down Lucy's arm, clasping her wrist to give it a soft squeeze before Lucy pulls away and heads out the front door with an "I will" murmured.

"Looks like it's settled. You're taking the house. I have some people coming this week who are interested in some of the furnishings I put on Craig's List."

"I'll buy them."

Her eyes narrow as her head inches side to side. "That's crazy, Emmett. You have furniture at your house. I assume."

"I'm going to rent out my house as furnished."

"Well ... still ... you don't want my things. It's my taste not yours. I don't think purples and velvet say bachelor."

She is my taste. I don't have a favorite color. I have a favorite person who loves purple and velvet. And I'm not a bachelor. I might not be married, but that doesn't make me available. I will never be with another person as long as Tatum is alive. It wouldn't be fair to someone else. There's no way I could love another woman the way I love her. My love for her is not contingent on her love for me. It's not even contingent on us being married.

Saying "I do" didn't make me love her more, it just gave her my last name.

"Emmett ... you need to move on." The pain in her voice is almost as bad as the contorted expression on her face.

"I'm not sure what you mean, Tatum. Last I checked, we were divorced. Last I checked, I'm no longer living with you. I have a job. I cook my own meals. I occasionally go out with friends. I do what I can for Lucy. I pay you child support and alimony. Until last week, we hadn't seen each other in nine months—short of a quick glance across an auditorium at Lucy's dance recital. If that's not moving on, then I don't know what you expect from me."

Hugging her arms to her chest, she stares at the floor between us. "I was happy to see you on a date. That felt like you were moving on. But I don't think some other woman will be interested in you as much if you're living in this house with the furniture *I* picked out."

"Nina is my neighbor. She invited me to dinner—as neighbors. So you don't have to worry about what she will think of furniture she will most likely never see."

"Well, if not her then—"

I sigh. "Tatum, it's my life. Moving on doesn't have to involve finding love again. At least, not for me."

"Emmett ..." Her gaze lifts to meet mine, and it drives that dagger into my chest another inch—a dagger that's been lodged in my heart since *that* day. "Lucy wants you to find love again."

"I have people I love."

She wets her lips and rubs them together. "I'm not talking about your parents or Lucy."

"Neither am I."

"Emmett ..." She shakes her head. "We're over. You know that."

"I do."

"Then why?"

"Because you brought it up." I run a hand through my hair before shoving that hand into my back pocket.

"You can't love me," she whispers.

"You can't tell me who to love."

"I can!" Her head shoots up, hands balled at her side. "I can tell you it's *not me.* You can't love me. I'm not yours to love anymore. And I hate ..." Her jaw clamps, but her unspoken words are felt between us.

"Say it," I whisper.

Her face reddens.

"Say it, Tatum. You've never said the actual words. So how can you expect me to believe them?"

"Don't ..." The muscles in her face quiver, falling victim to the pain—the truth.

Common sense and decency tell me to keep my distance, to not touch her. Yet, my hand makes its way to her face, and my heart twists at the way it still fits so perfectly in my palm. Hard knots in the pit of my stomach tighten when she shivers from my touch. "You *hate* one thing. And only one thing," I whisper.

Her gaze won't meet mine. It remains on my chest as my hand holds her face hostage. Even the tiny muscle in her nose twitches like it's always done when she gets angry.

"You hate that you love me."

"Let me go," she says on a shallow breath.

But my hand is no longer on her face. It's never been me holding her back. It's never been my hands keeping her hostage. I've always loved her with open arms. My love has never been forced. It's always been free. She's the one who cannot walk away. And she knows she needs me to take the blame for that too.

So I do.

Because that's how I love her.

THEN

EIGHT MONTHS AND FIVE DAYS.

That's how long we spent living out of an RV across the country. We combed beaches on both coasts and the Gulf of Mexico. We hiked mountains east and west of the Mississippi.

My parents thought it was the right decision. Always supportive. My brother thought I was incredibly irresponsible for leaving a good job. He warned me that I wouldn't be guaranteed a position upon my return. His wife, Andi, gave me a wink behind his back, ensuring me I would in fact have a job if I still wanted it.

I think she envied our chance at really living life where she quickly and unexpectedly had to settle into motherhood without having had a chance to sow wild oats.

Tatum's parents didn't disown her, but they were split on how they felt about her actions. Her mom found it romantic, but it made her nervous. And her dad gave nothing more than a grumble and head shake. But in the end, he gave her the longest hug goodbye and made her promise to call him if she needed rescuing.

Our adventure, although epic and unforgettable, didn't come without its hitches.

We fought. I spent more than one night sleeping in a dinky tent outside of the RV.

We made up. Sometimes that involved a look—a silent apology—that led to ripping off each other's clothes in places that were public, like restaurant bathrooms, dark alleys, under towels on a beach, or against a big tree just feet from main trails in the mountains. I have never felt as alive as I did in those moments.

Everything we did with so much passion, it felt like we were our own elemental force. We didn't just fall in love, we collided until our souls tangled, until we knew any attempt to live without each other would leave us crippled.

"Stop." Tatum rested her hand on my leg as I pulled the RV into my parents' long driveway, the end of our break from reality.

"What is it?"

She reached over and shoved the RV into *Park*. Then she climbed onto my lap as I fumbled with the seat to move it back to accommodate her.

"What's going on?" I laughed.

Frightened was the only word to describe the expression on her face. "Now what? I did it. I jumped off the cliff. I went all in. I took this trip with you, Emmett. And now we're broke and jobless. I can't crawl back to my parents like this. I willingly swallowed all of your *"don't worry about it's,"* but we are officially entering the gates of reality, and I need to know what's next. And you need to respect my need to have a plan."

I didn't share her level of anxiety. In fact, I was a little taken aback by her sudden rush of panic.

My hands slid from her ass to her back to her neck, cupping it as I feathered my lips over hers. "Can we at least park the RV before we map out the rest of our lives?"

"No." She closed her eyes and covered my hands with hers.

I chuckled. "Why not?"

Big brown eyes opened, and I felt something even bigger coming just from that one look. "Because I'm pregnant."

Fear bled from every pore on her skin. My reaction involved something a little more unexpected.

I killed the engine. "Get in the back."

Creases formed along her forehead. "Did you hear me?"

"Yeah," I said as I lifted her from my lap, pushing her toward the back as I unbuckled and maneuvered myself between the seats.

"Emmett—"

I grabbed her face and kissed her, walking her backward to the bed.

"What are you ..." Heavy breaths dropped from her lips while I kissed down her neck and peeled off her clothes, managing to get my shirt off—but my jeans and briefs only partially down my legs—before her back hit the bed.

"Emmett ... Jesus ..." Her breath hitched when I plunged into her, gripping her ass and pumping in long, hard strokes.

I couldn't explain it without it sounding ridiculous, but it pissed me off that she was pregnant and I wasn't aware of the exact time we made a baby. I was fine with living out of an RV with no plans for over eight months, but I wanted to fucking know when I was making a baby with her.

As she tightened around my cock, I lifted my head and watched her eyelids grow heavy, jaw going slack as she orgasmed. Mine quickly followed with her fingernails claiming the flesh of my ass, holding me as close to her as possible—as deep as possible while I spilled into her—looking into the depths of her eyes and memorizing this feeling to keep forever.

Our true beginning.

When she caught her breath, she grinned as I tried to keep my body from completely collapsing onto hers. "Um ...

I said I'm pregnant, not that I needed you to quickly get me pregnant before we parked the RV."

"I know," I said on a heavy breath as I dropped kisses along her face, content with staying buried inside of her for approximately eternity.

"And ... it *is* yours." She giggled some more. "In case this was your way of marking me or something like that."

My lips pulled into a grin just before I nibbled her ear, my hand caressing her hair. "Do I have to have a reason?"

"I suppose not. But you have to have a verbal reply to my news. That much I do need before we drive one inch farther down the driveway."

This woman was my everything. She made my world exponentially better. And while I wasn't insecure enough to think that I couldn't live life without her—a Romeo and Juliet scenario—eight months with her had shown me how incredible life was with her next to me.

"We do all the things." I kissed the tip of her nose.

"All the things?"

"House. Marriage. Chiefs season tickets. The important shit in life." I released her and slowly stood.

After we pieced ourselves back together, I pulled her into my arms. "By the way ... in case it wasn't implied, which it should have been, I'm so fucking elated that you're pregnant." I couldn't have controlled my grin in that moment had the fate of the whole world depended on it. "And it's a huge bonus that it's my baby."

She rolled her eyes and fisted my shirt as her expression turned into an incredibly fake scowl. "You big jerk."

Glancing over her shoulder, I reached into an overhead compartment and pulled out a zip tie. Then I took her left hand and secured it around her ring finger with the long tail of it sticking out. "Marry me, Tatum. Let me steal you for life."

She tugged at the end of the zip tie and glanced up at me with a raised eyebrow. "Emmett the Thief, I'm only saying yes to this ridiculous proposal because you knocked me up, and I want our parents to know we're committed when we tell them. But you'll have to trim the end of this, so I don't poke anyone in the eye when I show them how fucking cheap you are."

CHAPTER NINE

NOW

"When are you moving in?" Lucy asks as I load the last box that will fit into the back of the truck. She volunteered me to help them move out in spite of Tatum and Josh insisting they didn't need my help.

"After I get back from my work trip." I close the tailgate and tug off my leather gloves.

"Well, at least you'll get to enjoy the firepit area you constructed."

With a hint of a smile, the painful kind, I nod. "True. You know your mom said you can visit me whenever you want now. It doesn't just have to be Saturdays. You have a license and car. So if you feel like s'mores and talking about guys with your dad ..."

She laughs. "S'mores maybe. Guys no. You still haven't met Ashton."

"Yeah, where is he? If he's such a great guy, why isn't he here helping move your stuff?"

She shuffles her feet up the sidewalk to the front door. "He has soccer today."

"Sports guy, huh? I might like him. Does he play real football too?"

"Dad ..." she draws out my name as we head into the house.

"Okay, I think we're good. I'll meet you at the house," Josh says just before bending down to kiss my wife on the cheek.

Tatum's body stiffens a fraction. Is she not comfortable with him kissing her in front of me? Then maybe she should tell him to keep his lips to himself. I know I want to say those words to him. It's not that he's a bad guy. He seems nice enough, just not for my wife.

"Okay. I'm going to take one more look around upstairs. I'll meet you there."

"Lucy Loo ... you coming with me?" Josh thinks his name for my daughter is cute. Me? Not so much.

"My car has stuff in the back, so I'll follow you," she says.

"See you there." I give Lucy a wink.

When the door closes behind Lucy and Josh, I take a minute to look at my wife for possibly the last time standing in the living room of the home we built together. She can't even meet my gaze. Her nerves and scattered emotions thrum through the room with a palpable beat like someone's pulse as adrenaline shoots through their veins.

"I wanted you to make a clean break too," she mumbles, glancing around the room. "I hope living here doesn't haunt you. And if it does, I hope you can swallow your pride and just sell the place."

"There's nowhere I feel more at peace ... more at home ... than standing under this roof."

Her gaze locks with mine. "How can you possibly say that?" she asks with the wind knocked out of her lungs.

My mouth opens to vomit a million reasons why I want to live here, but I clamp it shut and clear my throat. "Let's have a look around and make sure you have everything you want. Of course, if you forget something, I won't change the locks. You are always welcome here." My effort to shift the conversation turns up fruitless.

I'm not sure she's blinked since my confession. Now things are just really uncomfortable. We have very different needs. I need to continue my scavenger hunt, the one where I'm hunting for the pieces to my life so I can put them back together, holes and all.

Tatum still feels the need to pound her fists and stomp her feet until the remnants of the life we created are nothing more than dust.

"Did you empty the hiding spot in the closet?" I ask and it brings her out of her state of shock.

She shakes her head. "Totally forgot."

I head toward the master bedroom on the main floor. We put a false wall in the back of the closet to hide important things, including Christmas and birthday presents. Tapping the upper right corner, it triggers the panel to release.

"Have you been in here since I moved out?"

When she doesn't answer, I glance back at her gaze affixed to something in the space. When I turn back around, I see what has her focus. A box wrapped in blue and orange wrapping paper with a big silver and blue bow stuck to the top of it.

Austin died two weeks before his fourth birthday. That was his gift. I don't know what's inside of it, but I remember

Tatum quickly handing it to me when Austin wasn't look-ing. I rushed it to the closet and hid it here.

Aside from the gift, there are a few shoeboxes of photos and a box of things we received over the years after our grandparents died. I ignore Austin's gift and nod to the other boxes. "Family photos? And I know that box has a quilt your grandma made."

Not a blink.

She shakes her head slowly, all color fading from her face as she takes slow steps backward.

"Tatum ..."

Turning, she runs into the bathroom and vomits in the toilet. I don't know what to do. I did what I could when he died, short of having godlike powers to bring him back to life or rewind time to change the outcome. She doesn't understand why I want to be here, but I understand why she needs to leave.

I wet the hand towel she left behind like so many other things in the house and press it to her forehead as I hunch beside her. She rips a wad of toilet paper from the holder and wipes her eyes and mouth before spitting into the toilet one more time.

"Sit back," I say, keeping the cold towel pressed to her forehead.

She eases onto her butt and rests her back against the wall, closing her eyes and squeezing out more tears that I know are no longer from vomiting. Hunching in front of her, I wipe them with the pads of my thumbs.

This hurts.

It doesn't hurt less than it did five years ago. Not for me. Not for her. I don't think it will ever hurt less; we'll just learn to navigate the pain better.

"It's a Build a Bear," she whispers while keeping her

eyes shut, but it doesn't hold in her tears. "H-he has a neon vest a-and a h-hard hat like ... his daddy."

Swallowing hard past the lump in my throat, I fight to hold back the emotion as my eyes burn. Austin was a daddy's boy. He loved going to work with me and riding in the big equipment. His voice echoes in my head every single day. "Daddy!" My favorite sound in the whole fucking world. Without it, I sit at home waiting for my Lucy day, trying to imagine it's real ... his voice. *Him.* I imagine he's really here and I just can't see him because he's hiding behind the curtains, in a closet, or under his bed. Without him, it's a world without music. A life without color. An eternity of numbness.

Tatum opens her eyes and continues to blink out unrelenting tears as her lower lip quivers. "Remember?" She draws in a shaky breath. "Remember when I called you from the mall and asked you to have him say the phrase 'Austin loves Daddy and dump trucks' slowly and clearly? And you asked why, but I said it was a surprise?"

I do. I remember.

But I can't fucking speak to tell her that, so I nod once and refuse to blink. When I'm with her, I feel like I don't have the right to miss him—not like her.

"That's what the bear says ... when you press its paw." Her body shakes with sobs. "In th-that box ... his v-voice is in that ... b-box."

My teeth grind as every muscle in my body tenses to hold it together. I clear my throat and stand, turning my back to her. "I'll get you a glass of water." As soon as I get to the kitchen, I rest my hands on the edge of the counter and hang my head as my jaw releases to let out the long hard breaths I'd been holding in the bathroom. I feel dizzy and my chest constricts like what I imagine a heart attack might feel like.

Lucy. This is for Lucy.

For her ... I pull my shit together, stand tall, take in as much oxygen as possible, hold it, and let it go slowly while filling a glass with water for Tatum. The kitchen sink overlooks the backyard.

"It's like a winter day ..." Tatum appears in the kitchen before I get the chance to head back to the bathroom. She wipes under her eyes with the pads of her fingers as I turn to face her. "The sun is bright in a cloudless sky. It's beautiful and all you want is to feel its warmth because it's been a long winter. And you know ... you know it's always been there, even on the days when you couldn't see it. But today you see it, and you close your eyes and try so hard to feel it. And sometimes you do. When it's still and there's no wind, you can feel its warmth, and it's everything you remember. It's life. But that moment is fleeting because in an instant the cold air kicks up and takes your breath away. And you can no longer feel the warmth of the sun. And you can no longer breathe."

Her gaze goes from the window to me. "I'm in this eternal winter, and Lucy is the sun." More tears fill her eyes. "And all I want to do is feel her warmth. But it's so cold. I can't shake it. The cold. The endless winter. Some days, I swear I could die from the cold all the while the sun is right there ... shining down on me."

After a few seconds of silence and neither one of us moving an inch, I take three steps and hand her the glass of water. Then I head toward the front door to drive my truck to their new house. "Don't stop," I say as I open the door. "When you stop and make the sun do everything, it's hard to not feel the cold. Remember when we'd go hiking in the mountains and you'd stop to take a break or snap some pictures? You'd get cold. I'd tell you to keep moving, but you just wanted me to hold you close to warm you up. So I did, but it was never enough. You had to keep going. Keep moving. You had to help yourself. And that's the hard thing to remember ... we can't ask too much ... even of the sun."

THEN

"WHAT DO YOU THINK OF THIS?" I called from the closet, feeling pretty proud that I'd figured out a way to use the wasted area beneath the stairs as a hidden storage space at the back of our closet.

"I think I have the world's sexiest handyman."

I glanced over my shoulder while standing on my knees to attach the removable panel. My jeans hung low thanks to my tool belt. Her gaze stuck to my ass. "I feel violated, Mrs. Riley. If your husband finds out you're gawking at the handyman's ass, he'll be pretty pissed off."

She rested her hand on her nine-month belly and grinned. "Serves him right. He's a thief anyway. Emmett the Thief. The guy is lucky I even gave him the time of day."

"I hear he's good in bed."

Her giggle ended in a snort. "He just has a humongous cock. But sometimes he gets a little lazy and doesn't use it to its full potential."

Lifting an eyebrow, I dropped the panel and stood. Unhooking my tool belt, I let it crash to the floor at my feet all while pinning Tatum with a look. "Then leave your big-cocked husband and let me show you what a real man can do."

Biting her lower lip, her cheeks turned bright red, the way they always did when she knew we were about to get naked. Only, we didn't make it that far. I kissed her neck and worked my way down her body. When I kissed her firm belly, she jumped and squeezed her legs together.

"Emmett ..."

I glanced at the floor and the puddle at her feet. Small amounts of fluid continued to drip down her bare legs. She pulled up the skirt to her sundress and revealed her soaked panties.

"If this is your idea of a golden shower, your aim is a little off."

"Oh my god ... oh my god ... it's time." She beamed with excitement, not showing an ounce of concern over the fact that she was in labor and would have to push something the size of a basketball out of her vagina.

She was my hero.

I stood tall and cupped her face, unable to move her grin one centimeter.

"We're having a baby," she whispered.

"So ... call the doctor or just go to the hospital?"

"Both. I'll call the doctor. You put my bag in the car and call our parents."

Before she could get away, I tightened my grip on her face and brought mine a breath from touching hers. "I love you. I love you more than should be humanly possible. And I will never love anyone or anything the way I love you."

Her eyes flooded with happy tears. "I love you too."

On the way to the hospital, I kept her distracted from her contractions with important facts about babies because she did in fact marry a nerd.

Babies are born with three hundred bones—ninety-four

more than adults. Those extra bones fuse together during development.

They also don't have kneecaps. The patella develops into hard bone between the age of three and five.

They can't taste salt (just sweet and sour) until four months. But they have three thousand taste buds compared to ten thousand in adults.

Sixty-nine is not just a great sex position, it's also the highest recorded number of children born to one mother. A Russian woman. Sixteen pairs of twins, seven sets of triplets, and four sets of quadruplets.

When we pulled up to the hospital entrance, she grabbed my hand and cut me off from finishing my last amazing fact about babies. I didn't realize until that moment that my body was shaking and hers was not. While we had a lot of things in common like the Chiefs and a love for traveling, we were complete opposites in many other ways. I was the storm—hard working but passionate about love and life. Sometimes to a fault. Tatum was the calm to my storm. Maybe it was the grace that came with her ability to dance and play music like her mom.

All I had to do was hold her hand and cheer her on, and I already felt like I might fail at that one simple duty. She had the hard job. She had to bring another life into the world by channeling immortal strength. And as her steady hand soothed *my* nerves, I knew she would be amazing.

I was so fucking proud of myself for stealing her.

I waited for her to say something, ask me for a favor, or just tell me to shut the hell up. She said nothing and did nothing except hold my hand. After a minute or so, I felt her calm energy wash over me. My shaking stopped. She smiled while releasing my hand and climbed out of the truck as a nurse greeted us with a wheelchair.

It took twelve hours of walking the hallways, squatting, swaying, back rubbing, ice chip eating, and a few tears of exhaustion before it was time to push.

"I should have said yes to the epidural," she murmured as another contraction hit, and her midwife told her to push.

"You're a rock star, Tate ... the headliner. The kind that sells out the biggest stadiums," I said with my lips at her brow as she squeezed my hand. "You'll always be my rock star."

She brought her other hand up to cup mine, face flushed and riddled with tiny creases of pain. "I need you to make me a promise?"

"Anything," I said without a blink of hesitation.

"Love this baby more. You have to promise to love this baby more than me ... more than us."

"Tatum ..."

"Promise me. You *have* to promise me. Parents are supposed to love their children more than each other. This baby is the best of us."

At the start of another contraction, the midwife gave me the just-say-it look. I returned several tiny nods.

"Of course, honey. Anything you want."

Minutes later, we welcomed Lucy into the world, and I instantly fell in love with her. Maybe I did still love her mother a tiny bit more, but my heart didn't feel it in a measurable way, and I prayed it would never matter. I prayed I would never have to prove that I loved Lucy more.

CHAPTER TEN

NOW

"How's the house?" Will asks as we walk down rows of large equipment, taking notes on things we want to bid on.

It's a work trip, but for us it's also a guys' getaway. The bummer part is I'm missing my Saturday with Lucy. I'm hoping she takes advantage of Tatum's willingness to ease visitation restrictions and decides to have dinner with me when I get back in town tomorrow.

"It's fine." I shrug.

"It's not weird?"

I shake my head. "Not to me. I realize nobody understands, but that's fine. I'm not asking anyone else to live there. And Lucy seems okay with it. Granted, it's only been two weeks, but we sat around the firepit last week, with her boyfriend, and roasted marshmallows."

"You don't think it will be hard to move on while living there?" he asks while climbing into the cab of an excavator.

"Move on? What does that mean? I'm so tired of everyone

using that phrase. I'm moving. I'm here. I work. I spend time with Lucy. I eat and shit. I clean and maintain my yard. Pay bills. Visit Mom and Dad at least once a week. I think what you're implying is that I need to forget about the past. But I don't want to forget the past. It's part of who I am today. When I moved out, I didn't forget about our parents or the rest of our family just because I was making one of my own."

"How's your dating life?"

I roll my eyes as Will climbs down wearing a smug expression like he's managed to make some genius point.

He hasn't.

"How's your golf game coming?" I ask.

"Shitty. What does that have to do with what we're talking about?"

"It's shitty because you have no desire to play golf or get better at it, even though a lot of your friends and business acquaintances play it. You're content with going to your grave a shitty golfer. Well, I'm content with going to my grave a single man. I have no desire to date anyone. I wasn't a big relationship guy before I met Tatum, and I've reverted back to that guy now that we're divorced. So what? Why is it so fucking important to everyone else?"

"We just want to know that you're okay?"

"Then I'll get a goddamn shirt that says I'm okay. If the vanity plates for IMOKAY aren't taken, I'll get them for my truck. Will that satisfy everyone's obsession with my psyche?"

"Jeez, man ... I'm just trying to help. Tatum has moved on. She moved out of the house, and you dove headfirst into your past. I get not wanting to forget him, but he's gone. You can't get him back. You can't get your wife back. So just love Lucy and love yourself enough to not waste the rest of your fucking life trying to live the life you wanted but do *not* in fact have."

"Spoken like an asshole who knocked up the boss's daughter then inherited his empire—like an asshole who has never had one day of true grief in his entire life."

He grabs my shirt bringing me close to his face, jaw set, eyes narrowed. "Wake the hell up! We *all* grieved Austin's death. And maybe if you would have been a little more fucking responsible, he would still be here."

Thwack!

I punch him in the nose and blood gushes out as he covers it and stumbles back a few steps. It's the first time someone besides Tatum has said those words aloud. It's the first time I've ever punched anyone that hard. As a glimmer of regret starts to filter into my conscience, my phone rings.

"Yeah?" I answer a little clipped as Will brings his shirt up to wipe the blood while mumbling, "The fuck, man ..."

"Emmett?"

"What, Mom?"

"Emmett ... there's been an accident."

"Dad? What happened to Dad?"

Will's eyes narrow as he pinches his nose and steps closer to me. "Dad? What's wrong?"

I shake my head slowly because I don't know—because Mom is not saying what happened.

"Mom? What's happened?"

"It's not your dad. It's ... Lucy and Tatum."

"What about them?"

"Oh, Emmett ..." Her voice breaks.

"For Christ's sake, Mom! Just tell me!"

"They were in a car accident." A sob escapes.

I can't fucking breathe. I just ... can't.

"Tatum is going to be fine. She has some cuts and bruises. But Lucy ... we don't know much yet, but she ..."

Emotion burns my eyes, intensifying Will's concern despite his bloodied nose. "She what?" I manage to ask without losing it.

"She's sustained a spinal injury, and she can't move her legs."

I pivot and start running toward the truck.

Six hours.

I'm a six-hour drive away from Lucy and Tatum.

My world is six hours away from me. And until I get there, I will not breathe. My heart will refuse to beat. The longest six hours of my life.

"Jesus, Emmett, tell me what she said!" Will chases me.

"Lucy and Tatum were in a car accident. And ..." I try to open the driver's side door but it's locked. "FUCK! Open the door!"

"I'm driving." He shoves me aside.

I glare at him as he unlocks the door. "Your nose."

"Screw my nose. I'm not letting you drive in your state. Now stop wasting time and get in."

Will drives and I want to yell at him to go faster, but he's already driving nearly twenty over the speed limit. His lack of knowing the truth about my past doesn't prevent him from putting himself in my shoes and hauling ass home as quickly as possible.

"I'm sorry," I whisper, breaking the three-hour silence. "About your nose." A sense of helplessness has calmed my nerves. I've allowed myself to consider the worst-case scenario because I've lived that scenario. But he died. Lucy and Tatum are not dead. That is everything at the moment.

"No. Don't apologize. I was out of line. I shouldn't have said it. I didn't mean it."

He did.

Maybe he didn't mean to say it the way he did, in the heat of the moment, but he meant it. He said what everyone thinks but never says.

When we make it to the hospital, I don't look back at Will or say one more word to him. Lucy ... I just need to get to my daughter.

And my wife.

"Emmett ..." my mom says my name as I pass the waiting room to the ICU where she and Dad wait with Tatum's parents.

"Not now." I shake my head. I can't talk to them. I have to get to Lucy.

The nurse escorts me to her room. Before she slides open the glass door, I see Tatum in a chair next to Lucy's bed, folded over, holding her hand and resting her cheek on it as Josh stands behind her, rubbing her back. He glances up when the nurse slides open the door, but Tatum doesn't move. With scrapes and bandages on her face and arms, she remains still, eyes closed.

Josh gives me a sad smile. "Emmett."

Still, Tatum doesn't move. And Lucy's hooked up to all kinds of machines.

Retrieving his phone from the pocket of his white lab coat, he reads the message and glances up at me. "I have a patient I need to check on. If either of you need anything, have them page me."

I say nothing. I don't even make eye contact with him because I can't tear my gaze away from my daughter and wife. After Josh and the nurse leave the room, I take slow steps toward Tatum.

Before I can speak.

Before I can touch her.

Before I can wrap my head around this horrific reality.

Tatum's eyes shut tighter, and her body starts to shake from tiny sobs. I peel Lucy's hand out of hers slowly and hunch beside her chair. With my other hand, I gently cup her cheek in my palm, being careful to not put pressure on her cuts or bruises.

"Emmett ..." She sobs and falls into my arms, knocking me off balance until I'm on my knees and she is too with her arms hugging me like I'm her only lifeline. Every cell in my body has missed this feeling ... the rightness of her in my arms. Yet nothing about this scene is right. We lost Austin. Losing Lucy would destroy us completely. I'm certain we would die right here if that happened.

"Shh ..." I rest my cheek on the top of her head and stroke her hair down her back.

"God can't have Lucy too. He just ... can't." Tatum cries.

I stand, pulling her up with me and easing her into the chair.

She doesn't look at me.

I turn and slide my hand under Lucy's hand as the fragile parts of my pieced together heart start to crack again. If it weren't for the machine keeping time to the heartbeat and the slight warmth of her hand, I would never know she's alive.

When I glance over my shoulder, Tatum slowly closes her eyes, sending more tears down her face. Why won't she look at me?

Is she upset with me? Does this bring back too many memories of Austin?

"I'm here, Lucy," I say while gently squeezing her hand. "And I'm going to make sure you pull through this. We have milkshakes to drink at the cafe and s'mores to roast. You ..." I choke on my words for a second. "You have to go to college and do great things. I have to walk you down the aisle. You have to make me a grandpa. You're not done being my world, baby. We've got this. Do you hear me?"

Tatum makes a choking noise behind me. When I angle to see her, she doubles over, nearly falling out of the chair. Releasing Lucy's hand, I turn and hunch down in front of her again, keeping her from falling to the floor as bone-rattling sobs arrest her body.

"Tate ... she's going to be okay. Don't you dare think otherwise."

Clenching my shirt in her delicate fingers, she buries her face in my neck and continues to cry out of control.

It's too much. Losing Lucy would be too much for her and too much for me. After losing track of how long we've remained in each other's arms, I ease out of her grip enough to see her face.

Still ... she won't let her gaze meet mine, so I put my finger under her chin and force her face up. She closes her eyes instead of looking at me, and her bottom lip trembles.

"What happened?" I whisper, clearing the tears from her face and the terrain of cuts and bandages.

Curling her lips together and drawing in a shaky breath, she starts to open her eyes just as the door to the room opens. Her gaze goes straight to Josh, and she sits back, forcing distance between us. I stand and take in a deep breath.

"What's her condition? What can we expect? I haven't really been told anything."

Josh gives Tatum a quick glance that she ignores before he returns his attention to me. "She suffered a spinal injury. Miraculously all of her other injuries are minor except for a concussion, but given enough rest, that should resolve and hopefully not leave any permanent damage. We'll know over the next few days."

"The spinal injury ..." I'm not sure what I'm really asking.

Josh nods slowly. "It appears to be an incomplete injury which means she has some function of her lower extremities, but not a lot. If we can get the inflammation down, we'll have a better feel for the extent of the paralysis."

"So she can't walk?"

Josh shakes his head.

"Is it permanent?"

"Again, we don't know yet." He makes his way to Tatum. "What can I do for you? Have you eaten? Do you need something for the pain? Your head must hurt. I could take you home for a few hours and drive you back here."

That's my wife.

That's my daughter in the bed, lifeless.

My whole fucking world is in this room, and Dr. Josh is trying to make a place for himself too.

Tatum stares blankly at Lucy while Josh rests his hand on her shoulder, giving it a little squeeze.

"Do you want me to have your parents come in for a little bit? I could have them make an exception for the number of visitors. I know they're really concerned about you and Lucy."

Not a blink.

Nothing.

I haven't seen Tatum like this since Austin died. She just ... faded away. Never in my life had I felt so helpless.

He died and I couldn't save him.

She blamed me, and I couldn't argue with her.

And every day she pulled away from me. It was like trying to hold water in your cupped hands. I fought to keep her, but the cracks were too big. Our love, our life we kept safe in a bubble ... it broke.

Josh nods at me toward the hallway, and I follow him out the door, closing it behind me. "She won't talk. She hasn't said one word to me since the accident. Her doctor, Dr. Mathers, got her to say maybe five words, but only because she said she wouldn't discharge her to see Lucy if she didn't answer a few questions."

I nod a few times, keeping my gaze over his shoulder to the room and Tatum's dead gaze on Lucy. They both look lifeless and limp. The only difference is Tatum's eyes are open, but fixed and unblinking.

"Do you think we should have her parents come talk to her?"

We.

So now Josh and I are a team? Great. Really great.

"Sure." I shrug. "It's worth a try. I just ..." I squint at Tatum.

"You just what?" Josh asks.

On a drawn-out sigh, I rub the back of my neck. "She's stable. Right? I mean, I guess what I'm saying is ... it's unlikely that she's going to ..." I can't say it. I can't even say the word *die*.

But I don't have to.

"They anticipate a full recovery from the concussion. They'll know more when she's awake again. They'll keep checking for any signs of memory loss or other neurological deficits. So to answer your question, no. It's highly unlikely that anything at this point would lead to death."

I nod slowly. Lucy will live. Austin died. Why does Tatum look like she's not going to make it?

"Do you know the details of the accident?"

Josh frowns. "Only what a few witnesses have told the police. Tatum hasn't been able to give her account of it yet."

"What did the witnesses say?"

I can tell from the indecision on his face and his quick glance over his shoulder to Tatum that he doesn't want to tell me.

"Just tell me."

"Witnesses said Tatum's car ran a red light."

"Who was driving?"

Again, Josh took a quick glance back in the room through the glass doors. "Tatum."

The light had to have been yellow, and she didn't want to slam on her breaks. There was no way she was under the influence. A yellow light. It had to be a yellow light, which means the person who hit them either ran a red light or they took off so quickly at the green light that they didn't see Tatum and Lucy coming through on the tail end of a yellow light.

"T-boned their car on Lucy's side."

"What about the person or people in the other car? Were they badly injured?"

"Minor injuries."

Tatum jumps out of her chair, and I realize Lucy's eyes are open. "She's awake." I push past Josh and rush to the opposite side of her bed. "Lucy ..." I press my hand to her cheek gently and kiss her forehead over the bandage. "Baby girl, I'm so glad you're okay."

Tatum grips her hand and looks on in a torturous mix of relief and pain. "Lucy ..." she says and Lucy's gaze slides in her direction. But before she can say anything more than her name, she starts choking on more sobs again.

"Mom ..." Lucy whispers through a dry sounding throat.

Josh rests both of his hands on Tatum's shoulder.

Lucy's gaze flits from Tatum to me then down her body. "I ... I still can't feel my legs." A little panic creeps into her words. "I thought it was temporary, but I can't feel my legs."

Josh takes out his phone. "I'll have the neurologist come in and do another exam. It's going to take some time for the swelling to subside. I don't want you to worry, Lucy."

"It's ..." Lucy gets teary eyed.

My girls are losing it, and I feel so helpless.

"I ... I don't like it. I ... can't ... feel them." She starts to panic.

I take her hand and run it over my scruffy face that I haven't shaved in over a week. She used to love running her hands over my face.

"Daddy feels scratchy. Daddy feels like a porcupine." She'd giggle.

"Do you feel this?"

Her hand moves as I continue rubbing it over my face, and she nods.

Bending forward, I run the inside of her arm over my face. "Do you feel this?"

She nods.

"Does it feel like a porcupine?"

"My—"

I shake my head. "Feel me on your hand. On your arm." I bend down a little more and rub my face on her cheek. "Feel me because I feel you. And you are going to be okay, baby. You just need to breathe ... and you need to be thankful for all the things you *can* feel. And eventually you'll be better. Just ... breathe."

"Daddy ..." she whispers as my face is next to hers so only I can hear her. She hasn't called me Daddy in years. "I'm ... scared."

"Don't be," I murmur softly back to her, turning my head until my lips brush her cheek.

"I deserve—"

"Shh ..." my lips move to her ear. "Don't. Not ever. It was an accident."

Tears fill her eyes, and I catch them at the corners before they have a chance to slide down her face.

"Mom." Her attention returns to Tatum as if it's just now registering that her mom was in the car too. "Are you okay?"

Tatum sniffles and swallows hard while nodding. "Fine," she manages to squeak out.

Another doctor comes into the room. The neurologist, I assume for two seconds before Josh introduces me to her.

"It's getting a little crowded in here. We'll step out for a few minutes while you do your exam," I say to the doctor but also to Tatum.

She looks to Josh for some sort of permission to leave or maybe just to not have to look at me.

"Go grab a drink and stretch your legs. I'll stay with Lucy." He kisses her cheek, and I want to grab her arm and yank my wife out of his hold on her. I am the thief. Not him. He's not allowed to steal what's mine. You just don't rob a thief.

Tatum heads out the door and straight to the waiting room before I can catch up to her. My parents stand and rush to me as hers do the same to her. While I field a million questions from them that don't really register, Tatum's mom fusses over her injuries and asks about Lucy.

I look at Tatum.

She looks at me.

There's something between us that's unspoken, but I don't know what it is. And I don't like the feeling it gives me. Even after five years apart, I know this woman. I know when she's hurting—which she is.

I know when she's angry—and I feel a little of that coming from her too.

But it's something more. A more I can't quite place.

"The neurologist is doing an exam. When she's done, I'm sure Josh can get you in to see Lucy." This gets my mom off my back with her long string of questions. "I'm going to take Tatum and get her something to eat. You should wait with her parents and see if they can go back with you in a little bit."

Tatum's unflinching gaze moves with me as I get closer to her.

"We'll be back in a bit. You can see Lucy soon when my parents go back to see her." I give her parents a small smile and rest my hand on Tatum's back to lead her toward the stack of elevators. We step on and the doors close.

As we stare at the digital numbers descending, I have to ask, "How red? How red was the light you ran? Was it yellow? Orange? A short light? The sun glaring?"

As soon as the elevator dings and the doors open, Tatum runs out and toward the nearest exit instead of the cafeteria. I follow her. By the time I reach the exit, she's around the corner by the lower-level parking with her head in a garbage can, hurling the contents of her stomach much like she did in the toilet the last time I saw her.

"Are you pregnant?" As much as it kills me to imagine her pregnant with Josh's baby, it's a slightly better alternative to the one I fear the most.

She lifts her head and wipes her mouth. "No," she whispers.

It wasn't yellow or orange. It was red. It wasn't a short light. It wasn't the sun glaring in her eyes.

"I just ..." Her whole face contorts as she chokes on her words while staring out at the entrance to the parking garage.

That's what the unimaginable looks like. I've seen it before on her face. *That's* the feeling I couldn't quite place, probably because I've tried to block it from my memory. Only this time ... she's not disgusted with me. She's not appalled and ruined by my behavior—by my mistake.

"My phone fell onto the floor. I ... I looked away for ..."

A blink. Maybe two. A breath. Maybe two. That's all it takes. That's all it takes to change your world forever. That's all it takes to go from the best parent to the worst parent.

She covers her mouth with her hand and closes her eyes.

"I forgive you. Lucy will forgive you. It was an accident." I don't mean to cause her more pain and grief, but that's what I'm doing. It's all twisted and etched into her face like she can't believe I just said that, like it was a bad thing to say. No ... like it was the worst thing to say.

Instead of taking back my words, elaborating, making excuses for her or for me, I pivot and head back into the hospital. This isn't Karma. This isn't gratifying or some weird sort of relief. It's tragic.

But ... it was an accident.

No matter how hard we try to be perfect, we are not. No matter how hard we try to do the right thing, the wrong thing manages to trip us up. No matter how undeserving one might feel of forgiveness, no one is unworthy of it.

CHAPTER ELEVEN

THEN

Austin was born on a Friday in the early morning hours of a hot August day.

Two.

We wanted two kids—a boy and a girl.

Just like our manicured lawn and meticulously painted fence, our life continued to be discreetly flawed yet picture perfect. We fought with passion. We lived without regret. And we loved to the depths of our souls.

It was why we took that RV road trip. It was why we ate ice cream for dinner every Friday night and followed it up with popcorn.

After Austin's second birthday, we took a trip to St. Louis to stay at a bed and breakfast—our first trip by ourselves since before Lucy was born. I took her to a fancy restaurant. Then we went dancing. I still couldn't keep a beat, but I gave it a solid E for effort because I loved Tatum and she loved dancing.

By the time we made it to the B&B, she was a little tipsy

from the wine at dinner and from me twirling her around the dance floor. That I could do ... I could twirl her, and it made her giggle like a child.

"Again!" She laughed and I twirled her again, ending in a dip and long kiss.

The room was quite nice with a big bed and a tub the size of a small swimming pool. After I locked the bedroom door, she turned, pulling off her silk scarf, eyes dancing with possibilities and cheeks sketched in shades of pink.

"Is it weird that I'm nervous?" She laughed it off, but it didn't completely hide the shakiness in her voice.

In some ways, I fell in love with her all over again in that moment. We'd become so lost in our roles as parents and responsible adults, that it was easy to forget we were still two crazy people madly in love.

"Nervous?" I shrugged off my suit jacket and toed off my shoes as if I had immunity to such nerves.

I didn't.

Tatum nodded. "It's been ... a long time since it was just us. Lights on. No hurry. All night to do ..."

I smirked. "Whatever we want?" I prowled toward her, loosening my tie.

Her gaze drifted to the floor. "I mean ... we usually just slide to the middle of the bed in the dark and do it in less than ten minutes."

"Well ..." I dropped my tie on the floor and started to unbutton my shirt. "I have plans for us that will last longer than ten minutes."

God ... I hoped I would last longer than ten minutes.

She still made me deliriously crazy with need from just one look. I *still* felt like the thief who got away with the world's greatest heist—in a bar.

I played it cool. That was my specialty. The manly man who didn't get butterflies in his stomach.

But I did. For her ... I always did.

"Plans, huh?" She peeked up at me through her thick, mascara-covered lashes.

I nearly died. Seriously ... I had the most gorgeous wife. How I stole her ... well, it was still a mystery.

"Like kissing you here..." leaning down, I lifted her hair and moved it off her shoulder before my lips found that sensitive spot just under her ear "...while I slowly undress you." My hands moved to the zipper at the back of her dress, inching it down.

When it pooled at the bottom of her feet, I stood straight again to get a good look at her in nothing but a black thong and a sea of flawless skin covered in goose bumps.

"You're shaking, Mrs. Riley."

She returned another nervous laugh as her hands covered her bare breasts. "I told you ... I'm nervous."

"Me too." I lowered to my knees, resting my hands on her hips as my lips ghosted along her abs to the edge of her panties.

"Why are you nervous?"

I grinned at her question, and my tongue teased her navel. "Because you're out of my league. Always have been. Always will be." My gaze lifted to hers.

She relaxed a bit, and it was us again—that crazy couple who met by unexpected fate, fucked about until she lost her job, traveled the country in an RV, had sex in public spaces, and got engaged via zip tie after an unplanned pregnancy.

Her hands slid off her breasts and landed on my head. As she laced her fingers through my hair. Her head did that puppy side tilt. "Emmett the Thief. Always stealing my heart. And every time it feels like the first."

She swallowed hard as I slid down her panties. She was mine. She would always be mine. What could possibly change that?

Only the unimaginable.

Her grip on my hair tightened as I guided her to sit on the bed ... to lean back ... to relax her knees as I spread them wide.

The tiny hitch in her breath cut through the silent room when my lips pressed to her flesh. Our intimacy felt like the most unbreakable bond. Again, how could I have ever imagined the unimaginable?

My tongue moved. She moaned and her hips lifted from the bed. I felt like a king. A king who could never be dethroned. Not a mere mortal husband who wore work boots and Carhartt clothes to work every day. Not a dad who spent most evenings picking up toys and washing dirty dinner dishes. A king.

"Oh Goddd ..." Her back arched so beautifully from the bed, and her knees collapsed against the side of my head. I could hear her heart beat and feel the pounding of her pulse. I'm certain it was as close as a man could get to Heaven on Earth.

We left the lights on ... and she undressed me the rest of the way, her hair mussed from my fingers tangling it while kissing her. And although I wanted nothing more than to be inside of her for the rest of the night, she had other plans.

Really *really* excellent plans.

I sucked in a sharp breath as she straddled my legs and wrapped her mouth around me—the warm, wet pressure. A feeling like no other.

The married-man-with-kids part of me considered protesting, insisting she didn't need to reciprocate like that. But the man in me—the one who had had maybe three blow jobs in nine years of marriage—he dug his teeth into his lower lip and let it happen for a few more seconds before pulling her up my body, before rolling us over, before sliding inside her.

I'd forgotten what it was like to watch the expression on Tatum's face as we moved together. Quickies in the dark were more for the endgame and much more tactile than visual.

The drunken lust as her mouth fell open.

The tiny breaths being forced out each time I rocked into her.

Yeah ... I still had it.

"Fuck ... me ..." I sighed after rolling onto my back, breathless and covered in sweat.

"Yeah ..." Tatum chuckled, no longer displaying any signs of nerves. "That ... definitely that."

And after a few minutes of catching our breaths, we glanced over at each other, naked on top of the sheets. Our eyes made a mutual inspection of the other one before we grinned and shared a knowing look that said one thing.

"Let's do it again!"

THE NEXT MORNING, we woke at nine-thirty—not a significant time to some people, but when you were used to getting up at five in the morning, and maybe six-thirty or seven on weekends, nine-thirty felt like noon.

"I'm starving." Tatum rolled toward me, molding her body into my chest and scissoring her legs with mine.

"Long night." I grinned.

She kissed my chest. "Mmm ... I can't remember the last time a *long night* involved something other than restless kids, vomit, nightmares, or years of marathon nursing and diaper changes."

"I know. Whose idea was it to trade in marathon sex for marathon nursing?"

Tatum giggled, running her big toe along my instep. "Says the guy whose response to me being pregnant with Lucy was to usher me to the back of the RV and stick your dick in me as if you needed to make sure I was pregnant. As if you needed to make sure we would have marathon nursing instead of marathon sex ... nightmares, vomit, dirty diapers ... that's on you, buddy."

I kissed the top of her head. "Says the woman who called me home from work with an emergency, which ended up being you desperate for me to put my dick inside of you because you were ovulating. Nine months later ... Austin."

"Fine," she huffed. "So we both agree that life is better with your big dick inside of me."

"Yes." I rolled on top of her and settled between her legs. "On that we do agree."

Eventually, we made it out of the room and downstairs for breakfast, after all, it was a bed *and* breakfast. I think we would have been content with just the bed. The owner started us off with coffee, fresh squeezed orange juice, and the local newspaper.

"Wow. I didn't know physical newspapers were still a thing." Tatum spread open the paper and thumbed through it. "Oh my god ..."

"What?" I asked just before taking a swig of my orange juice.

"This mother went to work and forgot it was her morning to take their nine-month-old to daycare. Left the baby in the car and it died from the heat. Can you even imagine?"

I shook my head slowly. "No."

She closed the newspaper, visibly shook by the story. "As a parent ... how do you ever get past that? How do you go on living?"

"Maybe they have other kids."

A frown stole Tatum's lovely face. "But still ... you never forget. It's not like an accident that was out of your control. I mean ... it was *her* fault. And their marriage. I just can't imagine how a marriage would last after that. Her husband would never look at her the same way again."

"It was an accident, not something she did maliciously."

"True." Tatum stirred creamer into her coffee. "But the mind does its own thing. I mean ... you could go through counseling, therapy, whatever, but he will always look at her and think about their daughter who would still be alive had she been focused. Clearly she put the child in his car seat. What could have happened between home and her work? Where was her mind?"

I shrugged one shoulder. "Like you said, the mind does its own thing. How many times have you walked from the kitchen to the bedroom to get something, but by the time you get there, it's slipped your mind? And maybe it wasn't her usual day to take the child to daycare. Maybe she wasn't even the one who usually took the baby. I can see how something so out of your normal routine might be hard to remember since our brains probably get hardwired for our normal schedule."

Tatum eyed me over her coffee cup. "You're a good man, Emmett. You think the best of people, and you're forgiving ... possibly to a fault. I'm lucky to have you in my corner."

I waggled my eyebrows. "And in your bed."

She smirked. "That too."

Everything was so perfect ... until it wasn't.

NOW

THE NEUROLOGIST CONFIRMS what Josh already predicted. We need to wait a few days to see if the medications decrease the swelling around her spinal cord. Then we'll have a better idea of her prognosis. So our parents go home for the evening, but not before bringing Tatum and me dinner which neither one of us eats very well.

"I'm off now, but I can stay if ..." Josh glances at me sitting in the other chair by Lucy on the opposite side of her bed as Tatum.

"I'm staying." I give Josh a look as if he's out of his mind to think for one second that I'm not staying the night.

My daughter.

My wife. And fuck him if he thinks otherwise.

"Get some sleep. You have to be alert to save the world." Tatum squeezes his hand.

He bends down to kiss her, and she stiffens when her gaze locks with mine a second before their lips meet. I don't know what the timeframe is for unloving someone. It's not five years. Not for me.

My love for her has not wavered one bit, so watching another man kiss her hurts as much now as it would have the day we got married. My heart doesn't understand that it's not okay for me to punch Josh in the face. All it knows is the love that's infiltrated all four chambers, every vein and artery, every cell is permanent. Our hearts, mine and

Tatum's, are still virtually indistinguishable from each other.

"Goodnight. Both of you try to get some sleep," Josh says.

I try to nod or look at him to offer some sort of acknowledgment, but I can't. It's her. It's always been her. It will always be her.

And doesn't that suck for me? Most of the time I don't mind. Most of the time it's comforting to love her. Not now. When she lets another man touch her intimately, it makes me wish that I could simply cease to exist.

The dimly lit room makes it hard to see her face, but I know she's watching me watch Lucy and her monitors. What must she be thinking? Is she thinking about the accident and blaming herself? Is she thinking about Austin?

"I'm in your corner," I say to Tatum while keeping my eyes aimed at Lucy.

When she doesn't acknowledge me, I question if she even heard me.

But then she murmurs something, and I have to give it a few moments to make sure I hear her correctly. "Well, you shouldn't be. You should be in Lucy's corner."

"It's the same corner."

Her head inches side to side. "I know you probably don't remember this, but when I was in labor with Lucy, I made you promise to love her more. Love her more than me. That's what parents are supposed to do—love their children the most. And in some ways, that was supposed to be the best way to show your love to me."

Oh, Tatum …

I remember everything. And I've always done exactly what she asked me to do. And I lost her because of it. Something she will never know.

"I do remember. And I promised you I would."

Her forehead wrinkles, and she clears her throat, shifting her attention to Lucy. "But you didn't."

Austin.

She means our son.

"But you can now. You can be in Lucy's corner. You can put her first."

"By what? Not forgiving you?"

Tatum drags in a shaky breath, and just as I think she's about to release it, she bolts into the bathroom and shuts the door. Lucy stirs a bit, shifting her head to the other side, but she doesn't open her eyes. Easing out of my chair, I follow Tatum, knocking gently on the door.

She doesn't respond, so I push down the lever handle and it cracks open. With her knees hugged to her chest and her head bowed, she occupies the corner of the bathroom opposite the toilet.

"I did this ..." she whispers. "And I'm so grateful that she's alive, but it could have turned out differently." Lifting her head, she doesn't even try to hide the wet trail of emotions running down her face. "I could have killed Lucy. And she may ..." She swallows hard. "She may never walk again. And you ... you are so quick to forgive me." Shaking her head, she closes her eyes. "That's not okay. That's not loving her more. Some things are unforgivable."

"It was an accident."

"No." She continues to shake her head, a tiny muscle in her jaw twitching as she bites back her anger. "It was negligence. There's a difference. You should know that."

There it is ... the accusation without actually saying the words. I should know that I killed Austin. That it was my negligence. That's what she means.

"Well, I can't divorce you. Do you want me to take Lucy

away from you? Has my penance been nullified by your actions? Am I now the 'fit' parent? Or do we let your parents or mine raise her? Will and Andi? What is the solution?"

Threading her hands in her hair, she rests her elbows on her bent knees. "How do you do it?"

"Do what?" I know what she means, but I need her to say it. After five years of looks, of the silent treatment, of hiding from me, I need her to say it.

"You know."

I shake my head. "I'm not sure I do know. Maybe you need to spell it out for me." Inside my half empty soul, there exists a need for pain. As much as I want her to love me without regret, I'll take anything she's willing to give me.

"If..." her face contorts "...she would have died, I don't think I would have been able to ..." She trails off, leaving me to fill in the blank.

"You wish I were dead? You think I should have killed myself?" My patience runs out, and I say it for her.

Tatum flinches at my candid interpretation of what I'm certain she's been insinuating since the day Austin died. When she doesn't answer, I fill in that blank too, even though I can't say it aloud.

It hurts too fucking much.

All these years, I've convinced myself that she's angry because as much as she wants to hate me, she can't. I've let my delusional conscience misguide me into believing that she loves me, but it just hurts too much.

But ... she doesn't.

I try to even my shaky breath as I search for oxygen in this stuffy little bathroom. My eyes burn with the brutal truth. And everything rains down on my heart, finding the already weak spots and chipping away at them. "Everything

I did or didn't do in the wake of his death..." my voice is so tight I feel like my words might break apart before they make their way past my chest "...was for Lucy."

And you ... but I can't say that anymore.

"I'm sorry if my existence in the world feels selfish to you."

She rolls in her bottom lip, but not before I see it quivering, and not before she sniffles. "Emmett ..."

"She lived, Tatum. Lucy is alive. So don't go slitting your fucking wrists. She will forgive you. She's in your corner too." I exit the bathroom before she can respond.

If anything short of perfection is unacceptable, then why did we have children? Why did we get married? Why are we even here? Tatum didn't love Austin more. She loved him like a mother. And she doesn't miss him more; she just doesn't know how to miss all of him. Her memories of him are stuck in a precise hole of time—the moment he died. If someone asks her about our son, she'll tell them that he died.

When someone asks me about Austin, I tell them about all the things that made him the most special little boy in the world. Then ... as if it's an asterisk at the end of a beautiful story, I tell them he died. I tell them I miss him dearly and that I don't regret a second of my life with him. I tell them he's my greatest memory, and for those nearly four years, the world was unquestionably a better place.

As I lower into the chair, pulled right next to Lucy's bed, she blinks open her eyes, fighting the groggy effects of her medications. Taking her hand, I kiss the inside of her wrist then press the back side of it to my face. She smiles as if to say, "Yes, Dad. I feel that. I feel you."

I smile back at her. "I love you, Luce."

"Love you," she whispers as Tatum emerges from the bathroom.

She's wiped off her face, and the poor lighting hides her red, swollen eyes. "Hey, sweetie. Do you need anything?" Depositing a kiss on Lucy's forehead, Tatum works to find a smile that's not too riddled with guilt.

"I'm good. Just … tired."

"Then rest," Tatum says.

"What time is it?"

I chuckle at Lucy's question. "Why? Do you have a date?"

"Ashton … does he know?"

"No. But I'll contact him tomorrow." Tatum sits on the edge of the bed and caresses Lucy's arm.

Her heavy eyelids fight to stay open as she mumbles something that sounds like "okay."

After Lucy's out and Tatum settles into the chair on the opposite side of the bed, she whispers, "What if she never walks again?"

CHAPTER TWELVE

The next morning, Tatum insists I go home to shower first. Maybe I stink the most. By the time I get toweled off and dressed, my parents are in my living room.

"Morning." Dad smiles as I make my way to the kitchen.

"We brought donuts." Mom nods to the box on the kitchen table.

"How did you know I was here?" I take a glazed donut and shove half of it into my mouth.

"We showed up at the hospital minutes after you left. Talked with Tatum for a bit. Then we decided to grab some breakfast and come here. It's a little more private than the hospital waiting room." Mom pours me a glass of orange juice that they must have picked up as well.

"Do we need privacy?" I raise a brow before taking a swig of juice.

"Sometimes it's easier to assess your emotional state when you're not putting on an act for other people."

I eye my mom while collapsing into the chair at the end of the kitchen table. "Well, assess away."

Mom's attention flits between me and my dad as if he's really going to weigh in on the matter. I'm certain the men in our family are not equipped with the necessary tools to make emotional assessments. He's really here for her emotional support.

"We know the accident was Tatum's ..." She stops as if the next word no longer fits.

I shake my head. "It was an accident."

"Yes, but as you know ..." Again, she trips and can't finish her thought. I might not be the one who needs their emotional state assessed. She's clearly struggling.

I let her silent pleas continue for a few more minutes before I empty the rest of my juice and stand, taking my glass to the sink and staring out the window to the backyard. "Austin's death was an accident. Tatum's and Lucy's crash was an accident. Sometimes people die from accidents. Sometimes they don't. We can't change the past. So the question is ... what do we need in order to continue with our future? Tatum needed someone to blame. And she needed that someone to not be a face she saw every day. That's okay. We all handle tragedy and grief differently. I don't love her any less for what she needed after Austin died. Lucy didn't die, but she might not walk again, which will feel like its own death. But I don't blame Tatum. I don't love her less. And I can look at her and see the woman I married. The mother of our children. My best friend. But that's just me."

"Had Austin not died on your watch ... would you be so quick to forgive Tatum?"

"Yes." I don't hesitate to answer. "What happened with our children ... it wasn't intentional or malicious. Just accidents. And I don't see Tatum as the reason for Lucy's situation. I simply see a mother who is beside herself with grief. And I hurt for her. I want nothing more than to take away that pain. But I can't. I'm not that person in her life anymore."

My mom wipes the corners of her eyes. "You're a good man, Emmett. I'm so proud of you. And my love for you has never wavered, not for a second. I hope you know that. The way you have loved Tatum is something far greater than I could have ever imagined. As much as your dad and I want to take credit for it, we can't. You simply have a soul that shines. It's pure. And your love is always ... always real. And Tatum ..."

"Is the love of my life. Now and always." I turn to face my parents, resting against the edge of the counter. "After Austin died, I made you promise to never blame Tatum for the end of our marriage. Nothing has changed. Part of her died that day with Austin. It changed her in a way no parent ever wants to imagine. It's not an emotion that can be tied into generic wedding vows. 'For better or worse ...' well, losing him was something so much more unimaginable than *worse*. And even though Lucy didn't die yesterday, I think Tatum lost another piece of herself."

"How do you do it?"

I narrow my eyes at my mom. "Do what?"

"Watch her love another man?"

There's no good answer to that question. Except ... "She was never really mine."

THEN

They said the second child would be super easy. We said more than eight years between kids would feel like starting over without the guarantee of an easy baby again.

We were right.

Lucy nursed. Slept. Pooped. Cooed.

Repeat. Repeat. Repeat.

Austin spit up nearly every ounce of breastmilk. Screamed (not cried, *screamed*). Slept in twenty-minute intervals. Needed to be held in a very specific way. Woke from the slightest noise or movement. Basically … he brought us to our knees for the first year of his life. Lucy essentially raised herself that year. She learned to spread peanut butter and jelly on two slices of bread and cut open a bag of precut apples from Costco for a snack.

A week before Austin's first birthday, I made the mistake of sharing a general observation with Tatum.

"My wardrobe is pathetic." She frowned as she stared into her closet after taking a shower while I put the kids to bed.

"You don't need to wear anything as far as I'm concerned." Standing behind her, I slid part of her robe off her shoulder and kissed her soft skin.

"Could you be anymore insensitive?" She whipped around, jerking her robe back up onto her shoulder.

I didn't see that coming, not even a little.

"I thought you told me to go enjoy a nice long shower while you put the kids to bed so I could destress from a long day and shave my legs at least once this month. But clearly it's all about sex … as if I don't have two kids demanding enough of me every day."

Whoa …

"That's…" I held up my hands in surrender "…not what I was thinking."

Her eyes narrowed. "Oh really? Can you honestly look me in the eye and tell me that you don't want to have sex?"

Such an unfair question.

"Listen, wanting and expecting are two different things. I'm not sure there's been a day since I met you that I haven't thought about sex with you. But for the record, I think about afternoon naps too, yet I rarely take one."

"Stop bullshitting me, Emmett. Can you just keep your dick in your pants for one night? Can you acknowledge for more than two seconds that I work my ass off taking care of the kids and that maybe I deserve to wash my hair and shave my legs without feeling the need to put out?"

Nine years of marriage ... and that was the first time she referred to us having sex as "putting out." And if I may add something else to the record, she didn't *put out* that often after Austin was born. More for the record ... I didn't expect much because I, too, was tired. Granted, she had the hardest role. She was the one who could soothe him. She was his food source. I changed a few diapers and took a few shifts of watching him so she could take a shower or run to the grocery store in peace and quiet.

Of course, I kept all those recorded details in my head. I was a lot of things, but not a complete idiot. Wordlessly, I backed away, before the flame reached the end of the fuse, and snatched my pillow from the bed and a blanket from the closet. Her clean hair and shaved legs could have the whole bed that night. I was fine with the sofa.

A little after two in the morning, a warm body nestled its way between me and the blanket. Familiar curves molded into me in all the right spots. Soft lips teased my neck. And lavender invaded my nose.

She was trying to give me an erection, and I feared it

could lead to divorce despite my lack of control over the situation.

With my lips pressed to the top of her head and my hands resting in the safe zone on her back, I whispered, "I'm sorry." The number one secret to a healthy marriage was to offer blanket apologies on a regular basis and hope you weren't asked to explain why you were apologizing.

"I'm pregnant."

I jackknifed to sitting, forcing her to straddle my lap and hold onto my shoulders. Her messy hair rolled down her back and chest while a few stray pieces clung to her face. Pouty lips parted, but what caught my attention was her swollen eyes. She'd been crying.

"You're ..." I dragged out that word because what came after it mattered. My reaction mattered. And I only had one shot to get it right.

Come on! Help me out.

She wasn't taking the bait. No tossing me a lifeline by filling in the blank. Just the opposite. She blinked slowly waiting for me to sum up her emotions and mine.

I was fucked.

"You're conflicted."

She made me wait for what felt like forever. Was conflicted the right word? Was it an insult? Of course she wasn't conflicted. She was a mother who loved her children and this one would be no different. I'd just set myself up to have to explain why I chose that word. Was I conflicted? Was I not excited to be having another child with her?

My truth involved cautious elation.

"So conflicted," she confessed, and my body sagged in relief. "I mean ... of course I'll love this child as much as I love Lucy and Austin. But it's so unplanned. And I'm so exhausted all the time. I'm not sure my body or my mind is ready for this." She frowned. "That's why I snapped at you. I'm sorry. Clearly, I'm already dealing with extra hormones."

"I for—" Yeah. I was on the verge of forgiving her. Such a close call. "There's nothing to apologize for."

Internal high-five.

She nodded several times. "We've got this. Right?"

"Of course. I mean ... we're not the world's best parents, but we're damn close." I smirked at the total lie. Perfection wasn't even in our realm of possibilities. We existed in survival mode twenty-four seven.

Tatum pressed her palms to my face. "Come to bed, baby. I miss you."

She didn't have to ask twice. I lifted her off my lap and carried her back to bed.

Two weeks later, she called me just as I was driving home.

"Hey, beautiful. What's up?"

"Emmett ..."

"I can barely hear you. Is everything okay?"

"Emmett ..." Her voice was mumbled and weak. It also sounded more like an echo.

"You're breaking up. I'm almost home."

"I'm not home."

"What?" I tried to make out her words.

"I'm at the doctor's. I ... I ... oh, Emmett ... I lost the b-baby ..."

I turned my truck around and sped off toward the medical clinic. "I'm coming. I'll be there soon."

When other people experienced loss, it was easy to give condolences, send a card or flowers, and go back to your own life. I didn't know how to handle the loss of a child. An unborn child.

The sight of my wife sitting in the waiting room—alone —felt like a dull knife being forced into my chest. She lost a baby, and they sent her to the waiting room. By. Her. Self.

She managed to look strong and unfazed. Face straight. Hands absentmindedly flipping through a *People Magazine* ... until she glanced up and saw me. Her eyes filled with tears, and she dropped the magazine, falling to pieces before I could get to her.

"I'm sorry, baby. I'm so very sorry." My eyes burned as I wrapped my arms around her, lifting her from the chair. We stood there unmoving for a few minutes, until she lifted her tearstained face.

"Let's go," she whispered.

I nodded, taking her hand and leading her to the parking lot. We didn't say a word to each other on the way home, but as soon as we pulled into the driveway, she reached over and rested her hand on my leg.

"Everyone is coming to our house tonight."

Oh yeah. I internally cringed. We hadn't told the kids or our families about the pregnancy. We were doing it that night. We'd invited everyone over for a barbecue. Tatum ordered a cake and T-shirts for Lucy and Austin, stating their big brother and big sister status.

"Where are the kids?"

"Andi's. I told her I forgot about an appointment and asked if I could drop them off. There was so much blood ..." Her voice cracked. "I knew something wasn't right."

"You should have called me." I squeezed her hand.

She shook her head. "I didn't want to worry you until I knew for sure."

"Still ..." I opened the door. "You should have called me.

We protect the kids. With each other ... we share all the burdens in life."

I walked around the truck and opened her door. "I'll go pick up the kids from Andi's. What can I do for you? Are you in pain or discomfort?" I helped her out of the truck.

Glancing up at me, her forehead tensed. "I lost a baby, Emmett. I'm ..."

That wasn't what I meant, but I also knew better than to try to defend what I did mean.

"I'm sorry." I kissed her forehead. "That's not what I meant. And *we* lost a baby. Your pain is my pain."

She shuffled her feet toward the door to the house. "Don't get the kids. Not yet. I just need ..."

When we stepped inside and shut the door, she turned toward me. My hands brushed her hair away from her face. "Anything. Just tell me what you need."

"I need you to hold me."

That I could do. It was my specialty. I wasn't an expert with the right words, but I could hold my wife and try to absorb her grief like a sponge.

We decided to keep the pregnancy and miscarriage between us. No need to burden anyone else with our loss. That left us with a houseful of family that night and a very anxious Lucy wondering about the mysterious surprise. I think most of our family anticipated a baby announcement. So the fact that we dug something else out of our hat was indeed a big surprise—something we had discussed but never really made a move to go forward.

"We're putting in a swimming pool!" Tatum managed to muster some enthusiasm, and only I could see past it to her unimaginable grief.

Explaining how an unexpected surprise like an unplanned pregnancy could cause such anxiety and grief one second then consume your world the next was hard. We loved that little peanut, and we grieved that little peanut. And if either one of us felt like fate acknowledged our unpreparedness for another child and took that child away, it was never openly expressed.

But ... I thought it.

CHAPTER THIRTEEN

NOW

Two WEEKS LATER, Lucy leaves her acute care at the hospital and receives several more weeks of care at a rehabilitation facility. Tatum spends the most time with her. I work. Shower. And spend every evening with her until bedtime.

Then the day finally arrives—she comes home.

No more assigning blame.

No more breakdowns filled with "what-ifs."

She can't walk on her own yet, but we haven't given up hope and neither have her doctors.

Her days will be filled with three to four hours of in-home therapy (physical and occupational) and online schooling.

"Stop," Lucy says to Tatum.

Tatum glances into the backseat while I keep my eyes on the road. "Stop what?"

"Pouting."

Tatum scoffs. "I'm not pouting. What on earth would I be pouting about?"

"I'm going to be at Dad's house and not yours."

All the bedrooms at Tatum's house are on the second level. I offered to put a lift chair on the stairs, but Lucy said she'd rather go *home*. That cut Tatum deeply, but she did a fairly good job of hiding her disappointment in front of Lucy. But clearly not good enough as Lucy calls her out on it.

"It's just temporary until you're running up and down the stairs again," her mom says, grasping for the positive side.

When Lucy doesn't respond, Tatum angles her body to get a better look at her. "Say something," she murmurs as regret saturates her words.

"I might not walk again."

Wow. This is the first time she's voiced those words. Was she putting on a brave face for weeks? For who? Us? The therapists?

I make a quick sideways glance just as Tatum swallows hard and blinks back her emotions.

"And that's life," Lucy continues. "I'm alive. Maybe I'll do something in the Paralympics. That would be cool. Right?"

When Tatum doesn't answer, because she can't, I jump into the conversation. "The coolest, Luce. Your mom would probably frown upon you doing Paralympic rugby, but I can definitely see you competing in archery or Boccia."

"Ooo ... archery would be cool. I'm pretty fantastic at darts."

"Stop," Tatum says so quietly we can barely hear her.

"Or tennis. I knew I should have gone out for tennis my

freshman year instead of track. What a waste," Lucy says, like she's not facing one of the toughest battles of her life.

There really are no words to describe how much I love this girl. She is and always will be my idol.

"It's never too late—"

"Stop!" Tatum cuts me off with an explosive response. "Stop talking about this like it's no big deal. Like never walking again is okay. It's not okay!"

I glance in the rearview mirror at Lucy, who shifts her attention out the window, and Tatum turns to look out her window too. When we get to the house, I help Lucy into her wheelchair and let her wheel herself up the ramp I built before we definitively decided whether or not she'd stay with me. For me, it has been and always will be her home, so I want to make sure she feels at home and a little independent when she is here.

We've added all the necessities with advice from her therapists. She has aids to help her use the toilet, shower, and get in and out of bed.

"Thanks, Dad." Lucy smiles as she manages to spin her wheelchair around in the entry to face me and Tatum. When her mom can't even look at her, Lucy clears her throat to get Tatum's attention. "I don't blame you. We all make mistakes that we'd give anything in the world to take back—get back that piece of the past—and have a redo."

I stiffen, a little uneasy about the reference. We all know she's talking about Austin.

The flinch on Tatum's face isn't missed by me. I see it. I *feel* it.

She takes a step toward Lucy and rests her hand on Lucy's cheek. "I'm grateful ... so grateful to God that you are alive."

Ouch ...

Lucy lifts her hand and rests it over Tatum's. "But it could have turned out differently."

"Lucy—" Tatum starts to pull her hand away.

"No, Mom." Lucy holds on to Tatum. "I'm here. But fate could have easily gone the other way. And you would have had to forgive yourself. Right?"

I want the floor beneath me to open and swallow me whole. Instead, I have to watch my daughter broach the subject I've avoided around Tatum for five years. And Tatum's discomfort is palpable. What does she say to Lucy? With me right here?

"I'm glad I don't have to think about that. It would feel quite …"

Unforgivable.

She doesn't have to say it. Not again anyway.

"I'm going to bring in your bag from the back of the car. The therapist should be here soon." I jab my thumb over my shoulder toward the front door and back my way out of this really awkward conversation. As I head toward the car— Lucy's car that we're using since it's too hard to get her in and out of my truck and Tatum hasn't gotten a new one yet —I think of all the things I will need to say to Lucy when Tatum is not around. Her need to soothe Tatum's conscience while trying to right the wrongs of the past is admirable, but it's a mistake. We've come too far. The things that are broken cannot be fixed, and it would only open old wounds to make such an unnecessary attempt.

She should forgive her mom and move on. That's the best move for everyone.

After we get Lucy's things unpacked and put away in the closet space I emptied for her in the master closet, the therapist works with Lucy, teaching her to live without the use of her legs in her home.

We watch as she learns and struggles. It's hard to not jump up and just insist we do everything for her. We can set her on the toilet and bathe her. We can put her in bed or on the sofa.

We can take another piece of her independence by not forcing her to rehabilitate and acclimate. That would be a bigger tragedy, so we leave her and her therapist alone for now, except when the therapist shows us things with which we might still need to assist Lucy.

After the therapist leaves, Tatum reheats one of the many dishes friends and family packed into our freezer to ease the transition home with Lucy.

"I was thinking..." Tatum taps her fork on her plate, having taken maybe two bites of her lasagna "...I'd like to stay for a few days just to make sure Lucy's sleeping okay. It's a king bed, so I can sleep with her."

"Mom, I'm—"

"I think that's a great idea," I say before Lucy can finish her protest.

"How's Josh going to feel about you staying with your ex-husband?" Lucy is relentless. She's Tatum.

I internally chuckle at the two of them butting heads.

Tatum lifts a shoulder into a casual shrug. "I'm not staying with my ex-husband. I'm staying with my daughter."

It's awesome the way they talk as though I—the ex—am not right here.

"Okay. But don't say I didn't warn you when Josh gets jealous."

Tatum rolls her eyes. "Jealous of what?"

"Thanks, you two." I stand, taking my plate to the sink. I'm feeling quite loved at the moment. "If you're going to talk about me, the least you could do is wait until I'm in the shower and do it behind my back like normal people."

A giggle escapes Lucy. "It's a compliment, Dad. I'm suggesting you have assets that might make another man jealous."

"Oh yeah?" I turn with my shoulders back, chest puffed out, and chin held high. "Such as?"

"Well, nobody grows a beard as quickly and as thick as yours."

Pursing my lips, I scratch my stubble covered chin. "I'm listening ..."

Another giggle comes out of Lucy, and it's the sunrise over the most beautiful sea. It's oxygen on the brink of suffocation. It's life. She's right ... the slightest twist of fate could have snatched her away from us. Even Tatum can't hide her grin as Lucy giggles.

"And your lawn mowing skills are way above average."

"True ..." I nod slowly.

"And your heart..." Lucy's tone shifts into one that's more serious "...is almost too big for your chest. It's almost too big for this world. And nobody knows that better than I do."

Well, fuck ...

The girl knows how to hit her dad squarely in the feels.

Tatum's grin fades, and she stands, taking her plate to the trash to scrape ninety percent of her dinner into the garbage. "I'm going to run home and get a few things packed. I'll be back in an hour or so. Okay?"

"Can you grab my extra charger in my nightstand drawer so I can charge my iPad and my phone tonight? I forgot to have you get it for me earlier."

"Sure." Tatum brushes past me without a single glance and kisses Lucy on the head before taking off.

When the door closes behind her, I sigh through my

nose while biting my lips together and giving Lucy a look. "Killing me."

"It's time."

I shake my head. "It's not."

"Then when?"

"When I'm gone. When I'm dead."

Her accident didn't affect her signature pout that was a direct genetic transfer from Tatum. "Why? Like ... I understood then. But things have changed."

"Things changed because of time, not just your accident. And there is no point."

"There's always a point to the truth."

I hate her advanced wisdom for a seventeen-year-old. It bites me in the ass when I least expect it.

"To set one free?" I reply in a mocking tone.

"Sometimes I think it would give her permission to ..."

"To what, Lucy? Hate you? Hate me even more?"

"To love you."

"I'm not sure Josh would agree with your theory or approve of your reasoning."

"Screw Josh."

My head jerks backward. "I thought you liked Josh—except for his incessant hand washing."

"I do like Josh. He's a great guy. A brilliant doctor. Handsome. He checks off all the boxes for most women."

"So what's the problem?"

"He's not you."

I chuckle. "And that's a bad thing?"

"It is for Mom."

"Why? A couple of months ago, you were encouraging me to date. You insisted I needed to get on dating sites."

"That was before the accident."

"So? How does your accident change my dating status?"

"She can no longer hate you."

"Mom?"

Lucy nods.

"I don't think it works that way. Two wrongs don't make a right. Tragedy and death don't make for an epic love story."

"I disagree. It's like you've never read *Romeo and Juliet* or listened to ninety percent of the songs on the radio."

I roll my eyes.

"Tell me you don't still love her."

"Who?" I buy time.

"Duh, Mom."

"I love her. I'll always love her. She was my wife. She's the mother of my children. That kind of love doesn't die."

"See! You do love her. If it were just a 'mother of my children' thing, you would have just said that. But you said you still love her as your wife."

"No."

"No what?" Lucy wheels her chair back from the table a few feet.

"No wrongs have been righted with your accident. It was tragic, and we are so lucky that it didn't turn out more tragically. But you need to stop looking at this as some opportunity to revisit the past. I only want you looking ahead to the future and getting better ... stronger ... walking again. Okay?"

Her enthusiasm dissipates like I just poured a bucket of water on her flames of hope. "Have you ever wondered about me? That maybe *I* need this?"

"I can't think about anything or anyone but you at the moment. And I want you to concentrate on you too. As happy as I am that you're in relatively good spirits after an accident that has left you temporarily in a wheelchair, I know you have some very challenging days ahead of you. Both physically and emotionally."

"What if there's a reason I didn't die in that accident? What if my time here wasn't over for a reason?"

"The reason you didn't die in that accident is because you have a bright and promising future, and the world needs you in it."

"But the world didn't need Austin in it?"

As hard as I try not to visibly recoil, I can't help it.

"The truth?"

Lucy nods once.

"I don't really believe there is a rhyme or reason for what happens in life. I think I believe in God, but I don't believe He dictates our lives. I believe we have free will which means our actions are based on instinct and impulse. Events are random. And luck is unpredictable and unbiased. The same mistake on any given day can have drastically different consequences. What's a close call one day can be utter devastation on another day. Luck wasn't on our side the day Austin died. I'm not even sure it was on our side the day you had your accident, but that's just differing degrees of unluckiness. For ... no particular rhyme or reason."

Lucy glowers. "But you said you thought meeting Mom ... *stealing* her was fate."

I shrug. "I like to think that. I also like to think that donuts won't give me a big gut and that we all get sports cars in heaven."

She doesn't want to smile. In fact, the grin she relinquishes is one of frustration. Much like her mom, she hates that I make her laugh when she's hell-bent on being pissed off about something. And she hates when I use such crazy examples to make my point. However, they *are* usually poignant.

"What's for dessert?"

I grin. "You name it. I know there's cookies, cake, ice cream, some sort of pudding and whipped cream concoction your friend's mom made."

"I'll try a bit of everything."

"Now we're talking."

CHAPTER FOURTEEN

I SLEEP on the sofa so I can hear Lucy and Tatum if they need me, but in the middle of the night, a glass clinking in the kitchen wakes me.

"Sorry," Tatum whispers. "I forgot to take a glass of water into the bedroom. And I'm parched."

Sitting up slowly, I rub my eyes against the light she turned on above the sink. "It's fine. Lucy sleeping okay?"

She takes a sip of her water. "Mmm-hmm."

When my eyes focus, I catch her gaze planted on my bare chest, and it makes me pause for a moment. Is she meaning to look at me like this? Or is she just really tired, and it's simply an absentminded look like when one spaces out? I choose to think it's the former, and I let my gaze take in her short nightshirt and toned legs.

"Don't look at me like that."

So fucking typical of her.

I lift a brow and pin her with a pot-kettle-black expression.

"I don't have my contacts in or my glasses on, so if you think I was looking at you, I wasn't," she says.

"Well, I don't have my glasses on either, so back at ya."

She chuckles, setting her water glass on the counter. "You have twenty-twenty vision."

"Not at night."

Rolling her eyes, she pads her bare feet toward me and curls up in the chair, shoving her legs up into her nightshirt. "Every time I wake up, I have this brief moment where I think everything isn't what it seems. There was no accident. Lucy is spending the night at a friend's house. And my biggest concern is making up a new routine for my dance students. Then I blink and the weight of my reality hits so hard I can barely breathe. So I close my eyes and try to get back to sleep where my dreams involve Lucy not in a wheelchair." Her gaze lifts from the floor between us to meet mine. "Do you ever have moments like that?"

I nod slowly. "I think the first time I remember feeling disoriented about reality upon waking was after your miscarriage. Sometimes I'd start to reach across the bed to rest my hand on your belly and catch myself at the last second."

Tatum looks away.

"I think when we sleep, our minds try to fill in the holes. The emotional wounds. And for a split second when we wake, everything doesn't hurt. For a few breaths, things feel right and normal. Then we blink and it all shatters like illusions do. Everything starts to hurt again."

Running her teeth along her bottom lip, her usual look of contemplation, she hums in agreement.

Silence settles between us, leaving only the soft tick of the clock on the bookshelf. It's funny how over the previous five years I imagined having a quiet moment like this with Tatum where she didn't look at me like I singlehandedly destroyed her whole world. There's been so many things

I've wanted to say to her. Yet, here we are, and I can't think of anything to say.

"I feel ..." She starts and then stops.

I glance up, waiting for more. It takes another minute or two for her to continue.

"I feel like there's something I owe you. Something I should say. But I can't figure it out."

My expression remains neutral, and my tongue remains idle.

"It's as if part of me feels like I should forgive you now. Yet ... it feels weird to forgive you just because I put Lucy in a wheelchair." She shakes her head and pinches the bridge of her nose. "God ... that sounds so awful. *Just* because I put her in a wheelchair. Like it's nothing. Like it's a scraped knee."

When she stumbles around for a few more seconds, I jump in and save her. It's what I do on instinct. It's what I've always done. "You don't owe me an ounce of forgiveness. The tragedies in our lives are not some "tit for tat" reconciliation. I have no desire to blame you for anything. Not for Lucy's accident. And not for the anger you've harbored since Austin's death. I know what it's like for *me* to lose a child. I know what it's like for *me* to have a child who can't walk. But I don't know what it's like for you or anyone else. There's not a road map for this. There's not a one-size-fits-all timeline for dealing with grief. If I could take away the guilt you're feeling, I would."

When she blinks, a tear escapes, and she swats her hand over her cheek to dry it. "It's not normal, Emmett. You *should* be angry. Lucy could have died. Now, she's in a wheelchair because of *my* negligence. If you love her the way you say you do, you should be angry for at least a moment. One fucking breath of anger to show you love her.

149

To show the fear you had when you got the call about the accident. The hurt … the pain … the anger … it's because we care. I need to know you care because the alternative is that I'm an unforgiving bitch who leaves her husband because she doesn't know how to deal with the loss of a child."

What am I supposed to say? I really don't know. Maybe things were easier when she didn't want to see me or speak to me.

"You need me to be angry with you? Hate you?"

"Yes."

I grunt a laugh and run my hands through my hair. "And that will make you feel what? Less guilty? Newsflash … it won't. Nothing I can do will undo what's been done. Not if I hate you. Not if I forgive you. And you should know that. It's been over five years since Austin died. And we're divorced. You've met someone else. You no longer live in this house. But all I have to do is look at you, and I still see the grief, anger, and resentment as strong as the day you asked me for a divorce."

More tears fill her eyes.

I slide off the sofa and crawl on my knees to the chair, resting my hands on her bare feet. "I'm not mad that you look at me the way you do. We've lost two children, and I know on an emotional level we will never be the same whether we would have stayed together or not. Nothing will fill that void. And I understand why you needed to find a way to simply not be reminded of it every day. This isn't a competition over who's more forgiving or who's best at pretending to function normally. It fucking hurts to breathe most days, but I breathe for Lucy."

And I breathe for you, Tatum. I don't say that, but god … I think it. "Memories are enough. Remembering Austin. And remembering the way you used to look at me. The way you used to love me. It's not ideal. It's not the dreams we imagined. But it's something. And when looking at what has happened to us ... *something* is enough."

Sniffling nose and lower lip trembling, she curls her hair behind her ears. "I grieve us too," she whispers. "It hurts when you're here. It hurts when you're gone. It hurts to love you. It hurts to hate you. We died ... and that just ... hurts."

Leaning forward, I rest my head against her shins and close my eyes. "I know."

Goose bumps shoot up along my skin the instant her fingers ease into my hair. It's the kindest touch I have felt since Austin died. She pauses when I shiver, but I don't say anything because I don't want her to stop. Can this be that dream that we don't want to wake from? Can this be that moment we try to find every time we close our eyes to escape our reality?

"I should get back in there in case she wakes up."

I lift my head and stand, quickly turning away from her so she doesn't see how her touch cut me back open, making all my old wounds bleed again. "Yeah, you probably should." I wipe my eyes and grab my blanket, giving it a shake out because I need to look preoccupied doing something other than looking at her with my longing gaze and chest wide open.

Her retreating steps stop, and I pause my motions with my back still to her.

"Emmett?"

"Hmm?"

"Thank you."

"For what?"

"For being in my corner."

Swallowing my pride, my pain, and a lifetime of emotions, I nod several times. "Always."

THEN

"I GO TOO!" Austin chased me to the back door, wearing his hard hat and vest.

My mini me.

"Not today, buddy. Maybe another day." I picked him up, and he grabbed his hard hat to keep it from falling off. My nose nestled into his neck.

"Daddy ..." He giggled and squirmed from my scruffy face on his skin.

He smelled of bananas and peanut butter from his toast that morning. When his little hand pressed to my face to push me away, I could taste the residual peanut butter. Austin always had a little extra on him.

Extra food.

Extra dirt.

Extra Play-Doh under his fingernails.

Extra toothpaste smeared on his cheeks.

"Such a heartbreaker." Tatum breezed past me, giving me a wink. She liked good cop bad cop. And with my little guy *always* wanting to be with me—at work, in the yard, in the shower, by the grill—that made me the bad cop most of the time because I had to say no so often.

Tatum made cookies, took him to the park, and played with him in the pool. Yet despite her efforts to be fun all the time, he still preferred mundane things with me like pulling weeds in the yard or riding in my truck to check on jobsites.

"If you let me hurry up and get to work, I'll hurry and get my stuff done so we can mow the lawn later?"

"I drive!" he squealed.

"You drive." I kissed his cheek and set him on his busy

little feet. Our yard was big, but not so big that we needed a riding lawn mower. But I bought one just so Austin could help me mow the lawn.

"Where do you think you're going?" Tatum asked as I opened the door to leave for work before Austin returned for an encore performance of "Take Me To Work, Daddy."

Before I could answer, her arms wrapped around my neck, and she forced me down for a long kiss. Our kids were used to our PDA, and we loved that it was the norm for them. We hoped they would have a love like ours for themselves someday.

"Thanks for the boner, babe," I whispered, adjusting myself as she stepped back, rubbing her lips together.

"Your parents said they'd take the kids for the weekend. I told them we had some organizing around the house to do. And the pool needed to be thoroughly cleaned."

I narrowed my eyes. "I thoroughly cleaned the pool last weekend."

Tatum frowned at my stupidity, my slow brain.

My eyebrows raised. We weren't going to organize anything. She made plans to be alone and naked with me. God ... I loved her. "Right. Good idea. You have no idea how badly I've been craving organization."

She chuckled. "Go to work. You have a lawn to mow later."

"Yes, ma'am." I winked and took off for work with an extra bounce in my step. As I walked out back past the pool, I spotted Austin's blue soccer ball on the ground. It wasn't meant for the pool, so I tossed it up onto the deck before continuing to my truck.

My morning continued to shine as we landed two new bids and hired a new welder with a lot of experience.

"You've put in over sixty hours this week," Will

informed me as I walked into the office to grab my keys before heading out to lunch.

"Time and a half." I winked at him because he'd been trying to get me to be salaried for years.

"Go home early. Paint your fence. Swim some laps."

I chuckled, tossing my keys in the air and catching them. "Clock out."

Will smirked. "Yes, get off my fucking time clock."

Not a bad Friday. In fact, it was feeling like the best Friday I'd had in a long time. On my way home, I stopped for a bouquet of flowers—pink roses and lavender—for my beautiful wife. I started to call her after I climbed back into my truck, just to let her know I'd be home early if she wanted to run some errands without the kids. Then I changed my mind since I was only ten minutes from home anyway. Why not surprise her?

Choices.

Adults made thousands of choices every day. Some could be as simple as how far to fill a water glass. Others could be as serious as quitting a job. Few choices felt like they could have a profound impact on our lives. What possible chain of events could happen as a result of filling a glass three-fourths full instead of half full? Using six squares of toilet paper instead of four? Coffee vs tea? Red shirt vs blue shirt?

Could thirty seconds change your life forever?

Yes.

As I made my way from my truck to the tall white gate of our backyard, I had no idea how all the choices Tatum and I had made that day would change the course of our existence forever.

As I locked the gate latch behind me, I started toward

the house with a huge smile on my face and a bouquet of flowers in my right hand.

A cloudless sky.

Almost ninety degrees.

The soft hum of lawns being mowed in the distance.

All the best things about summer.

I could envision the delight on Tatum's face.

The squeal of Austin running to greet me.

The lightning-fast glance of Lucy giving me a two second greeting from behind her iPad.

The sun's rays bounced along the glassy surface of our pool. For a split second I thought about our years of indecision. Pool? No pool? And I thought about the announcement we made to our family about it on the very day Tatum miscarried. The split second multiplied as did the ache in my chest. I hadn't thought about the baby we'd lost in quite some time.

We healed. We moved on.

With my free hand, I rubbed my chest. The pain felt real, like my heart knew something I did not.

And it did.

My gaze snagged on the white and orange hardhat Austin had been wearing that morning. It floated in the water not far from the blue soccer ball that I'd tossed onto the deck that morning.

Then ...

My. World. Shattered.

"AUSTIN!" I didn't take the time to unlock the gate. I jumped the pool fence and dove into the water to rescue my little boy—my mini me—from the bottom. "Austin! TATUM!" I gasped and cried for help as I pulled him to the edge and out of the water. "TATUM!" I yelled again while starting compressions. I didn't count. I just pumped his chest over and over. My mouth covered his mouth. He was so fucking cold. Tiny broken pieces of my heart ripped me apart inside as I tried to breathe life into his limp body.

"Breathe ..." I cried, compressing his chest over and over. "TATUM! Somebody! Call for help! PLEASE!"

Nobody called for help.

Nobody answered my desperate pleas.

It was just me and my lifeless world.

I compressed with one hand while I searched for my phone in my pockets that were wet and tight like goddamn suction cups as I tried to retrieve it.

"Dad? DADDY!"

I glanced up at Lucy on the deck, looking on in complete horror and shock.

"CALL 9-1-1! G-GO!" My words faltered as the growing reality of the situation came to rest in the wreckage of my heart, completely crushing my lungs. Every time I bent forward to breathe into Austin's mouth, I could barely find a breath to give him. "Breathe ... buddy ... p-please ... b-breathe ..."

I knew. I just ... *knew.*

Time lost its place in my life because I swear my heart stopped. It paused. It refused to beat without Austin's beating too. Like all the times he yelled for me, *"Daddy, I'm coming! Daddy, wait up!"* I waited.

I waited for him to breathe, so we could breathe together.

I waited for his heart to beat, so ours could beat together.

"I'll ... wait ... for ... you ..."

One two three four ... fifteen sixteen seventeen ...
One breath. Two breaths. Three breaths ...

My eyes squeezed shut, and I went through the motions. I swear to God I heard his voice.

Daddy, it's okay.

It wasn't okay. Why was he saying it was okay?

At some point the paramedics arrived and pulled me away from him.

They asked me questions.

I don't know if I answered them because I couldn't hear my own voice past the thundering of my heart. It was then that I realized it was beating again, and for a moment I had hope again, hope that it meant his was beating again too. I followed them toward the driveway as they worked in unison to save him.

"Dad ..." A small hand grabbed my arm.

I glanced down at Lucy and her teary eyes and quivering lip. "I'm sorry."

Oh my fucking hell, I thought. What was happening to my life? It wasn't real. It was supposed to be the best Friday ever. I was supposed to be mowing the lawn with Mr. Giggles helping me steer, my nose in his hair, inhaling his berry scented shampoo mixed with a little dirt and every snack he ate that day.

My ears rang. I could barely hear. Was I alive? It had to be a nightmare.

Wake the fuck up!

Lucy had watched. What must she have been thinking? Could her twelve-year-old brain process all that just happened?

"Luce ..." I squatted, holding her arms, putting us face-to-face. "Mom. Where is your mom?"

"I'm s-so s-sorry ..." More tears filled her eyes. "Will h-he be o-kay?"

"Lucy. Look at me?" I wiped her tears. "I need you to tell me where your mom is at?"

"S-she ran an e-erand. S-she said I ... I could w-watch Austin. F-for just a l-little bit. But Anna FaceTimed m-me. A-and I told him to w-watch a show and stay on the c-couch." She sobbed. "Is he o-okay? I'm s-scared."

I hugged her to me, cupping the back of her head.

"MY BABY!" Tatum's shrill cry cut like a jagged knife through the air. "NOOO!"

I released Lucy and ran out the gate.

"NOOO!" Tatum's arms reached for Austin as they loaded him into the back of the ambulance.

Before I could grab her, she climbed in the back. One of the paramedics tried to stop her for a brief moment.

"I'm his mother!" She cried more and the lady nodded, guiding her to the bench to sit while they continued CPR.

The doors closed.

The ambulance disappeared down the street crowded with police cars and a fire engine.

"Dad ..."

I turned and grabbed Lucy's hand. "Let's go. We have to get to the hospital."

"Is he okay?"

With no time to waste, I hoisted her into the passenger's seat of my truck. I couldn't answer her because ... I knew.

"She said it was only for an hour. She would be back in an hour. I told him. I *told* him to watch his show and stay on the couch. He knows he's not supposed to try to climb the pool fence."

As I raced toward the hospital, clothes soaked, mind numb, I rested my hand on Lucy's leg, and I kept saying, "I know. It's okay, Lucy."

Every time she said something, even when it didn't

really register what she was saying, I repeated, "I know. It's okay, Lucy."

But it wasn't okay.

Things would never be okay again.

The world would continue to turn, but it would always feel not quite right. Like amputating a part of your body. You can live, but not the same way.

When we pulled into the parking lot at the hospital, I messaged our parents. Had I called them, I would have lost it in front of Lucy. For her, I had to keep it together as long as possible.

Austin fell into the pool. He's in the ER.

I pressed send and turned off my phone.

"Lucy." Before I could say another word, my emotions robbed my ability to speak. My ability to breathe. It was nearly ninety degrees outside, yet I couldn't stop shivering. I swallowed several times and blinked to keep my tears in check despite how badly they burned my eyes. That lump in my throat swelled to something so unimaginably hard and big, I felt like someone was strangling me. I couldn't get a single word past it.

That was what realizing you have no control in the world felt like.

"He'll be fine, Dad. I prayed."

I fisted my shaking hands and nodded several times before opening the door. When we reached the emergency room, I asked to see Austin Riley.

The nurse smiled politely at me and then at Lucy. "Do you have other family here?"

"My wife."

With a wavering smile, she nodded. "Besides her?"

"My parents are on their way. Can I just see my son and wife?"

159

"Of course. Would your daughter like to wait with me until your parents arrive?"

"No, Dad. I want to see Austin too."

With a single look, the nurse confirmed what I already knew in the newly carved hole in my soul.

"Luce, the room is probably small, and there could be lots of doctors and nurses. Let me go check on him first, and I'll be right back to get you."

She frowned but nodded.

My feet dragged like cinder blocks. My pulse felt sluggish yet angry, like my heart was upset that it had to keep doing its job. The parts of me that didn't hurt felt hollow. I was a toxic mix of pain and nothingness.

"I'm very sorry for your loss," another nurse said as she left the tiny area behind the curtain, leaving me alone with Austin and Tatum draped over him sobbing—asking why?

As sure as I *knew* before they took him away that he would never open his eyes again, I also knew Tatum's question would forever go unanswered. Death held no accountability. We were slaves to its will. It was part of the deal in the game of life. We knew this when we decided to bring new life into this world.

There were no guarantees.

I sat on the edge of the bed and rested my hand over Austin's cold little hand. My other hand pressed to Tatum's back, rising and falling with each gut-wrenching sob. There was nothing to say, just emotions to be felt. A million questions with no answers that would ever make sense. Before facing Lucy and the rest of our family with the heartbreaking news, I let myself have that moment with my wife and our son —his body absent a soul and everything that made him ours.

Daddy, it's okay.

Holding my breath, I thought I could stay in once piece. My lips pressed together tightly, but it didn't work. I exploded. It hurt so fucking badly.

Take me with you, buddy. I silently begged him. He didn't deserve to be alone. I needed to go with him, wherever he was.

We would mow lawns and wear our hard hats. We would play in the dirt. I'd tickle his tummy, and he would giggle.

I let my own body shake with sobs.

I let hot, angry tears stream down my face.

I let the pain in, knowing I would soon have to stifle it and *all* of my emotions to be strong for Lucy and to be strong again for Tatum.

But for that moment, I bled out.

For that moment, I fucking hated the world and the very lonely place it had just become.

For that moment, my shoulders curled into my body as I convulsed with grief.

I didn't feel like a man, a father, or a husband. In fact, I had never felt so weak in my life.

Weak because I couldn't save him.

Weak because I didn't know what to say to Tatum.

And weak because I wanted to die.

I just ... wanted ... to ... die.

"It's not real," Tatum whispered with a scratchy voice after what seemed like a good half hour of the worst imaginable goodbye ever. Her cheek rested against Austin's motionless chest. Her gaze fixed to the curtain as I continued to stroke her hair down her back.

My tears had run dry, and I'd returned to my numb, hollow state.

When I didn't respond, she slowly shifted her red-eyed gaze to me.

"I wish it weren't," I whispered back.

"I ... don't understand." She started to cry softly again. "What h-happened?"

I eased my head side to side and worked to swallow past the thick emotions lodged in my throat.

He was there. Our little boy. Why couldn't he just open his eyes and start giggling, taunting the fact that he played dead and fooled us? That was one of his favorite games. He'd pretend to be dead until we'd say something like, *"I guess we'll have to go without Austin to get ice cream since he's dead."* And he would spring from his spot on the sofa or under his comforter and yell, *"Gotcha!"*

We'd laugh and then tickle him, his favorite form of punishment for his orneriness.

His laughter.

That big smile.

Rosy cheeks.

And boundless energy.

Everything about him was angelic.

But in that moment, it felt like someone told us heaven didn't exist and the sun would never shine again.

Tatum peeled herself from his chest, which only made her sob more as she covered her mouth and stared at him. I wrapped my arms around her waist, bringing her back to my chest, trying to hold her together when I knew she was already broken beyond repair. As was I.

"Excuse me..." a nurse peeked her head around the curtain "...I'm very sorry, but we need to move him to a different area. We can put him in a private room if you need more time."

More time.

Yeah, we needed more time with Austin. Approximately forever. Was that too much to ask?

Tatum turned in my arms and buried her face into my chest like suddenly the sight of him was just too much.

"We'll go see if the rest of our family is here," I said.

The nurse nodded. "I'll find you when we have him transferred to a different spot."

"Thank you."

With Tatum tucked into my side, I guided her toward the waiting room, feeling so much of her weight in my arms as her knees kept trying to buckle beneath her. I felt every ounce of her pain and weakness.

Would we ever feel strong enough to walk on our own again?

Would we ever feel the relief of a full breath?

Would the sun ever break through the clouds of our grief?

It was hard to imagine in that moment.

"Where's Lucy? I need to talk to her. She was watching him. I need to know what happened. How could this happen? How? I just don't understand." Anger seeped into Tatum's words. She needed answers. But more than that, I feared she needed someone to blame.

And while I knew she loved Lucy so very much, I also knew she wasn't herself, and the words she might say to Lucy would impact our daughter in the most profound and possibly tragic way imaginable.

They'd be words she could never take back.

They'd be words that would leave lasting scars on our young daughter's soul.

"Love this baby more. You have to promise to love this baby more than me ... more than us."

Tatum's words from twelve years earlier echoed in my

head, pushing aside my own unfathomable grief for Austin in order to make room for Lucy—for doing what was best for the child that we did still have. The *one* child we had left.

"Lu—" Tatum started to pull away from me as soon as she caught sight of Lucy in the waiting room with our parents.

I grabbed Tatum and turned her toward me, holding her arms, and forcing her to look at me with her back to them.

*"Love this baby more. You have to promise to love this baby more than me ... **more than us.**"*

Confusion and frustration played on my wife's tearstained face. And I took a deep breath, as deep as I could, and I made the decision to love Lucy more because that was what my wife asked me to do—that was the promise I made to her.

But more than that ... it was the right thing to do. I couldn't save Austin that day, but I could save Lucy.

"It was me. Will let me go home early. Lucy wanted to FaceTime with her friend. Austin was watching a show. And I decided to run out to the garage to check the oil in the lawn mower and fill it with gas. I told him to stay put and watch his show. It was ..." Tears reemerged, burning my eyes again because, while it was a lie, I knew the next part was most likely very true. "It was minutes. I only took my eyes off him for a few minutes."

Later we would learn a child Austin's age can drown in under thirty seconds.

Thirty. Seconds.

So much love. So much time. So many memories.

Gone in thirty seconds.

Tatum's face contorted even more as she slowly shook

her head and pried herself out of my hold. "How could you?" she whispered.

It was the first knife of many.

She turned and ran toward our parents and Lucy. Falling to her knees, she hugged Lucy like she was everything. And she was.

I kept my promise to my wife.

Yet she would never know.

And I would accept the consequences.

That was the day I lost my son, my wife, and in many ways ... Lucy too.

CHAPTER FIFTEEN

Tatum's parents took Lucy for the night. I brought Tatum home. She went straight to the bedroom and locked me out. I spent the night on the sofa listening to her cry. In the middle of the night, I walked around the pool, eyeing everything the police had already inspected. Austin pulled a chair from the deck to the fence to help him climb over it. It was a miracle it didn't knock him down the deck stairs. It was heartbreaking that Lucy didn't hear him because he probably shoved it down the stairs like he did whenever he wanted to move something from one level to another. He was a busybody, fearless and curious.

The next morning, I unlocked the door. Tatum had fallen asleep in a ball on her side of the bed, clothes still on, hands loosely fisted in her hair.

"I'm going to get Lucy," I said softly.

She didn't move, didn't say anything. But I know she heard me. I changed my clothes, the same ones that had been drenched from the pool and headed to Tatum's parents' house.

"Emmett." Tatum's mom pulled me aside as I stepped

into the foyer. "Lucy said it was her fault." Concern lined her face.

I could hear the TV on in the other room where I assumed Lucy was with Tatum's dad. "No. It was on my watch." My throat tightened with emotion.

Tatum's mom flinched, tears pooling in her eyes. "I'm sorry."

I nodded. "I'm going to take her home now."

"You left Tatum alone?"

"She was sleeping. That's why I want to get right back home." I headed toward the living room.

Lucy's gaze made a slow trip from the TV to me, a sign that she wasn't right, that she was still in shock too. I knew I had to fix it—fix her as quickly as possible before the damage became permanent.

"Let's go home, Luce." It had been a while since I'd picked up my daughter like a little girl and cradled her in my arms, but that was exactly what I did that day. Without another word to Tatum's parents, I exited the house and buckled her in my truck.

A few blocks from home, I pulled over and killed the engine.

"Look at me, Lucy."

She slowly brought her gaze to meet mine.

"I should have been home sooner yesterday. Had I been home sooner, Austin wouldn't have fallen into the pool. It's *my* fault. Mom knows it's my fault. Everyone knows it's my fault. If you tell people it's your fault, then Mom will feel like it was really her fault for leaving before I got home. But I should have been there. It was *my* fault. The blame is mine and only mine. I need you to tell me you understand this. I need you to promise that you will not ever try to make anyone think that is was your fault or your mom's fault."

"But …"

"No buts, Luce. It was my fault."

"But he's …" Her bottom lip moved uncontrollably as tears spilled down her cheeks. "H-he's dead."

I pulled her to me, hugging her tightly. "I know. It's my fault that he's dead. And I'm so very sorry for not being there. I'm so sorry I let this happen to our family. But we need to go home and be there for Mom. She's so heartbroken right now, and she needs you. Can you be there for Mom? Can you help her through this?"

In my arms, her head moved up and down a little bit. I didn't know if she could do it, if she could let her brain fully believe it was my fault and not hers, but I had to hope, I had to try.

When we arrived home, Lucy tiptoed into the master bedroom and crawled into bed with Tatum. I stood at the entrance and watched as my wife pulled Lucy into her arms and clung to her for dear life. As much as I wanted it to be me consoling Tatum, my arms holding her, I knew it had to be Lucy.

———

WE BURIED AUSTIN ON A TUESDAY.

Tatum clung to Lucy and her parents during every step of the way while I stood in the shadows, the guilty one. My wife couldn't even look at me. I kept my emotions in check as if my confession robbed me of all rights to grieve.

I woke early in the morning, from my new spot on the sofa, to take a jog. When I reached an open field, absent of anyone who could hear me, I screamed—roaring like an angry animal, so fucking pissed off at God for taking my son. For a few minutes, I let myself completely fall apart with anger and tears and the question *why?* Why Austin?

Then I'd walk home, taking time to catch my breath and regain my composure before sneaking past Lucy and Tatum in our bed, to take a shower before heading off to work.

Work ...

That was all I did.

Tatum didn't say it, she didn't have to, but I knew she didn't want me at home. She needed Lucy, and some days, her parents would come to visit and make them lunch.

After a week of sleeping with Tatum, Lucy decided she was ready to sleep in her own bed again, which meant she expected me to sleep with Tatum. So we did. We slept together with our backs to each other and an infinite chasm of grief, guilt, and blame between us. An ocean too wide to cross.

I knew it from the moment I confessed to her in the hospital.

"You need to get rid of the fucking pool," Tatum announced as she poured a cup of coffee a few minutes after Lucy got on the bus for her first day of school. It was the first thing she'd said directly to me since Austin died. With Lucy home as a buffer, she would say things to Lucy that I knew were meant for me.

"What's for dinner, Lucy? I'd make enchiladas, but we're out of chicken. And I'm tired of all the covered dishes clogging up the fridge and freezer."

That was her way of telling me to go to the store to get chicken without actually looking at me or addressing me directly. It was her way of telling me to ditch all the food friends and family had left for us.

Apparently, she didn't find it appropriate to tell Lucy to

get rid of the *fucking pool.* Lucky me. We were back on speaking terms—sort of.

Nobody loved that pool more than Lucy. Was it fair to get rid of the pool when it was her favorite part of summer?

"We shouldn't have ever gotten a ..." Tatum trailed off.

We shouldn't have ever gotten a pool. Of course, she thought it. I did too, along with so many other things we should or should not have done. I knew it. And I knew she did too, even if she couldn't say the words or even look at me to start to say them. I didn't blame her for not being able to say them, not when I couldn't say them. Austin died and we ran out of words. The unimaginable gobbled up our place in the world, leaving us stranded with no road map for navigating life after losing a child.

"Should we talk to Lucy first?"

"It was her idea," Tatum said, tightening the sash on her robe before taking her coffee to the bedroom where she shut and locked the door behind her.

So ... I filled in the pool. Built a firepit with surrounding gardens. And planted an apple tree (Austin's favorite fruit) with Lucy in honor of him.

I took care of the yard. Cleaned the house, washed the windows. I took care of the laundry and all of the grocery shopping, and I made most of the meals. Whatever I could think of doing, I did, asking absolutely nothing of Tatum.

It felt like everything, but it wasn't enough. No amount of work or good deeds could undo what had been done. In her eyes, I killed our son, and it was unforgivable. It was never a measure of her love for me; it was always a testament to her love for Austin.

CHAPTER SIXTEEN

NOW

Lucy has a physical therapist, an occupational therapist, and she still sees a psychiatrist. Now, they have more to talk about than just the loss of her brother. I might need to start seeing someone too—just to deal with the irrational feelings a certain doctor's Lexus parked on my street evokes when I arrive home from work.

It's been months since the accident, and the good news is Lucy wants to stay with me instead of having me make her mom's house wheelchair accessible. More good news? I get to see Tatum every day. She no longer spends the night, but she's here early in the mornings and doesn't leave until she's done helping Lucy get ready for bed.

The psychological bonus? Josh is here all the damn time too. Hugging, kissing, flirting with my wife. Talking to my daughter like she's his daughter. Cooking meat on the grill like it's his grill. However, he does nothing for me. Would it kill him to clean a bathroom or two? Rake the fallen leaves? Chop wood?

It's like Tatum looked for someone who is the complete opposite of me. I suppose the un-calloused hands of a surgeon can't risk getting a splinter or blister from manual labor.

Oh joy … with my late arrival today, they're already out back enjoying the firepit while the sky tries to spit a little fall snow. Ten bucks says Tatum had to start the fire, but now Josh is playing the manly role of letting my wife sit on his lap as if there aren't three other chairs around the pit since Lucy is in her wheelchair.

"Hey, Dad." Lucy smiles.

This girl … she's in a fucking wheelchair with an unknown future. She has therapy every day and works her ass off. It's her junior year of high school, and she hasn't once complained about online schooling or missing out on time at school with her friends. I'm not sure I'll ever be able to fully convey just how much of a hero she is to me. On my very best day, I don't come close to being half the person my dear Lucy has become.

"Luce." I kiss the top of her head. "How's my girl?" I emphasize the *my* just to make sure Josh remembers my daughter has a father and doesn't need another one. Fuck … it was much easier to deal with him when he wasn't in my face all the time.

"They're going to use these electrode things on my back to stimulate my muscles."

"Oh … did you have a doctor's appointment today?" I ask Lucy, but my gaze is on Tatum cuddled up on Josh's lap.

"It was last minute. Josh arranged it." Tatum shrugs like it's no big deal.

But it is a big deal because we agreed she'd take her to therapy now that she's going to an office instead of the therapist coming to the house. I can't take off work every single day, but I always make myself available for her doctor appointments.

"What's last minute?"

Tatum gives me a look, it's the "not in front of Josh and Lucy" look. I get it all too often from her.

"I'm going to shower," I say, giving her the "I'm pissed off" look.

"We saved you a hamburger," Lucy says.

I transform my face into Mr. Happy just for her. "Thanks."

After I wash my filthy hands in the mudroom, I inspect the remnants of dinner on the kitchen counter and the mess I'll clean up later when Josh skips out around nine o'clock with Tatum. He needs to do a better job of helping out around here. I'm not saying it will totally ease the sting of him fucking my wife, but at least I'll have a clean kitchen so I can spend more time playing video games with Lucy before climbing the stairs to sleep in her old bedroom.

"This morning."

I turn toward Tatum's voice as I throw the cold piece of meat onto a bun with some ketchup, mustard, and a slice of lukewarm cheese.

She crosses her arms over her chest and rests her hip against the counter. "It's a specialist who had a last-minute cancellation. I found out about it this morning, after you'd already left for work."

I take a massive bite and nod before mumbling over my full mouth. "If only I had a cell phone, you could have called me."

She rolls her eyes. "It's one appointment."

"One appointment about something I've never heard about."

"It's—"

"No." I grab a paper towel and wipe my mouth. "I'll wait for Lucy to tell me all about it."

"What's up with the mood?"

She doesn't want to get me started on all the reasons for my mood.

"No mood. I'm just tired. It's been a long day." I toss the rest of my shitty, over-cooked burger in the trash. Josh cooks everything extra well done. "And I have a kitchen to clean up. I'll have a fire to extinguish in the pit, crumbs around the pit to sweep up. And I need to do a load of laundry because I'm running out of work pants to wear. Did I mention I want to spend some time with Lucy too?"

And I'm going to have fucking pizza delivered because germaphobe Josh charred my dinner, but she doesn't need to know that. I've said enough.

When Tatum doesn't say anything, I head upstairs to shower. By the time I towel off my hair, slide on a tee and sweatpants, and jog down the stairs, Lucy's reading a book in the living room and the kitchen is clean.

"Please don't tell me you cleaned the kitchen," I say to her.

"Mom and I did it together after Josh left."

"Josh left without your mom?"

Lucy nods, keeping her focus on her book.

"Is your mom still here?"

"She's out back, covering the firepit and sweeping the crumbs."

I'm an asshole.

I sigh, pulling on my hoodie. "I'm going to see if she needs any help, then you're going to tell me all about your appointment."

"Sounds good."

After shoving my feet into a pair of loosely laced tennis

shoes, I step out back. Tatum glances over her shoulder at me while she finishes sweeping.

"I wasn't complaining to make you stay and clean up." I squat down by her feet and hold the dustpan while she sweeps the pile into it.

"No? Could have fooled me."

Standing, I take the broom from her and return it to the garage. When I return, she's not here.

"Did your mom leave?" I ask Lucy when I get back inside of the house.

Lucy shakes her head. "She's putting clean sheets on my bed."

"Well..." I take a seat on the sofa "...tell me all about your appointment."

She grins, curling her long hair behind her ears and telling me all about electrical stimulation and how it might help her walk again. I eat up her words and savor every second of her enthusiasm. I have no doubt that she will walk again. My Lucy is a fighter. As we're talking, Tatum slides past the living room and goes upstairs; I'm not sure why until she comes back downstairs with a laundry basket of my dirty work clothes.

I cringe, but I don't move because Lucy is still telling me about her appointment. When she's done, I kiss her on the cheek. "I'm so excited for you, Luce."

"Josh said it will be a game-changer."

I smile through my bitter response to his name. "Sounds like a game-changer. I'm going to check on your mom."

Down the hallway, Tatum's in the laundry room loading my dirty clothes into the washer.

"I'm an asshole. I admit it. You've made your point. Now go home to your boyfriend." I grab the laundry detergent and take the empty basket from her hands.

"I have no point, Emmett. You need help, so I'm helping."

"I don't need help." I dump the detergent into the dispenser and start the washing machine. "I just needed to vent because ..." I turn and lean against the washing machine, wearing a frown. "Because I'm an asshole."

"Let's get my house ready for Lucy so you don't have to come home to a dirty kitchen."

Pinching the bridge of my nose, I shake my head. "It's not that."

"Then what is it? Me? Josh?"

"Yes ... no." I run my hands through my damp hair and lace my fingers behind my neck on a long sigh.

"It's Josh," she says.

I blink and hold my tongue.

"All the more reason to have Lucy at home with me."

"She wants to stay here. Maybe you and Josh should hang out at your place. I'm perfectly capable of helping Lucy. She can get on and off the toilet by herself. The shower is wheelchair accessible. I'm not implying she doesn't want your help, but she can manage while you have your Josh time."

Tatum plants her hands on her hips. "It's not just about us having time together. It's the fact that he loves Lucy too, and he wants to spend time with her."

"Fine. How about he stops by once a week for a visit?"

She scoffs. "Once a week? That's ridiculous. He's going to want to see her more than once a week."

There are no words to articulate the anger I have boiling inside of me at the moment. "So we agree ... it's ridiculous to restrict someone to only seeing her *one. Fucking. Day. A. Week?*"

Tatum flinches as my words awaken the obvious.

"That's ..." She shakes her head. "Different."

"Because Josh isn't responsible for Austin's death?"

"Emmett ..." she shakes her head, unable to make eye contact with me.

"Because if mistakes—temporary negligence—is grounds for one-day-a-week visitation rights, then tell Lucy goodnight and that you'll see her next week."

Fuuuck ...

I don't mean it. I blame Josh and his hold on my family for bringing out the worst in me, for saying things to my wife that I would never say to her because none of it's true.

Emotion floods her eyes.

"I'm sorry. I didn't mean—"

"You did." She holds a flat hand up to me when I again try to apologize. "And you're ..." She bites her lips together and drags in a shaky breath as her gaze drifts to her feet. "You're right," she whispers. "I ... I don't know what happened to me after he ..."

After he died.

"I just was so angry at ..." She quickly wipes a tear.

"Me," I whisper.

"No. Yes." She shakes her head a few more times. "It wasn't as simple as that." Tatum pivots and pads her feet back to the living room.

Before I can swallow my stupid pride to go after her, the front door clicks. Lucy eyes me when I stand several feet from it, contemplating whether or not I should go after her.

"What did you say to her?"

I shake my head. "Something impulsive and stupid."

"Don't you think you should apologize?"

"Probably. I mean ... I did. I'll ... figure it out later, but not tonight."

"If we told her, things would be better between the two of you."

"There's nothing to tell."

"Dad ..." Lucy gives me a look with those unintentionally pouty lips of hers.

"I'm good. You're good and on the verge of epic with this new treatment."

She can't help but grin.

"Your mom and Josh are good. So what's the point of rocking the boat?"

"Because Josh will never love her like you do."

I let her words hang in the air for a few seconds before nodding. "True. But I think she loves him more than she loves me, so we have to let her be happy, Luce."

"But if she knew the truth, she'd love you more."

"The truth?" I shake my head. I don't want to think about Lucy's version of the truth. "No." I grunt. "It's not that. It's ... complicated."

I WAKE UP EARLY SATURDAY, peek in on a sleeping Lucy, and head out for a jog. I take the same route I used to take years ago when I lived in this house, pre-divorce. Only this time, when I get to the large open field where I used to scream and curse God, I simply rest my hands on my knees for a few seconds to catch my breath before straightening, my head back, eyes closed, and thanking God for Lucy.

As I circle around by the baseball diamonds, the wind picks up and thunder rumbles. Before I can pull my phone out of my hoodie pocket to look at the radar, the skies open and drop unrelenting sheets of rain. Squinting, I see a figure run into the dugout for shelter. I follow, opting to wait out the worst of it before heading home.

"So much for trusting the forecasters," I say breathlessly as I shake off the rain.

The person I followed turns, lowering the hood to her jacket.

"Tatum ..." I blink against the mist of water still hitting my face from the wind.

"Where's Lucy?"

"Sleeping."

"You left her alone?"

I chuckle. "Yes. Sleeping."

"What if she needs you? Or falls out of bed? Or—"

"Or what if she's still asleep when I get home, which she will be. And for the record, she's never fallen out of bed. She knows I go for a jog in the morning. And she knows how to get herself out of bed."

"Well ..." Tatum slips her hood back over her head and winces as the wind gusts. "I didn't know you jogged in the morning."

"You know I jog in the morning."

"No. I know you used to jog, when we were married."

"Well, surprise! I still jog. I didn't completely wilt into nothing after our marriage ended."

Tatum drops her gaze to her feet.

"Listen, about last night ..."

"It's fine."

"It's not fine. I said things I didn't mean."

"You meant them, and you had every right to mean them."

"Maybe, but not how I'm sure you interpreted it."

"And how did I interpret it?" She meets my gaze again.

"I imagine you focused on the part that made it sound

like I was blaming you for what happened to Lucy, instead of the part where I was expressing how much it fucking killed me to see my daughter one day a week for five years."

"Well, you get to see her more now."

"Yes, that totally makes up for those five years."

"That's not fair, Emmett."

"Life's not fair."

After a few seconds, she clears her throat. "Are we going to do this? Rehash all the things we would have done differently? Will it change where we are now?"

God ... she has no idea how long I've waited to see these tiny glimpses, these moments where I know she's feeling more than resentment. She's feeling guilt. Not just about Lucy's accident—she's fighting all the things that went wrong leading up to the moment Austin drowned.

"Josh is having a guy make his house wheelchair accessible."

"Oh? Is Josh in a wheelchair now?"

"Emmett ..." She frowns, but it's more of a scowl. "What is your problem with Josh?"

"He stole my wife." It comes out so quickly and so automatically, it takes me a moment to realize I said the words. Should I regret saying them? I'm struggling with this so much. How did this day come? The day that I have to feel guilty for loving her.

"I'm not your wife."

"You'll always be my wife." I can't help it. My heart won't let me lie about this.

Her head inches side to side. "You're delusional. You stole me from a guy on our first date. How ironic that you now feel like someone has taken something that you thought belonged to you. Poor Emmett."

180

Rubbing my lips together, I grunt. "Josh will never make you happy."

"You don't know that."

"I do." I shrug.

"Why would you say that?"

"Because you never would have married me if Josh was your type." I take two steps closer to her, and she squirms with nothing but a brick wall behind her.

"Don't touch me," she whispers.

I can't begin to describe what those words do to me. It's not so much what she says, but how she says it. Not a warning. It's a plea.

I think I could press my lips to hers and put my hands on places of her body that would make Josh feel sick to his stomach. I could do it, and she wouldn't stop me. She doesn't hate me by choice. She does it out of necessity. She knows we're everything or nothing, and right now, we've been forced into the middle where it's impossible to deal with the feelings—the emotional ones *and* the physical ones.

When she's with him, in his bed, in his arms, she thinks of me. That's the only way she can be with him.

"Please don't touch me," she repeats her plea, fisting her hands at her sides.

"I already am," I whisper.

Tatum closes her eyes as if she can will me away. I take pity on her, turn, and jog home in spite of the rain.

CHAPTER SEVENTEEN

THEN

ANDI HAD a friend who was a child psychiatrist. Tatum didn't see why Lucy needed to see someone. She thought she could mother her through the grieving process. Ironic, since Tatum could barely keep herself functioning after Austin's death.

Eventually, her parents and mine convinced her it might be a good idea, and Tatum agreed. We met with the psychiatrist before Lucy did. We—and by we, I mean I—went through the events of the day that Austin died. Tatum tried to hold it together while sitting as far away from me as possible on the love seat by the window overlooking downtown Kansas City.

"Could I have a few minutes alone with you?" I asked Dr. Kane when she said she had no further questions for us.

Tatum gave me a suspicious look that I ignored.

"I'll meet you in the car." I handed her the keys.

After another disgruntled look, she snatched the keys and headed to the car.

Dr. Kane shut the door. "You want to tell me the real story now ... don't you?" The very observant doctor gave me a sad smile and returned to the chair adjacent the love seat.

I rested my elbows on my knees, hands folded in front of me. "How did you know?"

"I have a gift for reading people. You were very easy to read as you told the version of the story that I assume you've decided is the best version for Lucy ..." She twisted her lips. "Maybe even for Tatum. I'm not sure it's the best version for you."

"So what's the real story?" I asked.

She crossed one leg over the other and folded her hands in her lap, long fingernails perfectly painted in light pink and white tips. "I don't know. That's what you're going to tell me."

"Is this confidential?"

"Lucy is the patient."

"I don't want Tatum to know."

"But Lucy can know?" She cants her head to the side.

"Lucy does know. Well, sort of."

"Please, Emmett ... enlighten me. We all want what's in Lucy's best interest."

I cleared my throat and started from the beginning, which was the day in the delivery room that Tatum made me promise to love our children more than her—more than us. Dr. Kane didn't flinch, didn't give anything away like my words surprised her. If anything, she nodded slowly a few times, conveying she understood and maybe approved. I wasn't sure.

"Did Lucy believe you? When you told her it was your fault? Or do you think she wanted to believe you because it meant she didn't have to take responsibility for it?"

"I ... I don't know. I guess I'm hoping that can be something you might discuss with her. But I don't want her to feel that it's her fault."

"I understand that, but if she knows, on some level that it was, in part, her fault, then that's something we need to deal with."

"Okay. But is there any reason Tatum needs to know?"

"I won't know this until I talk with Lucy. I don't think it's something you can keep from your wife forever. Have you thought about what that could do to your marriage? Have you thought about what it might do to Lucy if this does end your marriage?"

"Yes. I have thought about it. And every time I think about it, I come to the same conclusion."

"Which is?"

"In my unprofessional opinion, I think it would be easier for Lucy to live with divorced parents who love her instead of a mother who looks at her with anything short of complete love and adoration."

Dr. Kane did her slow nod again. "I understand your concern. And I will take it into careful consideration when I talk with Lucy. But you need to know that what might be best for her now, might not be the best for her in a few years."

"So you never keep secrets? All secrets are bad?"

"I didn't say that."

"Then what are you saying?" I started to feel a little agitation.

Dr. Kane returned a warm smile. "I'm saying ... I need to talk to Lucy."

TATUM DIDN'T SAY anything on the way home. We had two hours until Lucy would be getting off the school bus. I busied myself in the yard while Tatum cleaned the house, avoiding the locked door to Austin's room. She hadn't touched a thing, and she didn't want anyone else in there touching things either. When I took a break to grab a drink, she came down the stairs with a load of laundry tucked under her arm.

"Why did you need to talk to Dr. Kane alone?"

I thought I'd slid by with that one since she only talked to me on a need-to basis. Apparently, that was a need-to-know thing for her.

"I wanted to fill in some detail. I knew you were really struggling, so I didn't share everything when we were all together. I could tell you were needing out of there."

"What detail?"

I shrugged a single shoulder. "Just Lucy's reaction, when she saw me … in the pool."

Tatum swallowed hard. "Is that all?"

"Yeah."

After a beat, she pivoted to head toward the laundry room.

"Actually …" I stopped her. "We discussed us for a little bit."

"Us?"

I nodded once.

"What about us?"

"Well, our situation."

Her eyes narrowed. "What is our situation?"

Good question. I had no clue, but that was why I was fishing for her to give me some answers. "We discussed how a tragedy like this can be hard on a marriage." I stretched the truth. "Some marriages don't survive."

Tatum couldn't hold my gaze. It hurt. It spoke volumes without her saying a single word. When she wordlessly padded her way to the laundry room, I followed her.

"If you can't forgive me ..." I couldn't finish.

With her back to me, she loaded the washing machine. "It's not about forgiveness. Even if I could forgive you, I can't ..."

"You can't what?"

She closed the door to the washing machine and rested her hands on the top of it, head bowed. "I can't look at you," she murmured. "I can't look at you without seeing him. I can't look at you without thinking about you in the garage, not watching him, while he..." her voice cracked "...sank to the bottom of the pool. And I *hate* that I can't look at you. I *hate* this feeling so goddamn much."

My heart knew this day would come. And as much as I tried to prepare it to weather the hard punch of truth, it still left a hole, aching and bleeding. Swallowing hard, I kept my emotions in check, just barely. "It's not fair to Lucy. If you can't look at me, she will notice."

"I don't know what you expect me to do." She sniffled.

"Let go before you suffocate."

She slowly turned, cheeks streaked with tears. "Let go of what?"

With a sad smile that barely disguised my pain, I said, "Me. Let go of me."

"Y-you want a divorce?" She wiped her cheeks.

"No. I want you. I want Lucy. I want everything I wanted the day I met you. But I love Lucy more than us, and I love you more than me."

"Emmett ..." She choked and her face contorted as she tried to keep from falling to pieces. But I knew the truth.

She had already fallen to pieces, and I was no longer the person who could put her back together.

"This is on me. Not you. This is my failure. Not yours."

She covered her mouth and cried, eyes pinched shut.

Even if my arms no longer gave her comfort, I couldn't keep them from wrapping around her. Would she ever know I chose *her* in the moment? Would she ever know that giving her an out was the greatest love I could give her? I never imagined losing Tatum would be my most selfless act of love. You were supposed to fight for love. Right?

I pressed my cheek to the top of her head and whispered, "You were never really mine."

CHAPTER EIGHTEEN

NOW

WE FALL into a routine of online schooling, therapy appointments, and sharing Lucy with each other and her friends. The holidays fly by with splitting time between my family and Tatum's. By spring, her body is stronger, and we're closer to seeing her on her feet.

"Hey." I smile at my Lucy when I get home from work.

She's watching TV with a bag of potato chips on her lap. "Hey."

"I thought you were going to be with your mom and Josh tonight."

With a shrug, she shoves more chips into her mouth. "I can't."

After grabbing a Coke and downing half of it, I position myself between her and the TV. Her eyes are swollen and red. "Lucy, what happened?" I ask, leaning forward, resting my hands on my knees to put me at eye level with her.

With crumbs and salt stuck to her mouth and chin, her

lip quivers, and her eyes fill with more tears. "Ash ... Ashton broke u-up w-with me." She hugs the bag to her chest.

"Oh, baby ..." I take the bag from her and replace it with my body hugged to hers. "I'm sorry." I have a slew of things I want to say, starting with how undeserving he is of my Lucy. But something tells me she doesn't need that. The fact that she's here and not with Tatum and Josh must mean she needs something her mom wouldn't give her.

Tatum would boost her up. Tatum would tell her all the things I'm thinking. She's not mad at Ashton. I think she loved him. We don't like hearing anyone put down the people we love, no matter how much they've hurt us. I know this so very well.

Sitting next to her on the sofa, I pull her onto my lap like I held her as a young girl. Her torso may be longer now. She might have longer arms and legs, but she'll always be my little girl. And I will never stop protecting her with my embrace.

After a good ten minutes, when I start to question if she's fallen asleep, she traces the veins in my arm. "He said he doesn't want me waiting for him because he's so busy with soccer and he doesn't have much time to spend with me. But where am I going? My stupid legs don't work. Does he really think I have a lineup of other guys I'm turning down while I *wait for him*? Does he really think I'm that stupid? He wants a normal girlfriend to take to prom. He wants a girlfriend to have ..."

I clear my throat. "To have?" I'm afraid to ask because I fear I know the answer. And I hate that a terrible upside to her temporary paralysis is she can't be sexually active with assholes like Ashton.

"You know. Sex. He wants to have sex like every other

189

senior in high school. And don't act like you weren't having sex at his age."

I lost my virginity at sixteen. Ashton just turned eighteen. I can't talk, but it doesn't stop me from judging him. He doesn't play American football. This isn't the loss Lucy thinks it is.

"How was therapy today?" I go for the subject change.

"I didn't go. I told Mom I had an assignment that was due and I needed to skip."

"And she let you skip?"

She shrugs a shoulder. "She lets me do whatever I want because she feels guilty for the accident."

"Well, that's pretty crappy, Lucy. You're not going to walk ... you're not going to show boneheads like Ashton what they're missing if you're holed up in this house playing video games and eating chips. You have to keep working hard. Last week you stood. You. Stood."

"Then I fell right back into my chair."

"Lucy ..." I position her so she's sitting next to me instead of on my lap.

Her arms flail out to the side to steady herself. "Dad."

"Lucy, you stood. That means you will walk. That means you will not live the rest of your life in a wheelchair. That is infinitely better than school dances and ... other things." I smirk instead of saying sex.

"If I can walk, I can have sex."

Grimacing, I rub my temples. "Not what I'm saying, Luce."

"But it's true. If I can walk, I can have sex. I'm seventeen, Dad. You can't act like I'm your little girl forever."

"Yes. I absolutely can." I stand, which makes her wobble again on the sofa. Then I take her arms and put them on my shoulders as I grab her waist. "Now ... let's see you stand again."

"I'm not supposed to try it at home yet. PT's rules."

"Stand, Luce."

"What if I fall?"

"I won't let you fall."

"I can't." She shakes her head.

I grumble and take a deep breath. "If you can stand, you can walk. If you can walk..." I hate that I'm saying this, but right now, I'll use anything to motivate her "...you can have sex."

Her pout vanishes and she grins.

"When you're older. And married."

Rolling her eyes, she grips my shoulders with a bit of seriousness now. I lift her to her feet.

"Don't let me go!"

"I'm not, Lucy. I've always got you."

After making her stand several times in a row, I help her back into her wheelchair and make us dinner—steaks medium rare, baked potatoes loaded with butter, and green beans to even things out. Then we make a fire and assemble s'mores.

"I almost told her," Lucy says.

"Told who what?" I sandwich my marshmallow between the graham crackers.

"Mom. I almost told her the truth about Austin."

My gaze cuts to hers. "Why?"

"Because Dr. Kane thinks I'm ready. She thinks now that Mom's moved on and you're doing okay, that it would be fine to tell her. Mom feels responsible for my accident. I think she would understand now ... she would understand that what happened with Austin was an accident too."

"It was an accident. I messed up. Not on purpose."

"Dad ..."

I return my attention to the mess in my hands. Lucy and I just ... stopped talking about it years ago. At least the specifics of that day. I've assumed—hoped—that she's allowed herself to truly believe it was my fault and, not hers. But I've always known that look in her eyes. It's not sympathy for me; it's guilt. She knows what happened, even if I tried to color the picture to look a little different.

"Mom didn't think you were on your way home. He didn't die on your watch. He died on mine." Her gaze cuts to the side, lips pressed together.

I see how much her time with Dr. Kane has helped, something Tatum can't see because she has no idea there's more to it than a young girl who tragically lost her brother in a drowning incident.

"Dr. Kane asked me how I felt about you when I thought it was your fault. And I said I felt sorry for you because Mom couldn't forgive you. I said I forgave you. Then she said if I was willing to forgive you, I had to be willing to forgive myself or I wasn't ready to take responsibility for the accident. So I've tried, more than once actually, to tell Mom. But every time I choke. The words ... the emotions feel like they're stuck in my throat. It's not that I'm afraid she won't forgive me. I'm afraid to see the look on her face when she realizes that we've kept this from her for all these years. I think it will make her guilt even worse, like we didn't trust her with the truth."

"Then why tell her?"

She laughs a little. A painful laugh. "Because I want a normal life. And if I try to live with this secret, I will always need someone like Dr. Kane in my life, talking me off the ledge, helping me cope with the pain of keeping this from Mom."

"Maybe you should wait until you're walking again and she's let go of the guilt from your accident."

"Maybe telling her now will help her let go of that guilt sooner."

I shake my head. "That's not how it works, Lucy. There is nothing that will make your mom feel like her mistake is okay or less awful because another mistake somehow offsets it. If you tell her about Austin, it won't make her feel differently about me."

"She'd feel differently about you if she knew you're not the one responsible for Austin's death."

"I ..." I rub the back of my neck. "That's not how I want her forgiveness. I don't want her to forgive me because she believes I took the blame for his death. I want her to forgive me like she would if I truly was responsible for his death."

"And what if that never happens?"

I shake my head. "Then it never happens."

"But what if I have to tell her—for me?"

"Then you have to tell her. But do it for *you*, Lucy. Don't do it for me. Don't do it because you think I need her forgiveness. Don't do it because you think it's going to change my relationship with your mom. Do it only for you and what you need to live that beautifully normal life you talk about."

Just as she nods in understanding, the gate to the back-yard opens. Tatum makes her way toward us, hands tucked into the pockets of her long cardigan, hair in unruly waves down her shoulders.

"Just wanted to check on you. I tried texting, but you didn't answer. Did you get your work done?"

"Yes. Sorry. I must have left my phone inside. Dad made the most amazing dinner and started a fire, so I sort of forgot to bring it out here with me."

"That's fine."

Lucy wrinkles her nose. "You were at Josh's, weren't you? That's a much longer drive than if you were at home. Really, I'm sorry."

Tatum takes a seat in the chair next to mine. "Yes, I had dinner at Josh's, but it's fine. I had to drive home anyway. What's a couple blocks farther?"

"I assumed you were staying the night," Lucy says.

I stare at the flames because I'm not comfortable being in the middle of a conversation about my wife (ex-wife) sleeping at another man's house.

"I wanted to come home."

"Is everything okay with you and Josh?" Lucy has all the questions. Bless the girl's curiosity and natural ability to have a conversation, but enough with the Josh talk. We'll be going to Royals games soon. We should discuss that instead.

Tatum rolls her lips between her teeth and nods several times. Even if Lucy can't read it, I sure can. Something is not right with Josh.

"Okay. Well, I'm going to head inside and read awhile before bed." Lucy gives me a grin like she's pretty proud of herself for leaving us alone.

"I'll be in after a bit to help you get ready for bed." Tatum knows Lucy doesn't need her help. And Lucy knows Tatum likes that time with her. Brushing out her hair. Putting lotion on her legs and feet. Nurturing her baby girl.

"Tell me more about this awesome dinner." Tatum smiles after Lucy goes back into the house.

"She's overstating it. Nothing special. I threw some steaks on the grill and put potatoes in the oven. Green beans to check off the green vegetable box."

"Sounds good." She draws her knees to her chest, heels of her tennis shoes resting on the edge of the chair.

I stick more marshmallows on the end of the stick and roast them. "You can't let Lucy miss her therapy."

Tatum frowns. "I know, but she had schoolwork."

"She's a straight-A student. I think she's smart enough to multi-task. She's also smart enough to play on her mom's weakness."

"What's my weakness?"

"You ran a red light, and you feel guilty standing up to your daughter, who's now in a wheelchair."

"I'm protecting her. And I'm trusting her to know when she needs a break and when she thinks she can keep going."

"Protecting her from walking? Trusting her to stay motivated? Everyone needs a nudge sometimes. Today she needed a nudge not a break."

"That's a little harsh."

"Says the woman who works her dance students to death. How many times have you used the words, *no pain, no gain?*"

Tatum shakes her head. "That's different. My students aren't in wheelchairs."

"And if we keep nudging her, she'll get out of the wheelchair. Won't that be an amazing day?" I sandwich the marshmallows and chocolate between the graham crackers and hand the s'more to Tatum, giving her a genuine smile so she knows I'm not judging her; I'm just loving Lucy more.

"No pain, no gain." She grins, taking the messy s'more from me and squeezing it so she can take a bite.

"Everything okay with Josh?" I can't believe I'm asking this, but I know she's not talking about something.

"It's ..." she stares at her s'more and licks some chocolate before it drips onto her sweater. "Josh asked me to marry him." After a few more seconds of eyeing the marshmallow and chocolate, she shifts her gaze to me.

It's like losing her all over again. It's the night she stomped her way back to the bar after I told her I wasn't her real blind date. It's the day at the hospital when I told her Austin drowned on my watch. It's the day I signed my name on the divorce papers.

"And..." I clear away the thick feeling in my throat "... what did you say?"

"I said I need to think about it."

"What's to think about?"

"Lucy. She has one more year of high school left. And Josh has had some interviews at hospitals in Chicago. That's where he's originally from. So it could mean a potential move, and I won't do that to Lucy before her senior year. Plus her therapists are all here."

"She can stay with me. You can visit." I don't know why it gives me such satisfaction to play role reversal with Tatum. But she's breaking my fucking heart again, so I feel a little punchy at the moment. "I'd make sure she gets to her therapy appointments. Andi has offered to help a million times too, so I'd have lots of backup with family."

"I can't leave her." Tatum shakes her head. "I can't believe you're even suggesting it."

"Why? Because you think you love her more?"

"Jesus, Emmett, I didn't say that. I just thought you'd show a little more understanding for my situation. But no. You're ready to ship me off so you can have her all to yourself. I'm not leaving her. That's why I didn't give Josh an answer."

"Fine. Say, yes. Wait until she graduates. Then move to Chicago. Are you really going to let a year stand in the way of your happiness?"

Seriously. Fucking. Killing. Me.

This is not the conversation I ever imagined having with my wife.

"Just like that. You want me to say yes to Josh?"

"Sure. Why not?" I say with a little edge to my voice as I stand and pound my feet toward the garage to get the cover to the firepit.

Tatum is hot on my heels. "What is wrong with you? I thought we could have an adult conversation like friends."

I spin around just before reaching the rack with the cover on it. "Friends? Are you serious? I don't want to be your fucking friend, helping you plan your wedding to some other guy! I'M THE GUY! I'm your husband! I stole you!" Grabbing her face, I kiss her. There are no words to describe how it feels to kiss her again. I can't breathe, but at the same time it feels like the first real breath I've taken since Austin died. She's the air filling my suffocating lungs. I love this woman with every cell in my body.

It takes a few seconds for me to ease my grip on her, and that's when I realize it's not just me kissing her. She's kissing me back. Her hands claim my sweatshirt, holding me to her for a few moments before they wrap around my neck, fingers teasing my nape the way they did for twelve years of marriage.

The moment starts to fade because it's stolen. Stolen like Tatum. Stolen like so many moments, so many breaths in our life together. Some good, some tragic. Her hands slide back down to my chest, the fabric wadded in her tight fists as she drops her forehead to my chest and exhales slowly. I keep my arms around her and my eyes closed. If I open them, I know I will see regret in her eyes because my wife loves with her heart wide open. And no matter how much she loves me, I know she loves Josh too.

And he's asked her to marry him.

He's asked her to move to Chicago, something new and exciting and so many opportunities to dance.

He's a doctor who makes a good living without coming home with dirt under his fingernails or the stench of diesel woven into his clothes.

And he's not the face she thinks about when she grieves Austin.

The stolen glances.

The stolen kisses.

It's all temporary. I'm the thief who will have to give them back. I will have to admit they no longer belong to me.

"Emmett ..." she whispers. "I can't do this."

Threading my fingers through her hair, I ease her head up to look at me. She blinks huge tears, and I wipe them away. "Why did it have to be like this?"

My thumbs chase every tear.

Her voice shakes. "Why did he have to die?"

This time. This time I don't feel accused. I don't feel like she's trying to blame me. With the same disbelief that taking her eye off the road for two seconds led to Lucy in a wheelchair, she's wondering why our little boy wandered out to the pool in what was mere seconds—a minute or two at most—of someone not watching him. Why did we lose a child to a miscarriage? It's hard to invest in any sense of joy when you feel like it will be ripped away from you in the most unimaginable nightmare.

"I don't know. Most days ... I don't know anything," I say.

Tatum sniffles, rubbing her lips together. I know it won't change one thing. It will only carve more empty holes in my heart, but I do it anyway. I kiss her again. And she kisses me.

She tightens her hold on my shirt.

She cries more tears.

She opens her mouth to taste me—the familiar, the lost, and now ... the forbidden.

I wonder if she'd let me push her back two steps until her back hit my truck.

I wonder if she'd let me touch her in places that I've longed to touch her for as long as my empty heart can remember.

I wonder if it would change our future if she did.

Once, many years ago, I stole her. *I wonder* ... could I do it again?

"Dad? Mom?"

We jump away from each other—wiping our mouths, fixing our hair, and straightening our clothes.

"Uh ... coming, Luce," I call, snatching the firepit cover from the shelf while Tatum presses her hands to her rosy cheeks like she can extinguish the heat from them.

Maybe I won't win her heart this time, but now I know. She loves me. She's always loved me.

As I cover the firepit, Tatum flies past me into the house. I rub my lips together, tasting her, then I grin. While I clean the kitchen, Tatum helps get Lucy ready for bed. I don't mean to eavesdrop, but they left the door cracked open, and I can hear Lucy telling Tatum about Ashton.

Twenty minutes later, Lucy calls out, "Night, Dad."

"Night, Luce. I love you."

"Love you too."

When I put the last dish in the cabinet, Tatum steps around the corner. She fiddles with the rings on her fingers. Something she's always done when she's nervous. "Ashton is a real asshole," she says soft enough to keep Lucy from hearing her.

With an easy chuckle, I nod. "Agreed."

"Well..." she jerks her head toward the back door "...I'd

better get home. Thanks for the..." her cheeks turn pink again "...the uh ... s'mores."

A shit-eating grin settles on my face. "You're welcome. Anytime."

Tatum won't even look at me. She has the shyness of a teenager with a crush on her teacher. It invigorates my ego that's been down for the count for quite some time. She hasn't acted this way around me since we first met.

I should let her go, let her walk herself out to the car, drive home, and drown in a sea of guilt. I'm an adult who should have enough respect and decency to let her sort out her issues with Josh. I should be the better man and stay out of the way. After all, I had my chance with her.

"I'll walk you out." Yeah, I'm still the guy who stole her at the bar.

She opens the back door and shoots me a suspicious look. "Do you think that's a good idea?"

It's pretty much the best idea I've had in over five years.

"It's a dangerous neighborhood." It's actually the safest street in Redington. "I wouldn't be a gentleman if I didn't walk you out."

She struts her stuff to the gate. "I don't recall you ever being a gentleman."

I waited forever to have sex with her. How has she forgotten that? Although I don't think she thought I was being a gentleman at the time. She was too busy thinking I was still a virgin.

Tatum opens her car door and turns. "Thank you for walking me to my car."

I slip my hands in my pockets to keep from using them to grab her and kiss her. "You're welcome."

When I take a step closer, she shakes her head. "Don't

even think about it, Emmett. I have enough to confess to Josh."

I narrow my eyes. "You're telling him? About the..." I smirk "...s'mores?"

"Emmett, he's more than a casual fling. We've been together for over a year. And he asked me to marry him. And I ..."

My smirk dies. She shot it down with the word she hasn't said yet.

"Love him. I love him, Emmett. And tonight ... I was off. Confused. He caught me off guard with the proposal. And you caught me off guard with ..."

"The s'mores," I say with less humor to it.

"Yes." She draws in a shaky breath. "It's just been a very emotional and confusing day."

"Then drive home safely. Get some sleep. And I'll prepare myself to take a beating from Doctor Josh when he finds out about the s'mores."

Tatum shakes her head and tries so hard not to smile. She knows I'd level Josh in a blink. In fact, I've leveled him so many times in my head, I'm not sure it would even take a full blink. And it's not that I don't like him. I do.

I just don't like him with my wife.

"Night, Emmett."

"Night, Tatum."

I wait for her to pull out before bouncing back into the house on a completely irrational and likely impossible fantasy. But at this point, I'm good with irrational and likely impossible. It's way more than I had yesterday.

CHAPTER NINETEEN

THEN

"Why?" Lucy teared up when we told her that we were getting a divorce.

"Because we need space to heal after losing Austin," I say, squeezing her hand as she deflates, sitting on the edge of her bed between me and Tatum.

"You don't love each other."

"No, that's not true. We just don't know how to love each other the way we used to love each other. So we're going to take some time to figure it out," Tatum says as if we're taking a break and might get back together.

"But we're not going to be a family."

"We will always be a family, Luce. Nothing can ever change that. But not all families look the same. You know that. Katy's parents are not together, but she sees them. They are a family. They just don't live together." I wasn't sure she believed me or truly understood, but it was the best we had to give her.

"It's my fault—"

"It's *my* fault, Luce. We've talked about this. I made a mistake. You did nothing wrong."

"B-but ... it was an accident."

"Sweetie..." Tatum wrapped an arm around her "...it was an accident. But sometimes it's hard to forget about big accidents. But I know you will help both me and your dad feel better over time. You are the most important person in our lives, and we will never let you feel anything but completely loved. Okay?"

Lucy nodded slowly. "But someday, you'll get married again. Right?"

Our daughter was on the precipice of learning everything in the world we'd tried so hard to protect her from— the heartbreak of love and loss. How things like death and divorce were final. And the aching part of one's heart that was the tiny exception to unconditional love.

Kids would talk at school. She'd read more books with more realism in them. She'd watch more grown-up shows on television. We couldn't protect her forever, but we did our best to make things hurt a little less by giving them as much of a positive spin as possible.

Mommy and I won't live together, but that means you'll get twice as many birthday and Christmas presents. It was admittedly pathetic, but it was all we had.

"Lucy, we can't predict the future, so we're just going to take it a day at a time. And for now, Dad will live somewhere else, but you'll get to see him a lot."

That was the biggest lie. I already knew I wasn't getting to see her a lot. Truth? When we told Lucy, we had already signed papers. We had already gone before a judge to settle the custody arrangement. I had already been given one measly day a week with my daughter. After we decided to get divorced, something in Tatum changed. Her grief turned into pure anger. Anger at me. I thought my willingness to leave was the answer. I thought it would give her the space she needed.

I was wrong.

It sparked a new kind of rage and resentment. And I didn't understand it. I was so blind.

"So you're leaving today?" Lucy asked.

I nod. "I'm not leaving like going away. I'm just going to sleep at a different house. And this weekend you can come see it."

"Stay the night?"

"Maybe on special occasions." Tatum kissed Lucy's head. "You'll spend Saturday with your dad. The whole day. Then you'll come home to sleep. Dad's new home is pretty close, so it's silly to not just come back to your own bed to sleep. All your stuff is here."

It felt so incredibly cruel, but so did the environment we'd been living in since Austin died. Tatum forced every smile. And she rarely laughed. I thought with me out of the house, it might help her heal faster, and it might allow Lucy to see real smiles and real laughter. Something every child deserved.

"I'm going to finish packing a few things downstairs, then you can come and kiss me goodnight," I said, opting for a goodnight that felt no different than all the goodnights I gave her before I moved out.

"Okay." Lucy managed a half smile.

As I shoved the rest of my clothes into a second suitcase, Tatum came into the bedroom and sat on the end of the bed. "She's going to be okay," I said.

"I know."

"She's going to want to spend the night, on more than just *special occasions*. So you'd better figure out how you're going to handle that like..." I emerge from the closet after taking one last look through the drawers "...maybe actually letting her spend the night when she wants to."

"I can't," she whispered.

"Because you don't trust me?"

"Emmett ..." She stared at her folded hands. "It's not fair for you to ask me to trust you. Not now. Maybe not ever. I ..." My wife (ex-wife) wielded a sharp knife, and she knew how to slice my heart into tiny pieces. She glanced up. "I don't even know you anymore."

When I took the blame for Austin's drowning, I knew I'd lose a lot. But I didn't let myself fully believe that Tatum would no longer trust me with Lucy. I had to fight for one day—ten fucking hours.

"Will there ever come a day when you stop punishing me?"

"Will there ever come a day when Austin comes back? When everything that's happened is no longer real?" She narrowed her gaze at me, and I saw the hatred in her eyes.

I lost everything to save Lucy, and in spite of the pain I felt in my chest at that moment, the tears threatening my eyes, I knew it was the right choice. It was the only choice.

"I'll pick her up at eight on Saturday."

NOW

"I WALKED! DAD! I WALKED!" Lucy yells, the second I open the door.

It's been a week since she skipped her therapy appointment to mend her broken heart. It's also been a week since I've seen Tatum, which has been odd. She's managed to be gone just before I get home and arrives in the morning just minutes after I leave for work.

No joining us for dinner.

No putting Lucy to bed.

No s'mores.

Not going to lie … I miss s'mores.

But today, she's here, beaming right along with Lucy. Josh is also here. There's clearly excitement in the air, but is there also jealousy and anger? Does he know about last week?

"That is the best news ever!" I can't think about Josh and his feelings right now. I can't even focus on s'mores (even though that's all I've been thinking about) because Lucy walked today. I can't help myself. I have to pluck her from her wheelchair and spin her around in circles. "Lucy, you are my idol, baby." Burying my face in her neck, I kiss her and nuzzle her with my scratchy face until she loses control in a fit of giggles.

S'mores were great, but this beats that.

"Chad said he couldn't believe it. He said the first step is the hardest, and I took five steps!" Lucy says out of breath by the time I set her back in her wheelchair.

When I sneak a quick glance at Tatum on the sofa with Josh, her eyes shimmer with happy tears and what I can only imagine is relief.

"We're going to celebrate. Josh got reservations for all of us at some really fancy steak house in Kansas City," Lucy continues with her excitement.

I force myself to give Josh and Tatum more than a quick glance. "Is that so?"

Josh takes Tatum's hand and squeezes it like he's claiming her, but I don't sense any anger or jealousy in his face or demeanor as he nods. "Absolutely. If this isn't worth celebrating, then I don't know what is."

Well, I know what might also be grounds for celebration —Tatum leaving Josh and coming back to me. From the looks of their linked fingers, I don't think we'll be celebrating that anytime soon.

"Do I have time to grab a quick shower?" I point toward the stairs.

"The reservation is at six, so you have time." Tatum gives me a shy smile, but she can't hold eye contact with me for more than a few seconds before averting her gaze to Lucy, the floor, or basically anywhere but me.

I'm not sure how to read that, and I'm usually an expert on reading her.

After a shower, I dust off one of my good shirts and dress pants to wear for the occasion since Josh has on a suit, Tatum's in a dress, and Lucy has on nice pants and a sweater.

A little cologne.

A quick trim of my beard to even it out.

And a fake smile for Josh.

"Whoa ... you look *good,* Dad. You have a hot date tonight?" Lucy teases me.

"I do. She's a little young, but she's the most beautiful woman I have ever laid eyes on." I kiss the top of her head. "And she just took a really big step today."

"Aw ... Dad. Thanks, but seriously. We should take your picture in that for a dating app. I mean ... your beard is trimmed, which I haven't seen in forever, and you look kinda hot in that shirt hugging your chest like that. It's time. If I can take a step, so can you."

Oh, Lucy ... she knows how to pack a punch.

"I need to take this call, give me one second," Josh says, taking his phone into the kitchen.

"I'm going to check my makeup and grab my purse." Lucy wheels herself to the master bedroom.

I remain standing in the spot Lucy just vacated a few feet from the sofa where Tatum sits, rubbing her glossed lips together while staring at the floor.

"You look beautiful."

Her cheeks flush, and she forces her gaze to mine. "Thank you. Lucy's right; you look great too."

"It's just a beard trim. She's been insanely unrelenting about me getting on a dating site. I suppose I'll have to eventually give in and just do it."

Tatum swallows hard. "Y-yeah ... um ... you should."

We lock gazes for a few seconds.

"Do I need to be on the lookout for a fist headed for my nose?" I nod in the direction of the kitchen and Josh on his phone.

Tatum's brow wrinkles along with her nose. "I ... I didn't say anything yet."

I nod slowly. "Okay, well, when you do, give me a heads-up."

She bites the inside of her cheek and returns a slow nod.

"Are we ready?" Josh returns, slipping his phone into the pocket of his suit jacket.

"Lucy?" I call.

"Coming."

We load into Tatum's SUV that she bought for safety and to accommodate Lucy's wheelchair in the back, and we drive to Kansas City for a celebratory dinner.

Me.

My daughter.

My wife.

My wife's boyfriend.

"People are staring," Lucy murmurs as the staff at the restaurant adjust the table and chairs to accommodate for Lucy's wheelchair.

"Well, you're probably the first person they've ever seen in this cutting-edge invention called a wheelchair," I say, helping her get her chair adjusted in front of her place setting.

"Ha ha ..." Lucy rolls her eyes, but she can't help but relinquish a tiny grin.

As we glance over our menus, I nudge Lucy's foot with mine. She keeps her focus on the menu, but she grins because she knows I'm making a silent point.

She can *feel* me nudge her foot, which means she has feeling in her legs, which means she will not spend the rest of her life in this wheelchair.

"I guess we experience things for different reasons, right?" she asks while setting down her menu.

Tatum, Josh, and I give her our full attention.

"There are a lot of people who will never walk again. They will always experience pity glances and prolonged stares when they navigate in public. My time is short. Before long, I'll forget I was ever in a wheelchair."

Tatum's gaze cuts to mine. We're thinking the same thing ... this girl is life. She's the best of us.

"Yes. But you still have a long road ahead of you." Josh throws a bucket of cold water on the moment.

I'm sure his big doctor brain can't help it.

Tatum elbows him, and he gives her a what-was-that-for look. Brainy Josh figures it out after a few seconds and clears his throat. "What I meant, Lucy, is that you are doing great. We are so proud of you. And while you *do* have a lot of work ahead of you, I know you'll surprise us every step of the way."

"Thanks, Josh," she says with half-ass sincerity, which sparks a little pride in me.

We eat until our bellies just can't hold another bite. When the waiter delivers the check to our table, Josh grabs it before I can get to it.

"My treat."

I'm not stupid. It has to be close to a four-hundred-dollar bill with tip. If Dr. Josh wants to pay, I don't feel like less of a man for simply saying, "Thank you." When Tatum and I took our pre-marriage RV trip, we prided ourselves on finding free food, using coupons and BOGOs: basically any means to save a buck. Frugality is such an under-appreciated trait in this materialistic world.

"I'm going to use the ladies' room. Lucy do you need to use it too?"

"I'm good until we get home," Lucy says.

"I'll follow you." I stand and wait for Tatum to head toward the restrooms.

When we turn the corner, I press my hand to her lower back.

She stiffens. "Emmett ..."

"Tatum ..." I mock her.

She turns, eyes narrowed. "Have you been talking to Lucy? I feel like she was a bit standoffish with Josh tonight."

"I talk to Lucy, but we don't discuss Josh. If she seemed a little standoffish tonight, it's because he said all the wrong things."

"He had one misstep, and he corrected it." She folds her arms over her chest.

"He went into great detail about a routine appendectomy that took a bad turn, and he followed it up with the unsavory details of a miracle *bowel* resection he performed this morning. Just what I love to discuss while I'm eating. I think every word that came out of his mouth tonight was a misstep."

"You don't like him."

"I like him fine."

"You just don't like him with me."

Bingo!

"Doesn't matter what I like. The only thing that matters is what you like. If surgical stories are your foreplay, who am I to judge?"

She deflates with exasperation. "He saves lives."

"I saved a raccoon the other day when we were clearing an area for development. Ron wanted to toss it, and the whole family, into the grinder, and I said no. Three babies. Both parents. That's five lives in one day. Has Dr. Josh saved five lives in one day?"

She pinches the bridge of her nose like she's done for years when she doesn't want to laugh at something I say, but she can barely keep from losing it. "Emmett ..." Shaking her head, her lips part into a full smile.

"I'm going to use the restroom, but I just want you to think about that every time you're tempted to put Dr. Josh up on a pedestal like he's the only savior upon this earth. And it should be worth noting that I could have shared this heroic incident during dinner, or I could have talked about the sludge from the overturned sewer truck that we cleaned up this morning, but I didn't."

Keeping her head bowed, bridge of her nose pinched, and grin completely unharnessed, she says, "Noted," before I brush past her to the men's room.

CHAPTER TWENTY

I HAVEN'T RUN into Tatum on my jogs since the day it rained. I've felt certain it's because of the s'more incident, and she's probably chosen a different route and time just to avoid me. But this morning proves me wrong.

When I reach my open field, she's there, hands on her hips, breathing heavily, head tipped to the sky. What is she doing at *my* field? Does she know it's where I came when I had nowhere else to go to grieve Austin?

"This is my field."

She jumps, turning toward me. I'm instantly rewarded with a tiny smile.

"Why? Did you rob it of all its trees?"

I chuckle. "No. Well, Will might have done it before I started working for the company. It's been vacant for years. I heard they're finally going to develop the land next spring."

"I see."

Does she? Does she see through my idle chitchat to my nerves? She hasn't made me this nervous since our first date.

"Did Lucy tell you she walked across the therapy room yesterday with a walker?"

I grin. "You mean did she freak out and insist I order pizza and pick up ice cream? Yes."

"Did she tell you Josh is taking her to a Royals game this weekend? He has a friend who knows the owner and they're going to watch from a dugout suite."

Fucking Josh ...

"They? You're not going?"

"Two of my students made it to the finals in a local competition, so I'll be there with them. It's in the morning, and I'll be done before it starts, but just barely. I didn't want to hold them up. Half the fun is getting there early to watch the players warm up. Besides .... I have a dirty house that I desperately need to clean."

"I can go. I mean ... do we really trust Lucy with Josh?"

Tatum rolls her eyes.

"You know ..." I rub my lips together for a few seconds, contemplating the best way to ask my question. "You haven't said anything about your engagement. Can I ask what happened with that?"

She kicks at a few rocks while staring at her feet. "I said I couldn't make any life-changing decisions until I see Lucy making progress that might lead me to think she'll be walking by her senior year."

"She's already walking. Maybe with a walker, but she'll be on her own in no time."

Tatum nods slowly. "Yeah, I know. I'm just ..."

"Hey." I hold up my hands. "I'm not pushing you into anything. Just a question between friends."

She glances up.

I lift a single shoulder. "I mean ... we're friends, right?"

"Friends ..." she repeats like she's trying it on for size.

"I'm going to head home before Lucy wakes up." I jab a thumb over my shoulder.

"Okay. Make sure Lucy's ready Sunday by eleven."

"Will do." I jog back home, feeling a little high from our chance encounter and the indecision she feels for Dr. Josh. I wish I could take credit for it, but I know it's just her. She's not spontaneous by nature; it's how I've conditioned her to be over the years. But now I'm not part of her daily life, nudging her closer to the edge and telling her to just close her eyes and jump. And I'm sure as fuck not going to encourage her to go all in and marry Dr. Josh.

───────

AFTER I GET Lucy loaded up with Josh, and in the kindest way possible let him know he'd better take good care of my whole damn world, I clean the bathrooms, aerate my yard, and ... think about Tatum. It doesn't take much thought before I find myself in her driveway unloading my aerator.

She's not much of a yard keeper, and clearly neither is Dr. Josh. Granted, he doesn't live with her, but if you're going to spend time between my wife's legs, you sure as fuck better at least aerate her yard and throw down some fertilizer. It's just human decency.

"Can I ask what you're doing?" Tatum stands on the porch with her arms folded over her chest when I shut off the aerator.

She looks incredible in her leggings and long fitted tee, but it's that signature pouty face that she passed on to our daughter that gets me every time.

"You can, but I'll have to answer you with a 'duh' because it's obvious that I've aerated your yard."

"It's not your yard."

FOR LUCY

I keep pushing the beastly piece of equipment back to the truck and run it up the ramp into the bed. "Which makes it even more pathetic. Really, you should feel ashamed of yourself. You're going to have a weed infestation and a thatch nightmare if you don't get started on this early."

"Are you going to mow my lawn this summer too?" she asks with a very mocking tone to her words.

"Probably. After all, I plowed your driveway all winter."

"You did it so I could get out of my driveway to take her to therapy."

I roll my eyes. "You have four-wheel drive."

"Then why did you do it?"

"You know."

She doesn't respond right away. "Was Lucy pretty excited about the game?"

I grin at her changing the subject. "So excited."

"She just sent me a text with a photo of their fancy suite. Want to see it?"

"Nope."

"Why?" She giggles.

"Because I can be happy for her without torturing myself that she's there and I'm not."

"Get over here, Emmett, and come see the smile on our daughter's face."

I pause my motions.

Tatum holds up her phone—of course I can't see it from where I stand. She's baiting me to stop working in her yard, and I have fertilizer yet to spread.

Lucy wins. She always wins. So does her mother for that matter. I drop the bag of fertilizer and pull off my leather gloves as I clomp toward her in my boots to get a

JEWEL E. ANN

closer look at the photo. Taking two steps up onto the porch, I grab her phone and look at the picture.

"She looks happy. Like she's having a good day," I say while reminding myself that it's just a game, and my daughter is too smart to let Josh win her over with a suite.

"I have some leftover banana bread from yesterday. Can I heat you up a piece?"

Handing her back her phone, I narrow my eyes. "I'm going to finish your yard."

"Yeah, yeah ... I know. But you can take a break for banana bread." She heads back into the house, and after a few seconds of deliberation, I follow her.

"How was the dance competition?"

Tatum glances over her shoulder as she sticks the partial loaf of bread into her toaster oven. The Royals are on the TV in her living room. "Amazing. They took first place. I'm so proud of them."

I browse around her main floor, mostly watching the game. Her kitchen is smaller than mine, so is the living room. There's a tiny office with a simple desk against one wall and standing bookshelves along two other walls. A half-bath and a back door to the garage. All of the bedrooms are upstairs along with the laundry room and the full baths.

"I haven't cleaned anything yet, so stop inspecting my house." She cuts me off, just as I reenter the kitchen, and hands me a mug of hot chocolate with lots of whipped cream on top.

"Thanks." I take a sip.

Her gaze lands on my mouth, and she grins. "You have ..." She points to her own mouth to mirror where I have whipped cream on my upper lip.

I wipe my mouth with the back of my hand.

"Now…" she laughs "…you've just smeared it." She rubs the pad of her thumb along my upper lip.

I grab her wrist, and she jumps. Then, I slowly suck her thumb into my mouth.

"Em … Emmett …"

I don't stop with her thumb, because I can't stop. I run my tongue along her palm and press my lips to the inside of her wrist.

Her mouth opens, releasing a heavy breath.

"Why didn't you tell Josh about the s'mores?"

"It … it was a mistake."

I shake my head, walking her back a few steps until she hits the edge of the counter. "We're an accident, not a mistake. But I want to touch you on purpose … be with you on purpose …"

"We … we can't."

I kiss her neck, brushing her hair away with my fingers. "Why not?"

I'm a little afraid of her answer. If she says Austin's name, the moment will end. But over the past few months, she hasn't looked at me like I single-handedly killed our little boy and obliterated her whole world.

"Because it's wrong," she whispers while her fingers thread through my hair, keeping my face in the crook of her neck.

She's my wife. Was. Is. Always will be.

Touching my wife isn't wrong.

We kiss and she claws at my back.

I start to lift her T-shirt, and she mumbles, "No. It's wrong."

Yet she keeps kissing me. Being her favorite kind of wrong does all the right things to me.

I grip her ass with one hand, and she moans, sliding her

tongue deeper into my mouth. When my hand tries to slip under the waistband of her leggings, she mumbles, "Uh-uh, it's wrong."

We had sex in other people's homes—while on the clock. We used to shoplift trivial items just to see if we could get away with it. When did she start living by a moral compass?

My lips keep moving with hers as I fight to hold back my grin. Thank the god of mercy that she doesn't think that us kissing is wrong because it's life at the moment. We are more than two terrible people who can't control our physical instincts. We were married for twelve years. We've made three babies together. And maybe that doesn't matter to some people, but it sure as hell matters to me.

Since it's wrong to put my hands anywhere but along the outside of her clothes, I return them to her face, kissing her harder. After a few more seconds, I feel her on my leg.

She's ... grinding against my leg.

Taking a chance on her protesting, I lift her onto the counter. She wraps her legs around my waist. There—if she's going to grind against me, I want to feel her *there*, not on my leg. It's been over five years since I've had sex, and it's not my thigh that aches with need.

We kiss deeper and harder, sharing soft moans and vibrating groans. Holding her ass in my hands with it barely touching the edge of the counter, I move her over my erection. Had I known aerating would turn into dry humping, I wouldn't have worn denim. It's like wearing ten condoms at once. But I'm *so* neglected in this area, it doesn't matter. I'm fully clothed and seconds away from an orgasm.

"Emmett ... Jesus ... Emmett ..." she tears her mouth away from mine and bites my shoulder, working her pelvis overtime against me, nails digging into my back.

I'm close, but getting no help from the counter or the cabinet six inches away from her back, so I carry her to the sofa. With her still wrapped around me, I lay her down and pistol my hips at such a desperate pace my heart might explode before I release. When I do orgasm, just seconds after she does, I wonder how we got to this point. Twelve years of marriage and no dry humping—until now. At the moment, it's all so backward.

"This ..." she says out of breath "... is getting complicated."

All two hundred pounds of me is limp on top of her, my face pressed to her neck. I should get up before she can't breathe.

"And I don't need complicated," she adds just before I peel my body away from hers, getting no farther than on my knees beside the sofa.

I rest my hands on my thighs, catching my breath as she sits and straightens her shirt before combing her hair with her fingers. It's not complicated to me. Never has been. She's my wife, even if she decided to abolish the legal part of our marriage. I love her, even on the days she hates me. And this—what just happened—is who we are, have been, and always will be. It's the reason she lost her first job as a realtor. It's the reason she got pregnant before we were married, and it's the reason Josh will never have all of her, no matter how much she thinks she loves him.

And here's the thing ... I feel sorry for her. I really do. I know she feels some degree of love toward Josh. He was there when she needed something in her life that made her feel *alive* again. Losing a child feels like you're dying every single second of every single day, but you don't actually die. You live. And that's so much worse.

"I have to tell him this time." Her face contorts into

something painful to look at. "He needs to know that I'm messed-up right now. That his proposal jumbled my thoughts, and since then I've been out of control and impulsive."

"You make me sound like an STD you picked up while on a bender."

"Emmett ..." She shakes her head.

"Can I be there? When you tell him? I'm dying to hear the words *dry humping* come out of your mouth."

Her cheeks turn bright red. "I'm not saying that." She gives me a shove and marches into the kitchen, pulling the banana bread out of the toaster oven.

I'm so fucking stuck. I can't really dive into this subject without bringing up the tragic reason we separated in the first place. And I can't do that ... I can't even say Austin's name around her yet.

She hands me a plate with two slices of banana bread on it and butter oozing off the edges of the crust. "Lucy ... her accident really messed with my head. I can't even look at her without thinking 'what if?' What if the car that hit us would have been going a little bit faster? What if it would have hit her door at a slightly different angle?" She leans against the counter, resting her hands on either side. "Do you ever think that? What if?"

She's no longer talking about Lucy.

"No. I don't."

Tatum frowns.

"What-if's go nowhere but to crazy town. They answer nothing. They solve nothing. They fix nothing. At least when they're referencing the past."

"So ... you have no regrets?" She narrows her eyes.

"Of course I have regrets. I bet I do at least one thing a day that I regret."

Her gaze shifts to the sofa.

"I don't regret that," I say.

Her eyes make a quick redirection to me. "You don't have to explain yourself to anyone."

"Neither do you."

She scoffs. "You don't want to know why I just allowed that to happen?"

Chewing the last bite of the banana bread, I shrug a single shoulder. "In all our years together, did I ever ask *why* after we had sex?"

"We didn't just have sex." Her hands shift from the counter to crossing over her chest.

"Sorry ... do I want to know why you were so eager to dry hump me?" I scratch my chin. "Hmm ... nope. I'm a guy. Not everything in life requires an explanation."

"Oh ... and you weren't eager?" Her head tilts to the right.

"Why are you trying to pick a fight with me? Are you afraid I'm going to provoke you again, but this time you won't stop me from taking off your clothes? Can't we just enjoy this banana bread and have a civil conversation about something like the weather?"

"The weather? You want to talk about the weather?"

I nod. "Sure. In spite of a lack of rain, I was pleasantly surprised to find things here at your house are quite moist after all. Pretty wet actually."

"Not funny."

"It's a little funny." I set the plate on the counter beside her, allowing me to invade every inch of her space. "Josh is a lucky guy."

CHAPTER TWENTY-ONE

SINCE I'M A TRUE GENTLEMAN, I finish fertilizing the lawn instead of watching the game. Then I fix the broken fence and cut down a few dead tree branches before heading home. By the time I get out of the shower, Lucy arrives home with a wide grin and the smell of victory. The Royals won.

"You should have been there." She's glowing as she wheels her chair into the living room with Josh right behind her.

"Not gonna lie; I'm a little envious of your seats." I kiss the top of her head.

"I told Lucy we should all go next time I get an offer to watch from the suite. I felt bad Tatum couldn't make it. I'm sure she's exhausted after the dance competition and cleaning the house."

I don't think I'll be invited to any games with Josh after Tatum tells him that she *is* exhausted because I stopped by to give her an orgasm and have a couple slices of banana bread.

"What did you do all day, Dad?" Lucy asks.

"I did some work around here, and then I went over to your mom's to aerate, fertilize, and fix a few things."

"Oh? Tatum didn't tell me she needed help around there. Now I feel bad." Josh frowns.

He should feel bad that he's not observant enough to see that stuff on his own without Tatum having to ask him.

"No need to feel bad. I took care of it."

I took care of her.

"Thanks, I appreciate it."

You won't for long …

"Thank *you* for taking Lucy to the game."

"Anytime. See ya, Lucy."

"Bye, Josh. Thanks."

The door closes and Lucy gives me a funny look.

"What?" I ask.

"You were at Mom's house?"

"Yeah." I shrug. "So?"

"So … since when did you become Mom's yard keeper?"

"Since I fell in love with her eighteen years ago. Since she gave me a beautiful daughter who is very nosey. Sometimes marriages fall apart for reasons that don't involve falling out of love."

"So you *do* still love her." Lucy smirks like she just solved a big mystery.

"Always, Luce. I will always love your mom." I wink. "But I love you more."

Her smile fades a fraction as she moves herself from the wheelchair to the sofa. I lift her legs onto the ottoman.

"I'm ready to talk about it."

"It?" I sit, angling my body toward hers.

"That day … the day Austin died."

My throat immediately starts to constrict. "Okay."

"Why did you tell Mom it was you? I mean, I know, but

I *don't* know. Did you think she would hate me? Did you take the blame so she wouldn't hate me?"

I shake my head. "I knew she could never hate you. She loves you in ways I can't fully describe. But losing Austin … that moment after we left him, left his body, she wasn't herself. And I saw this look in her eyes, like she needed answers. After all, when she left he was fine, and by the time she got home, he was already gone. Imagine how you felt when Ashton broke up with you … now take it times a million and take that times infinity. That's how your mom felt. I knew she would say something to you, but it wouldn't be the right thing, and no matter how many times she might have apologized, it would never erase her words from your memory. I felt in my heart, so deeply, Luce, that I failed at saving Austin, but I knew I could still save you. And not just from your mom. I wanted *you* to believe me too. I didn't want for you to feel responsible."

Lucy blinks several times and finally nods once. "Dr. Kane said you were protecting Mom too. After all, she was the one who left Austin with me. She might have blamed herself too."

"Yes," I whisper.

"You let your marriage end … for me. And for Mom." Lucy wipes a tear.

I never wanted this day to come, the day she allowed herself to completely acknowledge and accept the events of that day. As her father, her greatest protector, I wanted to shield her from the pain and grief—if possible, forever.

"She would hate this," Lucy continues. "She loves you. I mean, she loves Josh too, but I know she still loves you. When I talk about you, she smiles. She didn't used to, but now she does. I wonder if she ever wishes she were still with you instead of Josh."

"Well, I don't know the answer to that, but I do know that time can change people. Josh seems to love her, and if she loves him too, we have to accept that. It's not tragic." (I lie) "It's life. She's moved on. After Austin died, I was so afraid she would never be the same, never recover from the loss. So in a small way, I celebrated her meeting Josh."

"He's not you."

I laugh. "I think that's the point. I think she had to find someone who is nothing like me."

"So … when you're with her, like today, what do you talk about?"

I swallow and clear my throat. "Um … just stuff. I spent most of my time in the yard and fixing the fence, but she did offer me some banana bread and she had the game on. We talked about you and how wonderful you are." I grin. "And how exciting it was for you to get to go to the game today. She told me a little bit about the dance competition. Her students won."

Lucy returns a slow nod. "So you talked like adults, like a married couple." The grin that appears on her face is sly and mischievous.

We fucked about like adults—actually like teenagers— but it felt nearly as good.

"You have to look at the whole picture, Lucy. It's no longer just about me and your mom. Things have changed a lot. Josh is a very important part of her life now. As for me, I'm just really happy that she can look at me and it doesn't make me feel like the worst person in the world. We have to focus on the small victories instead of being greedy and wanting the miracle."

"You wanted me to walk again. That's a miracle. Why weren't you satisfied with me being alive? What's wrong with wanting *everything*?"

This girl …

I reach over and squeeze her leg, and it moves. It jerks in response. We grin. "You're right. Shoot for the stars. Why not, right?"

———

AFTER DINNER, Lucy's friends stop by to take her for a walk, basically to wheel her to the skate park where I know several of them smoke. My protests don't hold up to the "I'm almost eighteen" speech or the "I'm still in a wheelchair. Do I not get to have friends anymore?" speech.

I take a seat on the porch swing. It's not that I'm impatiently waiting for her return … Okay, it's one hundred percent that. Within minutes of taking a seat with my cold root beer, Tatum turns into the driveway on her bike. What are the chances of us having alone time twice in one day?

I grin. "Your tires are flat."

She gets off her bike. "I know. That's why I'm here."

Setting my root beer on the railing, I make my way down the ramp and turn toward the garage. "Did Josh not come by after he dropped Lucy off?"

"He did." She follows me with her bike.

"And he couldn't fit your bike into the back of his vehicle to get air in your tires?"

"He didn't know I was going for a bike ride. And he got called into the hospital."

I flip on the compressor and fill up her tires. "There you go."

"Thanks." She gives me a reserved smile, not like the one she gave me earlier today before we kissed. "Emmett?"

"Yeah?" I wind up the hose and turn toward her.

"I told Josh that something happened between us." She scrapes her teeth over her bottom lip several times.

"Okay," I say slowly. "Do I need to sleep with one eye open?"

"He gave me an ultimatum."

"An ultimatum? Like ... you can never see me again? Because that's not realistic with Lucy."

"No. It's not that. He said if I was truly sorry, and I really did love him, that I had to make a decision."

"A decision?"

"Emmett ..." Her face does that painful contortion thing. "We ended. We ended tragically. And while I'm glad we can be friends now, that in some ways I can forgive you, I know it's fragile. We're fragile. If I stare too long at you, all I see is him."

Him. She still can't say his name.

"And when I see him, I'm reminded of the events of that day, and the resentment comes back. And I know ... I really do know that I have no room to point fingers, not after what happened with Lucy. But maybe that's the ultimate sign for both of us. You should be able to look at someone you love and not think of their greatest mistake. And I should be able to do the same thing."

"When I look at you, I don't think of your mistakes."

"Emmett ... how can you not? How can you look at Lucy and not think about me fumbling my phone and a car crashing into us? You're a strong man, but nobody is that strong, that perfect."

"What is the point to your speech?"

She sighs. "Before dinner, Josh made me decide if we're forever or if we're over."

My gaze goes to her hand and the diamond ring on her finger. "Jesus, Tatum ..."

She brings her hands together, covering up the ring. "I love him. He's emotionally good for me."

"Sounds safe." I shoulder past her back toward the front of the house.

"I'm sorry. I shouldn't have let you kiss me. And today … that never should have happened."

"For Christ's sake, Tatum …" I grab my root beer and sit back down on the porch swing. "You don't have to do this with me. You don't have to belittle us to justify marrying Josh. If you want to have a safe marriage void of true passion and live with a guy who can't start a fucking lawn mower, then by all means, go for it."

She sets the kickstand and stomps her feet up the ramp. "He can start a lawn mower. He just doesn't have time for it, so he hires someone else to do it for him."

"So … you've never actually seen him start one?"

She shakes her head quickly. "That's not the point. And for the record, we have passion."

"No…" I take a sip of my root beer "…you don't. If you had with him what you had—what you *have*—with me, then what happened this afternoon between us would have never happened. Tell me … did you fuck him? After he put that ring on your finger, did you fuck him?"

"That is *none* of your business!" Her cheeks flare with shades of red as she parks her fists on her hips.

"That's a no. Do you remember what I did to you before I put that zip tie on your finger?"

"That's different. You did it because I was pregnant with Lucy."

"Had you not been pregnant with her, and I would have proposed in a more traditional way, I would have been inside of you just as quickly. I would have sealed the deal in the most intimate way possible. That's how I love you. I love you with my whole fucking heart. I love you with my entire body. I love you emotionally, physically ... passionately."

"Loved," she whispers. "That's how you *loved* me. In the past. Before Austin died."

Tatum said his name, and it gives me pause for several moments. She has to blame me. If she can't blame me, then she has no reason to not love me in all the same ways that I love her.

"No. You *loved* me, Tatum. But I *love* you now. I loved you then. I will love you always. I love you in ways you can't even imagine. And maybe that's the problem; you can't imagine why there would still be love between us. So you're right. Josh is the answer. He is the anti-me. But that fucking sucks for you because you deserve the guy who would steal you. You deserve the guy who's smart enough to see that if the woman he loves kissed another man the way you kissed me today, she doesn't really belong to him."

After a silence settles between us, she says, "Where's Lucy?"

"At the skating park with her friends."

"I'll tell her tomorrow, then."

"She'll be thrilled." I give her a fake smile before taking another long swig of my root beer.

Tatum squints. "Lucy likes Josh. He took her to a game today. They had a great time."

"Agreed. Josh is a great guy."

She maintains her narrow-eyed expression. "But?"

I shrug. "No buts. He's a great guy."

"Then wish me well, Emmett. Don't be such an ass about this. Be happy for me. I think I've earned a little happiness in my life."

Keeping an idle tongue is really hard right now, but I

bite it and smile. "Yes. You sure have. Congratulations. Have you set a date?"

Distrust hangs heavily in the air between us as she attempts to gauge my level of sincerity.

"Early summer. He's taking two weeks off."

"His idea or yours?"

"His. Why?"

He wants to expedite the wedding before she has a chance to change her mind, before I have a chance to change her mind.

"Just curious."

"It will be just close family and friends."

"Good thing I'm your friend." I give her a toothy grin.

"Emmett ..." She stares at her feet. "I can't have you at my wedding."

"Why not?"

"Because Josh knows we did things."

I'm in blissful denial at the moment. It's how I can joke about this. It's a joke, right? She's not really marrying Josh. She didn't just accept his proposal hours after I gave her an orgasm. Right? RIGHT?

"What about Chicago? Is he taking a job there? Are you moving there?"

"I don't know yet."

"You didn't discuss it?" I stare at the amber bottle in my hand.

"We discussed different possibilities. If Lucy doesn't want to move before she graduates—"

"Of course she's not going to want to move before she graduates."

Tatum shoots me a scowl. "*If* she doesn't want to move before she graduates, then I'll stay here with her and go to Chicago most weekends."

"I'm here. You don't have to stay."

"That's not an option."

I laugh. "Not an option? Why? Because you still don't trust me?"

"No. Because she's my daughter too, and I'm not okay with two days with her and five days away from her."

God ... this woman infuriates me. I love her. I love her in the most self-destructive way, but she still infuriates me. "That does suck ... only seeing Lucy two days. But actually, I can't attest to that because I didn't get two days with her. I got one fucking day with her. Ten hours to be exact."

"Emmett ..."

It's always my name. Like her saying it should bring me out of my state of mind, wake me up to see her version of the truth.

"You can *Emmett* me all you want, but that's still the truth. I would never hold your mistake to such an insane level of inhumanity. I would never go in front of a judge and insist you be disqualified from ever driving her anywhere again."

Tatum tears up, and it usually gets me. A punch in the gut. But not today. She can't kiss me the way she kissed me and still play the fucking neglectful parenting card. Not ever again. She thinks she's earned a chance at happiness, but what about me?

"I can forgive you and you can forgive me, but it doesn't change the past."

I shrug. "I'm not trying to change the past."

"Oh, that's right. You're just trying to live in the past. That's why you wanted this house. That's why you refuse to date."

Drawing in a deep breath, I hold it and let it out slowly through my nose. "You're right. I like the memories this house holds. That's why I wanted the house. And I don't date because my heart still belongs to the woman standing in front of me. And it's not a switch I can turn off."

"Don't do this, Emmett ..." She shakes her head. "I don't want you to love me."

"Well, I'm sorry. It's not your choice. And it's not even my choice. I don't wake up every morning and spend an hour practicing loving you like taking a morning jog. It's automatic. It's like my heart beating. I don't think about it. So maybe when I die and other things cease ... like the beating of my heart ... then maybe you'll be set free of my love. So there's that. Something to look forward to. *Oh good! Emmett finally died, now I don't have to deal with his love.*"

She bats away a tear.

"Chicago will be good for you."

"Why?" She sniffles.

"Because I'm not there."

She winces. "It's not that I don't love you. I just ..."

"I know."

"I wouldn't marry Josh if I didn't love him."

"I know."

"And I do want you to be happy."

I give that a little thought. I'm not sure she does want me to be happy. I think she wants me to be okay. Okay for Lucy. Okay for her conscience. But not happy. I think she feels like my life falling just shy of true happiness is my penance.

CHAPTER TWENTY-TWO

THEN

Tatum rarely called me. She used Lucy to send her messages, sometimes she'd shoot me an email, but a phone call was rare.

"Hello?" I answered my phone at a jobsite, one hand holding the phone while my other hand covered my ear to hear her as I walked away from the machinery toward the parking lot and my truck.

"Emmett?"

"Sorry ... just a sec." I jogged to my truck and climbed inside. "I'm at a jobsite and couldn't hear you. Is everything okay?" I asked Tatum.

"Yeah. It's ... I ... well, I just wanted to call you and tell you something before I tell Lucy and she tells you."

"Sounds complicated. What is it?"

"I ... met someone."

It was one thing to know something, like death was inevitable. And it was another thing to *know* something, like someone died. The thing you knew would eventually happen *happened.* And you realize that nothing could have prepared you for it. As much as you tried to ready your heart, guard it from complete destruction, you underestimated the force, the real impact.

"That's ... um ..." I pinched the bridge of my nose and squeezed my eyes shut. "Who is he?"

"He's a doctor. Not mine. Funny thing, actually, Alice and Derek introduced me to him. Not Cody," she said with a nervous laugh.

I wished I'd found the same level of irony, but I didn't.

"Anyway, we've gone out a few times. He's really nice."

She had no clue how little I cared about Dr. Nice.

"I'm going to tell Lucy about him when she gets home from school this afternoon. And I'll introduce her to Josh ... that's his name ... this Friday. We'll all go out to dinner. And since you'll see her on Saturday, I didn't want you to be blindsided by the news."

Too late. I was blindsided. Ran over with a truck speeding down the interstate.

"Emmett? Are you still there?"

"Yeah. Thanks for the call." I ended the call. "FUCK!" I pounded the palm of my hand against the steering wheel several times before gripping it and dropping my head between my arms.

I wasn't delusional, at least that was what I told myself. I knew we were over, hence the divorce. I just thought she'd live out the rest of her life as a lonely grieving mother the way I was living the rest of my life as a lonely grieving father and ex-husband. In my head, we would both be miserable. And maybe that felt fair to me whether it was right or wrong.

"Want to talk about it?" My dad asked as we watched the Royals play at his house.

"Talk about what?"

"Your mood?" He handed me a beer.

That was the clue that I wasn't okay. I rarely drank real beer, usually just root beer.

"Tatum has a boyfriend. She called me about it earlier in the week—a heads-up. And Lucy gave me the scoop yesterday."

"You're divorced." He sat in the other recliner.

"Thanks, Captain Obvious." I took a long swig of my beer.

"I'm just saying, you knew it might happen. She's a great lady. Of course, some other guy was going to eventually snatch her up. I know it's hard on you, but you have to deal with it. What does Lucy think of him?"

"Hard to say. She wasn't overly excited. More matter-of-fact about it. He's a surgeon. Never been married. No kids. He drives a nice car. He's polite. And he likes to hold Tatum's hand and whisper things in her ear that make her laugh."

"Ugh ..." my dad grumbled, wrinkling his nose.

"Exactly." I focused on the game.

"Is it serious?"

I shrugged. "Must be serious enough for her to tell me and introduce him to Lucy. And now Lucy is on me more than ever to find someone for myself. To get out there and date. To set up a profile on some crazy dating app. It's like she needs to know I'm okay, and the litmus test for that is me having a girlfriend."

"Well, she might not be entirely wrong about that."

"No." I shook my head. "She *is* entirely wrong. I don't need a girlfriend or another wife to be happy. I have Lucy.

And you and Mom. Will, Andi, and their kids. I mean ... why the fuck do I need anything more?"

My dad chuckled. "Companionship. Sex ..."

I tried not to grin, but my dad's timing on talking to me about sex for the first time was laughable. "I don't need a girlfriend to have sex."

"Whatever does it for you, Emmett."

What did that mean? I wasn't sure. Did he think I meant I was having sex with myself? My hand and some internet porn? Or did he think I meant randomly hooking up with someone, like someone I met at a bar. *That* was what I meant, even if I was just saying it to make a point. I wasn't actually looking for anyone at a bar or anywhere else for that matter. And so what if my hand did the job when I needed a release?

"I had a lady drop her dog off a few months ago. A widow. About your age. Nice looking gal. She mentioned being a big Chiefs fan. And she lives in Redington. When she returns next month to pick up her dog, I could see if she'd be open to me giving her your number?"

No offense to my dad—after all, he made a solid living freeze-drying animals. But I wasn't a freeze-dried animal kind of guy, so I already had no interest in that woman. Not to mention the idea of my dad fixing me up was just ... too weird.

"Thanks, Dad. But I think I'll pass."

"Suit yourself."

"I will."

"She's not coming back to you. You know that right?"

I rolled my eyes.

"Your mom and I had this conversation years ago when Lucy said something to her about you and Tatum living together again someday."

I didn't know Lucy said that.

"Your mom said what happened with Austin severed something between the two of you that can never be mended, no matter how much you love each other. She said if she were in Tatum's shoes, she would have done the same thing. She would have left me. So it's not just her. Tatum wasn't trying to punish you. She's doing what she needs to do to survive and be the best mom she can be for Lucy. It's not that she can't or won't forgive you, Son. It's that she can never forget. Your mom said it would be like living with someone who has PTSD, only worse because she blames you."

I just wanted to watch a game with my dad. How did the guy, who rarely said more than "yes, dear" and "okay, dear" turn into Dr. Phil?

"I'm deliriously happy for her, Dad. Really. If she's moving on, that means she's no longer feeling like the world is over. That's good for her. That's good for Lucy. Why wouldn't I be happy about that?"

"I'm proud of you, Emmett. You've always accepted responsibility. You've always put Lucy and Tatum first. I know a lot of men who would have drunk themselves to death had they experienced what you did."

Bless his Dr. Phil heart. Really. My dad tried to say and do the right thing around me. But I wasn't so sure the right thing to say was that any other man would have drunk himself to death, so kudos to me for not ending my life.

The crazy part? After years of taking the blame, working so hard to convince Lucy that it was actually my fault, not just a coverup, I started to believe it. I had days of feeling guilty for Austin's death. The lie became my truth.

CHAPTER TWENTY-THREE

NOW

TATUM: You need to come now. Lucy is in the middle of therapy and she's having a moment.

I stare at Tatum's text. A moment? Did she have a setback? Tatum usually refers to Lucy's "moments" as times when she has an emotional breakdown.

Emmett: On my way.

I jump out of my truck and jog into the physical therapy building, feeling an uneasy sense of urgency. Usually when Lucy has a breakdown, Tatum does too.

Sure enough, when I round the corner from the waiting room to the large open area filled with therapy tables and equipment, Tatum's wiping tears from her face.

"What happened? Where is she?"

Tatum nods behind me.

I glance over my shoulder at Lucy *walking* toward me with nothing more than a single cane for balance.

"No need to load up my wheelchair anymore." Lucy beams ... she fucking *beams*. I've never seen her smile so big.

If Austin's death was the deepest depths of Hell, this is the absolute infinite height of Heaven.

"Chad said I've been ready to walk on my own for weeks; it's just been a lack of confidence holding me back. But yesterday at the skating park, I met this cute guy and he asked me out. Dad ... he asked me out, and I was in my wheelchair. No way am I going out on a date in a wheelchair."

Oh fuck ... that smile. It wasn't about simply ditching the wheelchair; it was about a guy. And our conversation comes back to haunt me.

"If I can walk, I can have sex."

Tatum will kill me.

"Luce ..." I shake my head. "I'm speechless."

When a hand touches mine, I glance down. It's Tatum squeezing it. Tears in her eyes. And that "our baby is walking" look on her face.

My life is a mess. A complete shit show, but no one person knows all of it. Lucy knows things that Tatum doesn't know. Tatum knows things that Lucy doesn't know. And I'm the keeper of all the secrets. It's not a great job.

"Can we go shopping? Please? I want some new jeans since I've lost so much weight in my legs. Nothing I have fits me right."

"Of course we can go shopping." Tatum releases my hand and hugs Lucy.

"I guess I'll head back to work."

"No! We *have* to celebrate. Cake pops after I find new jeans. Maybe Josh can come. Is he working?" Lucy asks Tatum.

Tatum shoots me a wary look, and I return a tight smile. "Um ... I think he's working, but I can call him."

"Yes! Call him." Lucy takes off toward the exit with

nothing but her cane and a new lease on life.

"Does she know about the engagement?" I ask.

Tatum's thumbs slide over the screen of her phone, and then she curls her dark hair behind her right ear and holds the phone up to it. "Nope." She gives me a slightly panicked look. "Hey, sorry to bother you, but Lucy had a good day at therapy, and she was wondering if you could meet us later for her favorite cake pops?"

After a few seconds, her nose wrinkles. "Well, yes, *us* means me, Lucy, and her dad."

Her dad.

I don't have a name anymore. *Emmett* could be Tatum's friend or her dirty lover. Josh would never choose to be in the same room as *Emmett*, but maybe he'll deal with Lucy's *dad* for fifteen to twenty minutes of cake pops and celebrating Lucy no longer needing a wheelchair.

"No, I was going to tell her tonight. Maybe it's a good time to tell her. Yeah ... okay. I'll text you when we're done getting her new jeans. See you soon. Love you too."

"Everything good with your fiancé?" I ask.

"Everything is fine." She heads toward the door like everything is not fine.

After I buy Lucy not one but four pairs of new jeans, two new sweaters, a purse, and boots she couldn't live without, we meet Dr. Josh for cake pops.

He's at a table when we arrive, cake pops already purchased and waiting for us.

"Lucy Loo!" He jumps out of his chair when he sees her walking toward the table. "What is this?" He hugs her. "Oh my god! I'm so proud of you, darling."

Darling? She's not his darling. What the fuck?

"Thank you. Looks like we can sit anywhere we want at the next Royals game."

Fantastic. He's now her game buddy.

She takes a seat next to me as Josh kisses my wife.

Yes … I'm still calling her that. Stubborn as hell? Probably. But I've run out of fucks to give by this point in my life.

As Lucy devours her first cake pop, Tatum reaches deep into her handbag. "Lucy, Josh and I have something to tell you."

Lucy glances up, licking her lips. "What's that?"

Tatum pulls out her diamond ring and slips it on her finger. "We're engaged." She smiles and so does Josh as he slides his arm around her, claiming her.

And I'm okay with that for now. I'm still certain her last orgasm was with me.

"Engaged?" Lucy says like she's never heard the word. "You're … getting married?" Her nose wrinkles as she cocks her head to the side.

My thoughts exactly.

Tatum chuckles. "Yes. That's what engaged means. I thought you'd be happy for us, sweetie."

"I'm …" Lucy shifts her attention to me as if I'm going to share my thoughts.

Tatum and Josh also stare at me, but they clearly don't want my thoughts on the matter.

Clearing my throat, I find a fabricated smile. "So much great news in one day, huh, Luce? It's almost too much to take."

Her eyes narrow at me. I'm not sure what she expects me to say. But more than that, I can't figure out what's going on in her head, but it gives me chills because I know she's been holding on to her little secret, waiting for the right time to share it with Tatum.

I don't think now is the right time.

"Lucy …" Josh reaches across the table and rests his

hand on hers. "I should have asked for your permission." He shakes his head. "I ... I don't know what I was thinking. But you need to know that I love your mom more than anything. And I love you like you're my own daughter. So I hope you're okay with this."

Oh ... where to start ...

First, he doesn't love her more than I love her. Not even close.

Second, he doesn't have kids, so comparing his love to her like a love he'd have for his own daughter is just nonsense. It would be like loving the neighbor's dog like my own when I've never owned a dog. You just can't make those comparisons. I realize it might sound like I'm splitting hairs here, but the details matter. At least ... they matter to me.

Again, Lucy looks to me like she might consider being okay with it if I'm okay with it. So here we go again ... I find myself lying to Lucy to make her feel better about something and to make Tatum feel less guilty. This martyr shit is exhausting.

"They're thinking early summer for the wedding. I'm sure that means a new dress for you," I say to Lucy.

Lucy continues to inspect me. I really don't know what else to say. After a few seconds, she nods slowly. "Well, congratulations."

That's my girl. I internally laugh because her congratulations is about as sincere as my enthusiasm for her getting a new dress to wear to a wedding that makes my soul feel drained of its life.

Josh bites. Hook. Line. And sinker. "Thank you, so much, Lucy Loo." I think he has actual tears in his eyes.

Tatum doesn't buy it, but she also doesn't call Lucy out in front of Josh. She just smiles through gritted teeth.

I drive Lucy home, and no shocker, Tatum follows us. I hope she can let this day go back to being about Lucy and her walking. But something tells me, she's on a mission to make Lucy be happier for her—which is just sad that Josh doesn't make her happy enough so she needs everyone else's approval and enthusiasm.

"What's Mom doing?" Lucy asks as we pull into the driveway, and she sees Tatum pull in behind us.

"I think she's just a little concerned that you weren't sincere enough with your congratulations."

Lucy rolls her eyes. "She loves *you*, Dad. Like ... what is she even doing? Josh is nice, but he's not you. Why would he want someone else's sloppy seconds?"

"Lucy!" I put the truck into *Park* and gawk at her. I don't know whether to be grateful that she's on my side or mortified that she just referred to her mom as sloppy seconds. Maybe I don't understand how her generation uses that term, but it doesn't exactly sound like a compliment to Josh or Tatum.

"You know what I mean."

I don't actually, but before I can confess my ignorance on the slang meaning, Lucy climbs out of the truck slowly, using her cane to steady herself as her feet reach for the ground one right after the other. I grab her bags from the backseat.

"Hey, Mom. What's up?" Lucy plays the innocent role, but after her "sloppy seconds" comment, she's anything but innocent.

"I thought we should talk, just the two of us." Tatum follows Lucy into the house.

"Sure. About what?"

Tatum shoots me a look—it's not exactly a friendly one. "Let's talk in your room."

"I think I'll move upstairs soon. Chad said stairs will be my next big obstacle. Then Dad can have his bed back ... you know ... in case he wants to hook up some night. Then he won't have to use my twin bed."

Okay ... she's officially gone off the rails. Now she's full-on baiting Tatum.

"Is he hooking up in your twin bed now?" Tatum asks, gritting through her teeth as she shoots me one last evil glance over her shoulder before shutting the bedroom door behind them.

I chuckle to myself. Lucy is something, stubborn like her mom and a complete pot-stirrer like me. I've always enjoyed ruffling Tatum's feathers.

While they talk, I make dinner. I'm fearful that Lucy is spilling her guts, putting it all out there just to shatter Tatum's world again, but there's nothing I can do about it. It's no longer just my secret. And I agree with Dr. Kane; Lucy needs to do whatever she feels is best for her.

"Night, sweetie. I love you," Tatum says just as the bedroom door opens.

I sigh, knowing Lucy didn't tell her. Tatum would not be this controlled had she told her.

"Please make sure she's in bed safely before you go to bed or hook up with some stranger in your daughter's bed," Tatum says to my back as I stir the pasta on the stove.

"I always do."

I love that she's feeling a hint of something resembling jealousy. Welcome to my world for the past five-plus years.

After a few seconds, the front door clicks shut.

"You're going to let her just marry him? Really?" Lucy takes a seat at the kitchen table, setting her cane on it and narrowing her eyes at me.

I give her a quick glance and a slow shrug. "She didn't

ask for my permission. There's not a lot I can do."

"Tell her you love her!"

"She knows."

"Not if you don't tell her."

"Lucy ... I've told her." I shake my head. "What did you two discuss in there? I assumed when your mom left all was good. Now, you're giving me the third degree like this engagement is my fault. A result of something I didn't do or say? Really, Luce?"

"I ..." She deflates. "I was so close to telling her, Dad. I even said that I had something to tell her. Then I chickened out and asked her if she'd go with me to get on the pill instead."

Fuck. My. Life.

"What did she say?" I drain the pasta.

"She said yes, of course. But that's not what I wanted. I just made that up because right when I started to say it, to tell her that it was me who was supposed to be watching Austin, not you, I froze. I thought of why you said you lied in the first place. That look on her face. And I got scared that even now, she might look at me like that ... like I killed him. And ... I couldn't do it. Now I feel like a complete chicken with no backbone. I mean ... she won't hate me, right? Not now?"

"She wasn't going to hate you then, and she won't hate you now. But I understand your apprehension. I'm not exactly relishing the idea of her knowing either. But you just have to be prepared for if or when you do tell her. She's not going to just laugh it off and hug it out with you. Your confession will turn her world upside down again. And I don't actually know what she will say or do, but you have to be prepared for the worst. And maybe that worst means for a split second she looks at you like you killed Austin. Or maybe she has a knee-jerk reaction and says something to that effect. I really don't know, but you have to be prepared to let it not scar you because, however she reacts, it will be temporary. How you perceive it will be permanent."

"So I should tell her, but I need to ignore how she reacts?"

I shake my head, rinsing the pasta before turning to face her. "I'm not telling you to tell her. I'm not telling you to *not* tell her. I'm also not telling you to ignore her reaction if you do tell her. I'm telling you to anticipate something that might be a very knee-jerk reaction and not what's truly in her heart. If you tell her, please remember she loves you more than anything or anyone. She always has and she always will.

"When you were a little girl, we grounded you after you used permanent marker on your mom's computer screen, and you blacked out all of her keys. You ran to your room and screamed just how much you *hated* us. We knew you didn't really hate us. It was a knee-jerk reaction."

Lucy nods. "I understand."

"Listen, Luce ... I made a decision the day Austin died. And I knew that decision would likely change my life forever, but I was okay with that. I'm *still* okay with that. It's not fun watching your mom fall in love with another man. But today ... when you walked with very little assistance, I didn't think about Austin and I didn't think about your mom marrying Josh. All I could think about and all that mattered was that girl walking toward me with so much pride in her smile.

"So here's my point ... tell your mom. Don't tell your mom. But whatever you do, it has to be for you and only you. Not for me. Not for your mom. Not for your therapist."

She nods again. "Okay."

CHAPTER TWENTY-FOUR

"How do I look?" Lucy asks, her hand on her cane a little more shaky than usual.

"Too good for this skate park kid," I say without a smile.

Tatum scoffs. "Oh stop. She looks amazing, and yes, too good for any boy, but we're going to be nice to said boy when he arrives. Right?" She shoots me a stiff smile.

Lucy's too skinny. She needs to build up the muscles in her legs. And what if she trips or falls ... is this kid going to catch her? I don't like this. I've never been a fan of her dating. And now that I know she has sex on the brain, it makes this situation even worse.

"*The boy* has a name. It's Racer. And he's very responsible."

I'm certain no boy named Racer can be responsible.

"And what are you and this Racer kid doing?" I ask, my eyes narrowed.

"Not *Racer kid*, just Racer." Lucy makes her way to the front window to watch for him. "We're grabbing dinner, then we're going to hang out with some other people."

"A party?" I ask.

"No. Just hanging out."

"Emmett, you need to relax a bit," Tatum warns as she sits in her paisley chair, hands folded in her lap like she's not at all concerned about Lucy's date.

"Will there be alcohol?"

"Dad ..." Lucy says my name, dragging it out in a long, exasperated sigh.

"Sex?" There. I said it.

"Emmett!" Tatum's jaw drops. "Would you please stop? This is our daughter you're talking about. She's not going to have sex on a first date. Why would you even ask her that?"

I can only see Lucy's side profile as she keeps watch at the window, but she's grinning because she knows why I asked. "He's here." She turns and heads toward the door.

"You're not running out to his car. He's coming to the door to get you."

"Dad, I can't run yet. And you have to promise to not say anything but 'Hi. Nice to meet you.' Can you handle that?"

As she wraps her hand around the doorknob, she eyes me with that secretive smirk still stuck to her face.

"Do you need me to give you a condom?"

"Oh my god! Emmett!" Tatum jumps out of her chair, enraged over my question because she doesn't know what motived our little girl to walk, but I do.

Just before opening the door for Racer, Lucy turns to me and rolls her lips between her teeth to hide her knowing grin. "I'm good, but thanks."

"Ignore your dad, Lucy." Tatum wedges herself between us and hugs Lucy. "Just have a fun time. You look beautiful. And if you get tired and need me to come get you, just call. Okay?"

"Thanks, Mom." She opens the door.

Racer has long blond hair just past his chin. It looks like he doesn't make a great effort at combing it. His jeans ride too low, and his shirt is three sizes too big. But what do I know? I'm just the dad.

"Racer these are my parents, Emmett and Tatum. This is Racer."

"Nice to meet you. Enjoy your evening." Tatum rests her hands on Lucy's shoulders. "Oh, do you need some money?"

"Dad gave me money," Lucy says.

"Be safe," I say, eying only Racer. "Be smart."

Lucy shakes her head at me. "Let's go, Racer."

We stand at the open front door until they've pulled out of the driveway in his pimped-out Ford Focus.

"What was that all about?" Tatum turns toward me, arms crossed over her chest.

"What was what all about? The sex talk? The condom offer? It's called I know my daughter is seventeen. I know what seventeen-year-olds do. I was seventeen once. The question is what's wrong with you? Do you prefer to turn a blind eye to the obvious?"

"She's recovering from a spinal cord injury, Emmett. I don't think she's thinking about sex."

"Well, then you need to rethink." I shut the door and head to the kitchen, opening the fridge to survey my options for dinner.

"I can't believe you think Lucy is acting like what you were at seventeen. Just because *you* clearly had sex on the brain doesn't mean she does. I was embarrassed for her. I would have died had my dad offered me a condom. And it's like you were giving her your blessing. That makes no sense. Don't you feel any sense of protectiveness toward her?"

Pulling out leftover chicken, I shut the fridge door and

grin. "I'm pretty sure offering her the condom was a protective measure." I grin.

"It's not funny."

"It's a little funny." I retrieve a plate and slap two pieces of bread on it.

"Why do you have condoms to offer her anyway? Are you dating again?"

I pull pieces of chicken off the bone and put them on my bread. Why does her question give me such pleasure? Why does she care?

"I don't think dating is a prerequisite to using a condom."

"Jesus ... so you're just having random sex with women? Does Lucy know? God ... I hope you don't bring them here."

"So ... how are the wedding plans coming along?" I put the rest of the chicken in the fridge and grab the barbecue sauce.

"You're changing the subject."

"Yes, from my sex life to yours."

"So you *do* have a sex life?"

I glance over my shoulder at her. "I think you can kiss me, hump my leg, and ask about my sex life ... *or* you can marry Josh. But you can't do all four. So what's it going to be?"

She winces at the humping my leg statement. "Lucy is standing up with me. We're getting fitted for dresses on Saturday."

"Sounds lovely. I'm so happy for you." I shake some barbecue sauce out of the bottle then screw the cap back onto it.

"Are you really?"

Taking a bite of my sandwich, I nod and chew. "Your happiness is mine," I mumble.

"Don't say that, Emmett. I know you don't mean it."

"Why can't I mean it?"

"Because I know you still have feelings for me."

"And you still have feelings for me, but you're marrying Josh anyway. So why can't I have feelings for you but still want you to be happy?"

She bites the inside of her cheek.

"Unless you're not really happy."

She scoffs and turns, gazing out the front window. "I've lost two children, and I nearly lost Lucy. I'm not sure happiness is the right word. I'm moving on, searching for something resembling joy in my life."

"So Josh isn't your happily ever after? He's just a bit of joy? That's sad, Tatum. Why marry a guy unless he makes you deliriously happy? Why marry a guy unless he ignites passion?"

"What makes you think Josh and I don't have passion? You've said this more than once." She turns back toward me.

Taking another bite, I shrug. "Just an educated guess," I mumble.

"You know what your problem is? You think you're the only man for me. You've always had this arrogance about you from our very first date."

"I'm quite aware that I'm not the one for you. Maybe I was never the one for you."

She flinches. "That's …" She shakes her head. "That's not what I meant. You were the one for me until …"

"Until I killed our son?" It's the first time I've ever said those words aloud. I've taken the blame. I've accepted responsibility. But I've never said those exact words.

"I couldn't grieve." She releases a slow breath, sending her gaze to her feet. "With you here, I couldn't grieve. I was so angry and devastated, but I felt like every tear, every aching moment of heartbreak was slowly destroying you. And I would have been angry and devastated no matter what the cause would have been of his death. And we would have been angry together. We would have grieved together. But we couldn't. And I started to resent not only the fact that he died on your watch, I resented feeling guilty for grieving in front of you."

"Tatum, I never expected you to not grieve or hide your emotions from me. I expected you to be angry with me. To hate me. To ..." I shake my head.

To leave me.

"But that's just it!" She lifts her gaze to meet mine. "It wasn't just about you. It wasn't just about assigning blame. It was that I lost my son. And I had a daughter to console. And I couldn't do it while tiptoeing around your feelings. I felt like you were always here ... always waiting for me to yell at you. Beat my fists against your chest and tell you how much I hated you and how I should never forgive you. But I didn't need someone to blame. I needed someone to hold me. To ..." Her eyes fill with tears. "I felt like you were waiting for me to console you. To tell you that it was okay. That I didn't blame you. And *that's* what angered me more than anything. That he *did* die on your watch, but I somehow had to be the one to forgive and forget, to accept and move on."

Tatum quickly wipes the tears that escape. "I couldn't *grieve* him like I needed to. And then ... you said I should let you go. And I felt so fucking abandoned. And then I just got ... angry. I hated you for giving up on us. I ... *hated* you for everything," she whispers.

All this time, I had no idea. I wasn't waiting for her to

console me or forgive me. I was waiting for her to *leave* me. And I couldn't see past that impending doom of my marriage to realize that she needed space, not separation. I handed her the divorce. I think I silently asked for it way before it ever crossed her mind. And that anger ... when she fought me for custody of Lucy ... she was mad because I was letting our marriage end.

"I ..." My head eases side to side as her words continue to settle into my conscience, piecing those months after Austin's death together. Right now, I hate myself too. "I never expected anything from you, except for the divorce. I knew my presence not only in this house but in your life was a painful reminder of the child we would never hold again. I just didn't know what my role was in your life or what you wanted me to do. I honestly felt like my existence in your world was unbearable. And I would have left. I would have left and given you space had I not felt like Lucy needed me too during that time. But never ... ever did I expect you to console me or forgive me or anything like that. And I thought you wanted out ... of the marriage. I didn't want to make you ask for it."

Tatum gives me a sad smile. "It's in the past. We can't change anything. I'm just glad we can be here for Lucy and that things feel civilized again. For years I wondered if we'd ever be able to be in the same room and not feel the pain."

I still feel the pain—the pain of losing not only my son, but my wife. Maybe she doesn't feel it because she doesn't feel like she lost me, or maybe she has Josh now and that's enough for her *joy.*

It's so hard to find a breath right now. Did she really just confess that she didn't want the divorce? Did I blow up my whole fucking world when all she needed was some space?

I eat more of my sandwich because I don't know what to

say. For the first time, I feel Lucy's conflict over telling Tatum our secret. It won't change the past, and I'm not sure it would change the now or the future in a positive way. I'm not sure it's fair to expect it to change anything.

"Cold chicken and barbecue sauce." She smiles. "I feel like we lived off that for a good year or more after Lucy was born. You'd grill a bunch of chicken and we'd eat it the rest of the week until we splurged and ordered pizza Saturday nights."

I inhale her words, every stolen moment that she allows herself to reminisce about the good times in our life. We had a lot of them. And we should have had more.

Stupid fucking me.

"Taco pizza." I grin.

"Is there any other kind?" She winks.

"Want a sandwich?"

"No. I'll grab something at home."

"So yes. You want a sandwich." I set my plate on the counter and get the chicken and barbecue sauce back out of the fridge.

"I don't want to eat your food."

I laugh. "You can have Lucy's portion."

After I assemble her sandwich, she takes the plate. "Thank you." She sits at the kitchen table while I grab a root beer for myself and a glass of water with no ice for her.

"I offered her a condom because a while back she voiced her motivation for walking. Basically, if she can walk, then she can have sex."

"What?" Tatum mumbles over her bite of sandwich. "Are you serious? Did she actually say that?"

"Sadly, yes. And I wasn't thrilled. But I also desperately wanted her to walk again. I think I would have been fine with *anything* that motivated her."

"So what did you say?"

I shrug. "Not much. I simply related the fact that she had already said ... if she can walk, she can have sex."

"So you gave her permission?"

"Yes. I gave her permission to walk."

"Emmett ..."

"No. You don't get to *Emmett* me on this one. She's seventeen. I knew there was a good possibility that she might not walk until she turned eighteen. How was I supposed to know that it would motivate her to walk this quickly?"

"She asked me about birth control, but I didn't actually think ..." Tatum takes another bite of her sandwich and slowly chews it. "Wow ... where did time go?"

I internally laugh. I'm not sure where her time went, but mine flew by in ten-hour-a-week increments that felt cruelly insufficient and always passed in a blink.

"Josh took the job in Chicago."

Oh, Josh ... stealer of my wife, imposter in my life.

"And you?"

"I don't know yet. I haven't told Lucy. But now that she's dating again, I think it's highly unlikely she'll be willing to leave here before she graduates. So now I have to decide if I live here and visit Josh on the weekends for the next year or so ... or if I'll live there and come visit Lucy on the weekends. I can't imagine not being here for Lucy. I can't imagine not asking her about her day. And she's not done with therapy. I don't know when that will be. But I told Josh I won't leave her if she's still needing therapy."

Instead of telling her that I can handle it, which is what I want to say, I play the observant *friend*. "Looks like you have a lot to think about."

"What would you do?"

I chuckle. "You're asking me? Really?"

She shrugs.

Now I *really* have to bite my tongue. I wouldn't marry Josh. That's what I would do. I would focus on Lucy. I'd put her first ... love her more.

"I think you know the answer. You're just afraid of it."

"And what's the answer?"

"If I tell you, then the decision won't truly be yours. You have to make this decision, and no one can make it for you. No one else can be your excuse if you regret your decision later." I stand and disappear down the hallway.

"Where are you going?"

I return with Mancala and unfold the board on the table.

"Wow. I haven't played this in years." She grins as I sort the stones.

On our epic pre-marriage road trip, we played Mancala all the time.

"I assume you're staying here until Lucy gets home."

Tatum gives me a look that confirms I know her very well.

"So I thought we could do something besides plan your future."

With another man. I don't say that, of course.

Three hours of Mancala, and two bags of microwave popcorn later, we hear a car pull into the driveway. Tatum jumps up and runs toward the window. I shut off the lights.

"What are you doing?" she asks.

"If you're going to spy on her, you can't have the lights on so she sees you spying on her." I stand behind her and gawk at my daughter and Racer in his car. It's too dark to see much until one of them opens a door just enough for the lights in the car to illuminate.

"She's smiling," Tatum whispers as if Lucy can hear us. "That means she had a good time."

"Or that means she's really relieved the date is over." I offer a better explanation.

"No. I know that smile. She's smitten. Oh ... look ..."

I wrinkle my nose. I don't want to look at Racer leaning over to kiss my Lucy. "I think that's long enough. He doesn't need to clean her teeth with his tongue."

Tatum giggles. "Stop ... it's just a kiss. Looks like a good kiss."

Racer's hand slides from her face to her neck, from her neck to her shoulder, from her shoulder to her ...

"Time's up!" I rush to the front door and turn on the living room lights, and I flash the outdoor lights several times like an emergency signal.

"Emmett! What are you doing?"

"Teaching the kid a lesson. A kiss. That's all he should expect on a first date."

"You're embarrassing her. That's not teaching him a lesson. You offered her a condom, Emmett. What did you think they were going to do with a condom?"

"Nothing in my driveway." I watch Lucy get out of the car. At least Mr. Handsy has the decency to open her door and help her.

"Get away now." Tatum pulls my arm, dragging me away from the window and down the hallway just enough to keep us out of sight as they walk to the front door.

I cross my arms over my chest and eye her. "Now I can't see if he's making a move on her again."

"I doubt he's going to grope her at the front door with all the lights on."

"I groped you in very well-lit, public places."

Her cheeks pink. "I think now that I'm officially

engaged, we should refrain from discussing things we did in the past. It's disrespectful to Josh."

"Josh isn't here. Or ..." I cock my head. "Are you under an obligation to discuss everything we do or talk about? Come to think of it ... does he know you're here?"

Tatum averts her gaze, wetting her lips. "He's working tonight. He knows Lucy has a date."

"And that you were planning on staying with me, *alone*, until she got home from her date?"

"I didn't know I was staying with you until she got home. You're the one who got the game out and popped popcorn."

"So ... you're going to tell him we were alone?"

"Yes. No. I don't know. We didn't do anything that he would be upset about."

The door opens.

I start to rush toward it.

Tatum grabs my arm again. "Count to ten," she whispers. "Just play it cool."

I roll my eyes and mouth—one, two, three, four, five, six, seven, eight, nine, ten—as fast as I can.

"Hey, Luce. How was your date?"

She sets her purse on the ground and sits on the sofa. "It was good until my dad went crazy flashing the lights. Mom ..." Lucy eyes Tatum behind me. "You're still here?"

"Of course. I wanted to hear all about your date."

Lucy's gaze ping-pongs between us. "So ... you've been here all evening alone with Dad?"

"We played Mancala." Tatum sits next to her.

"Okay ..." Lucy continues to eye me, as if I'm the child. "Well, we had pizza, then we hung out with some friends. Then he brought me home."

"Will you go out with him again?" Tatum grills her.

"I hope so. He's nice. And polite."

"And handsy," I add.

"And you were never handsy with Mom?"

"Not in her parents' driveway." I give her a tight smile. Then I think of all the times I used a napkin on Tatum's lap in restaurants to hide my hand down the front of her pants. But we weren't teenagers.

"Well, I'm glad you had a good time. We can talk more tomorrow when your dad's not here to shame you."

"I offered her a condom." I feel the need to remind them. I was never going to actually give her one, but she doesn't need to know that. Had she said yes to my offer, I would have grounded her until her eighteenth birthday.

"Goodnight, Lucy. Love you." Tatum kisses Lucy's cheek and hugs her before grabbing her handbag and car keys. "Thanks for dinner, Emmett."

"Anytime." I smile.

She blushes again. Why ... why is my wife marrying another man when I still make her blush? Life is so cruel.

CHAPTER TWENTY-FIVE

LUCY

It's weird.

Getting fitted for a bridesmaid's dress for my mom's wedding is weird. Kids aren't supposed to attend their parents' wedding, just like parents aren't supposed to attend their children's funerals.

It's backward. It's wrong. And it's weird.

"You always look amazing in that color of blue." Mom smiles at me as a lady places a few pins to alter the length of the dress. "I'm going to try on my dress. I haven't shown anyone yet. You'll be the first to see it."

"Okay." I give her a fake smile. I want to see my mom dig out her old wedding dress, the one she wore when she married my dad. I want to see her get excited when it still fits her. Then I want my dad to walk into the room and give me a glimpse of the smile he had on his face the day he married her.

Five minutes later, she steps out of a dressing room in

her white strapless wedding gown. It's beautiful. She's beautiful. But it doesn't make this less weird.

"What do you think?" Mom steps in front of a cluster of mirrors, lifts the flowing skirt, and makes a slow turn.

"You look beautiful, Mom." I give her a true smile this time because she does look beautiful. But she always looks beautiful.

"You think so? Is it too much? For someone my age? Should I pick something that shows less skin?" She stares in the mirror at her bare shoulders.

When I don't reply, her gaze in the mirror shifts to me. "You don't like it." She frowns.

The lady unzips my dress and helps me out of it as I use my cane to steady myself, then she helps me get my arms threaded into a robe.

"I like the dress," I say when we're alone.

"You just don't like it on me?"

I shake my head slowly. "It's ... not that."

"Then what?"

I take a seat in a white fabric chair and fiddle with the sash to the robe. "It's just the whole wedding, I guess."

"You think we should just elope? I wondered if the wedding was too much since I've been married. But this is Josh's first marriage, so I didn't want to take anything away from him and his family."

"No, Mom ... it's not that. It's ..." I don't know how to have this conversation with her. I've played it out in my head a million times. It's different now, in person, with my nerves making me a little nauseous.

"Your dad told you. Didn't he?"

"Told me what?"

"About Chicago?"

I shake my head. "What about Chicago?"

She cringes as if she now regrets mentioning it. "I've been meaning to talk to you about this. I suppose now's as good a time as any. Josh has taken a job in Chicago."

"I'm not moving to Chicago."

Mom nods. "I know. I'm not asking you to move to Chicago. At least, not now. I know you want to stay here and graduate with your friends. And you'll have to decide on a college at some point, if you're going to college. But I need to decide what's best for us in the interim. Do I stay here with you and visit Josh on the weekends? Or do I move to Chicago and visit you on the weekends? But I'm not even thinking about moving until you're done with therapy, and Josh knows this."

"Then why are you getting married? Why now? What's the rush?"

Her face wrinkles. "He asked me. I said yes. We're in love. I'm not asking you to sacrifice anything, Lucy."

"Are you sacrificing anything?"

She narrows her eyes. "What do you mean?"

"Do you love Josh like you loved Dad?"

"Lucy, where is the coming from? Do you not like Josh?"

"I like Josh, but I'm not the one who's marrying him."

"I just told you we're in love."

I nod. "But I asked you if you love him like you loved Dad?"

"It's ..." She shakes her head, gathering the skirt of her dress and taking a seat in the chair adjacent to mine—her Champagne glass and my sparkling juice glass on the table between us. "It's a different kind of love. Your dad and I had this young, passionate kind of love, like together we could conquer the world. We made bad decisions and learned only by making mistakes over and over again. We figured out how to be parents by just jumping in and doing it, no matter how inept we felt at the time. But with Josh, it's a mature love. We became friends first. We both came into the relationship with so much more life experience and realistic goals—not only for our lives separately but for our future together. When I'm with Josh, I don't feel so impulsive. He grounds me."

"Sounds boring."

She chuckles. "Lucy, I've had enough happen in my life to make boring seem like a dream come true."

I fight with the words in my head. There's just no easy way to say them. I keep hoping she'll say something that will make it easier to just blurt it out. But she's too protective of something ... Josh? Her heart? Me? I don't know.

"What's really on your mind, Lucy? I can see it on your face. What aren't you telling me?"

This is it. This is as good as it will get. She's asking me. It's time to tell her.

"Dad wasn't home when Austin drowned."

Her head inches back, confusion distorting every inch of her face. "What? What are you talking about?"

"He wasn't. I was the only one home. I was the one who was supposed to be watching him." Tears sting my eyes. "It was only for a minute or two. I told him to stay in the living room watching his show so I could FaceTime with my friend in the bedroom. It was only minutes—it felt like seconds. And I heard Dad's voice. I heard him screaming. It was like nothing I had ever heard before. I ran out onto the deck, and he was soaked, kneeling beside Austin, doing CPR. He told me to call 9-1-1."

Mom blinks and a river of tears rush down her face.

"He told you it was him because he was afraid you might say something to me that you wouldn't mean, that might have been hard to forget—hard to forgive. But he didn't tell me that at the time. He made me believe it. He made me believe it was his fault, that he was supposed to be there to watch Austin. And ... I believed him because he's my dad. And I trusted him. And I think..." I wipe the tears from my face "...I needed to believe him. I didn't want it to be my fault."

Mom's hand covers her mouth as she squeezes her eyes shut and cries. I didn't tell her this to make her cry. I told her this because it's the truth. And I don't want any of us living a lie any longer.

"If you need to blame me, I can take it. I've talked a lot with Dr. Kane. And I'm ready to take responsibility. I know you love me, and nothing will change that. But I also under-stand that you might feel angry right now. And that's okay. I'd be angry too."

I move the glasses aside and scoot my way from the chair to the table so I can wrap my arms around her the way she's done to me so many times in the past. She says nothing ... she just cries.

***

EMMETT

I GLANCE at my phone as I head toward my truck at the end of the day. There's a message from Lucy that halts my steps.

Lucy: She knows.

Before I have time to generate feelings about her

announcement, I glance up, and I'm transported nearly two decades earlier, to a time when Tatum was sitting on my tailgate, waiting for me. Sometimes she was there to read me the riot act. Sometimes she was there because she couldn't wait to see me.

Today, seeing her on my tailgate, I don't know what to expect. After a few seconds of staring at each other from twenty yards apart, I force my boots to move toward her.

She's wearing sunglasses which tells me her eyes are red and swollen behind them. Lucy ripped open some old wounds and poured salt onto them.

"Hi," I say as I approach the tailgate.

She says nothing.

I deposit my bag and lunch cooler in the backseat and close the door.

When I plant myself in front of her, hands in the front pockets of my jeans, she whispers, "Why did you do that?"

My instinct is to play dumb. Why did I do what? But I haven't seen her look this deflated and broken in a long time.

"For Lucy. And because you asked me to do it."

Her head inches side to side. "Wh-what are you talking about?"

"When you were in labor with Lucy, you made me promise you that I would love her more. After Austin died, I saw the look on your face. The anguish and the confusion. The natural desire and need to understand—to assign blame. I knew you would never intentionally say or do anything to scar Lucy for life. But we often do the most damage to people by complete accident."

Her lower lip trembles. She's probably thinking about the accident and spinal cord injury.

"So I took it. I took the blame. I saved Lucy from the part of you that wasn't really you. I loved her more because ... that's what you asked me to do."

"Jesus ..." she sobs, wiping the tears that fall below her sunglasses. "Y-you had n-no right! I love her. I-I would never ..." She pauses, as she should.

Never is a strong word. It's absolute. It's all encompassing. And it's nearly impossible to say with any truth. *Never* is the embodiment of the unimaginable. So is *always*. There is nothing absolute about our lives. Who we are lies in the space between always and never.

Austin's death was unimaginable. We thought we'd *always* be together. We thought there would *never* come a day when we would choose to divorce. We failed to make room in our heads and in our hearts for the unimaginable.

"He drowned on Lucy's watch. That's unchangeable. But he died because we had an uncovered pool. He died because we didn't take the proper measures to ensure his safety. And we can spend the rest of our lives blaming ourselves, but it won't bring him back. And that will *never* change, but it will *always* hurt. We set Lucy up to fail. Not you. Not me. *Us.*"

She hops off the tailgate and wipes her eyes under her glasses, turning her back to me. "*We* may be responsible for his death," her voice shakes, "but *you* are responsible for us. You didn't give us a chance. You didn't give *me* a chance. You didn't trust me. You let Lucy watch our marriage end. You let me fall in love with another man. You stood idle with the truth hidden from me ... from everyone."

"Yes," I whisper. I don't have a case to plead anymore. She knows what I did. She knows why I did it. And if I had it to do all over again, I'd make the same decision. I'd do it for Lucy. But not because Tatum asked me to love Lucy more. I think I knew from the moment she was born that loving her more wasn't a choice. Our children have been the best of who we were, who we are, and who we will be.

"It's unforgivable, Emmett," she says as she walks away from me.

CHAPTER TWENTY-SIX

On the way home, I stop by the field, my field, and I allow myself a good ten minutes to yell at the wind, the clouds, the cruel god who took my son. I allow myself ten minutes to cry and grieve one last time.

Grieve Austin.

Grieve Tatum.

And also ... open my heart to the relief that Lucy no longer has this secret to keep.

When I arrive home, Lucy's in the kitchen eating pizza at the dining room table.

"You ordered pizza?"

She nods, wiping her mouth. "Figured you might be too emotionally exhausted to make dinner."

I wash my hands. "And you? How are you, emotionally?"

"Well, today I made my mom cry ... a lot. And from the look of your eyes, I'd say I made you cry too. That kinda sucks." She shrugs. "But I've shed a lot of tears today too, so I guess we're all having ... a day."

"But do you feel better?" I grab a root beer and sit on the opposite side of the table.

"*Better* is a tricky word to define right now. I honestly don't know how I feel. I thought I'd feel relieved, but watching Mom cry … it was hard to feel anything but pain and guilt. I second-guessed my decision so many times, but it was too late. I couldn't un-tell her. All I could do was hug her as she collapsed into my arms, wearing her wedding gown."

I grunt something like a laugh and shake my head. "Good timing, Luce."

"I know." She frowns, slowly chewing a bite of pizza. "But I just didn't want her to marry Josh and move to Chicago without knowing how she got to this point in her life … really *knowing*. And maybe she still marries him and moves to Chicago. I didn't tell her because I don't like Josh or I don't want her to marry him. I told her because it was eating away at me, and the only time that would have felt more unfair to tell her would have been after she married him."

"It was the perfect time. Really. I was just kidding you. I told myself a while back that if or whenever you decided to tell her, it would be the right time for you, and that's all that mattered. I know it, and in time, your mom will know it too."

"What did she say to you? I know she must have called you."

"She met me at work. She was sitting on the tailgate to my truck."

"Was she mad?"

"Hurt." I take a bite of pizza and mumble, "And a little mad. But I know her anger was because of the pain."

"So I made things worse between you two?"

I shake my head and take a drink of root beer. "We're divorced. She's marrying Josh. You're almost eighteen. What can she do at this point?"

"But what did you say?"

"The truth. I told her it wasn't your fault, even if it was technically on your watch. It was our fault for not having a protective cover over the pool, or cameras, or some sort of alarm. We naively thought we'd always keep a close eye on him. We naively thought the fence would be enough, in spite of watching him climb *everything*. And honestly, we blinked. There were times that he headed toward the door to go outside while I was working in the garage and I had to chase him, pulling him off the fence as he reached the top in a matter of seconds. There were times when I saw your mom chasing him because he snuck out while she was making dinner.

"We blinked too, Lucy. And that's all it takes. One blink and thirty seconds. It takes thirty seconds for a child his age to drown. That's it. *We* allowed this to happen. And the really awful part? We put you in the terrible position to be the one who blinked at the wrong time. So yeah ..." I swallow past some residual emotion and clear my throat. "Today it felt raw again. Today your mom and I faced the *real* truth."

"But Mom is still mad ... at you?"

"She's grieving again through a different light. She's grieving the loss of Austin all over again, and I think she's grieving the loss of our marriage and our family. She needs time. So we give her time."

"What if she never forgives you for lying to her?"

"Then that's sad for her, isn't it? We forgive other people for our own sense of sanity and peace. I've never asked for her forgiveness, and I never will."

"So we're not supposed to say we're sorry when we do something wrong?"

"*Sorry* isn't the same thing as asking for forgiveness. When you accidentally bump into someone, do you say, 'I'm sorry. Please forgive me?' Or do you simply say you're sorry?"

She grins. "Good point."

"So did you say you're sorry?"

"No. I'm not sorry for lying. I would do it again because I love you more, Lucy. I'm sorry and regretful that it happened at all. I'm sorry we didn't do more to be responsible parents and pool owners. I have lots of sorries to give, but protecting you is not one of them. Don't apologize unless you mean it, unless it's something you would take back. Otherwise, you're just being insincere."

She reaches across the table and rests her hand on mine. "I want to be you when I grow up."

That makes me cry.

I DON'T SEE Tatum for nearly a month. It's the longest I've gone without seeing her since Lucy's accident. She manages to pick Lucy up for therapy and drop her off here all while I'm at work. Lucy's gone on a few more dates with Racer, but Tatum hasn't felt the need to be here for those comings and goings. One night she dropped Lucy off after she and Josh took her to dinner, but I was in the shower and they didn't come inside the house.

I miss her. I think I've missed her since the day Austin died. After Lucy's accident, I was reminded how it felt to see Tatum almost daily. I got a few smiles, stole a few kisses, and imagined for a brief moment that we *were* bigger than the most unimaginable tragedy. We were stronger together.

Like all brief moments of hope, that one has faded.

I love my wife. That will never change. I will always feel protective of her. And if anyone ever judges her for ending our marriage, I will lose it. Unless you've lost a child to an accident, you don't know what that does to your heart. One can imagine, but that imagination will fall short. Death robs your soul of reason and purpose. Tatum has a pass for the rest of her life to act without reason and purpose, and I will always be her fiercest defender of that right.

"We tasted cake today." Lucy sits down in the chair next to mine as I roast a marshmallow.

"And what did you decide?"

"Well…" she shoves two marshmallows onto a roasting stick and laughs "…it wasn't supposed to be my decision. However, Josh couldn't make it because he was stuck in surgery. And Mom seemed to not care. She's been so off this past month, but every time I ask her if she's okay, she nods and smiles. I'm so tired of her nods and smiles. Like … if she's upset with me, just say it. Right?"

"I doubt she's upset with you. She's had a month to process it all. Maybe she's just stressed because of the wedding."

"I chose raspberry cake with white chocolate frosting."

"Good choice." I assemble my s'more.

"What cake did you have at your wedding?"

"Vanilla. Vanilla frosting."

"Boring."

I laugh. "Probably. Your mom and your grandma picked it out. I didn't have anything to do with it. I didn't have anything to do with ninety-nine percent of the planning."

"Because they didn't let you?"

"Because I didn't care. Most guys don't care. Heck, Josh probably didn't have surgery today. He just didn't want to taste cake and act like it mattered to him."

"I'm going to marry a guy who cares about the details."

I lift an eyebrow at her. "Marry a guy who cares about you. Screw the details. They don't matter."

"Mom said you're not invited to the wedding. When I asked why, she said because it would be awkward having her first husband at her wedding to her second husband. But that's just stupid. You guys have hung out and played a game together when I went on my first date with Racer. You've done yard work for her. You've had dinner with Mom and me and Josh more than once. I think it's awkward that you're not invited. Don't you?"

"Not really."

"Or do you not want to go so you're not acting like it's a big deal?"

"Aside from seeing you in your dress, which I can see pictures later, I don't have any huge desire to be there."

"Because you still love her?"

"You know the answer." I lick my sticky fingers.

"Then fight for her. The whole choose-me-love-me thing is very romantic. What happened to leaving it all on the field?"

"I've been benched. I have nothing to leave on the field."

"I don't buy it. You're too scared to leave it all on the field. You're afraid that you'll put your heart out there, and she'll still choose Josh. Right?"

"The dresses have been ordered. And I'm gathering the cake has been too. She's not choosing anyone. She's already chosen."

"You stole her once. Do it again." I love how the story of how we met always makes Lucy smile.

"I think stealing her from a blind date, whom she had never met, is a little different than stealing her from her fiancé."

"You won't know until you try." She smirks.

"Stop. I don't like how invested you've become in an *us* that no longer exists. It wouldn't just feel like my heart on the line. It would feel like yours too. And I'm not feeding into that illusion. I'm not taking a chance with your heart where there is *no* chance."

"You're running out the clock and walking off the field."

Shaking my head, I laugh. "There's two minutes left in the game and I'm down by three touchdowns. It's statistically impossible."

"Hail Mary."

This girl makes me smile so damn big.

"It could be epic." Lucy doesn't take the time to sandwich her marshmallow between graham crackers and chocolate. She shoves it into her mouth, making a sticky mess of her lips and fingers. "So epic," she mumbles.

I think *she's* epic. So epic.

"If it helps, her yard is a mess. It needs to be mowed, the weeds need to be pulled, and the shrubs by the front door have taken over. You'll cringe."

"You think I should tidy up her landscaping and take care of her yard? Just ... show up unannounced? Because if I call her and offer, she'll say no."

"Well, duh ... you need to do it when she's gone. Like this weekend. She has a dance competition all day Saturday. I'm going with her."

"I see. I'll transform her yard from a mess to a neatly

manicured oasis. She'll come home, see the yard, and break off her engagement with Josh."

"Exactly." Lucy nods with a hundred percent more confidence than what I have.

"I hate to break it to you, but I've played the gardener and Mr. Fix It role before. It didn't work."

"Well ..." She licks her fingers. "I'll think of something."

"Or ... you could think of nothing and let your mom live her life without anyone trying to keep her from marrying Josh."

"But what if she loves you more?"

"What if she doesn't?"

"Well, that's just it. We need to know."

CHAPTER TWENTY-SEVEN

On Saturday, I don't play gardener to Tatum while she and Lucy are at the dance competition. With two weeks until the wedding, I feel like the nicest thing to do is to let her get married and move to Chicago.

As I make dinner, Lucy messages me.

Lucy: Don't be mad. Mom thinks you had a woman stay the night last night.

I narrow my eyes at her message.

Emmett: Why would she think that?

Lucy: Because I told her.

Emmett: Why?

Lucy: Because we have to know.

Emmett: Know what?

Lucy: If she's really ready to let you go forever.

Emmett: By lying to her?

Lucy: You can tell her the truth. She's dropping me off at Racer's house.

Emmett: I think you need to tell her the truth and then come home so we can talk about your issues with acceptance.

Lucy: She's really bothered by it. She hasn't said anything to me on the way home.

I stick her filet of salmon in the fridge and sit down to eat mine along with green beans and rice. Two bites into my dinner, the doorbell rings.

"Just great." I sigh when I see Tatum's car parked in my driveway. "Hey." I give her a tentative smile when I open the door.

"I'm not okay with you having random women stay the night when Lucy's living with you." She barges past me.

"Come in," I mumble. "Random women?" I shut the door.

She pivots, hands balled at her sides. Her unruly dark hair partially pulled back with strays all around her face, clinging to her red cheeks. "Lucy told me there was a half-naked woman in the kitchen this morning when she awoke. AND ... she heard you and said half-naked woman last night. She called her a screamer."

Dear lord ... Lucy is quite the storyteller. A screaming woman?

"Screaming is a bit of an exaggeration. Maybe deep moaning, but not screaming." I don't know why I'm playing this game. Maybe because I didn't expect Tatum to be so enraged. Lucy's seventeen not seven.

She flinches. "It's inappropriate."

"Dating? Having sex? Have you not had sex with Josh with Lucy in the house?"

"That's different?"

"How so?"

"Because Josh isn't some random guy I brought home."

"What makes you think this woman was random?"

"Uh ..." She drops her jaw. "Because Lucy said you couldn't even remember her name. Emmett! What is wrong with you? Why would you even sleep with someone if you didn't know them well enough to remember their name in the morning?"

Oh Lucy …

This story just keeps getting better.

"I'll make sure it doesn't happen again. I'll write my date's names on my palm so I remember in the morning."

"Who are you?" She juts her head backward.

"Her name is Laura. I didn't forget her name. I just didn't want Lucy to grill me on our relationship. It's early."

"Not early enough to sleep with her."

I rub my lips together to keep from grinning. "We didn't do much sleeping."

"I hate you." She stomps to the front door and grabs the handle, but not before I grip her other arm.

She hates me? That's a strong word she's only used in regard to our past. But now … because of some made-up one-night stand, she *hates me*?

"You don't get to *hate* me for having sex. Not after the kisses in the garage. Not after the orgasms we had together the day Josh took Lucy to the baseball game. And definitely not when you're two weeks away from marrying the wrong fucking guy."

"Well you …" She rips her arm from my grasp as angry tears build in her eyes, red and feral. "You did this. ALL of this! You lied to me about Austin. You let us get a divorce. You let me grieve the loss of us. You let me fall in love with another man. Then kissed me! And you let that *moment* happen the day of the game. And you never said one goddamn word! Now you're screwing some random woman in *our* house. In *our* bed. With *our* daughter just upstairs. That's NOT OKAY!"

"Why?"

She shakes her head as the tears pool to the point of release. "You know why."

"No. I don't know why. Because you still think I deserve to be alone for the rest of my life? Because you don't think I'm worthy of that kind of pleasure unless you're the one doling it out on your terms?"

"You were mine." The tears fall in fast streams down her face and onto her shirt and my floor. She doesn't make any attempt to stop them or wipe them away. "I let you think you stole me, but I gave myself to you, and in return you were mine. My husband. My lover. My friend. My children's father. My strength. My fucking *everything*. And you let us end."

I've waited *years* for this moment. For everything to be out in the open. For all the excuses to be gone. For it to be me and her with nothing but the truth no matter how much it hurts. And boy ... does it ever fucking hurt.

"I did it for Lucy."

"You had no right!"

"I did it for Lucy."

"You did it because you didn't trust me to do the right thing!"

"I did it for Lucy," I say again, my voice calm and even.

"You didn't know how I would have reacted!" She's lost all control, and her hand covers her mouth to catch a sob.

"I did it ... *for Lucy*," I whisper.

Her body shakes, eyes closed, sobs muffled. "I ... know ..." she says with a broken tone of surrender, the difficult submission shattering each word as they fight past her throat. "W-we ... we d-didn't p-protect him ... w-we didn't p-protect Austin. I s-shouldn't have l-left. I ... I did this ..."

Taking a step toward her, I open my arms and she falls into my chest. After several minutes of letting go of all that's been building up over the past month—or maybe the past six years—she sniffles and glances up at me with red, swollen eyes and a puffy face.

"Tatum—" I start to say something. I start to tell her the truth, that I wasn't with anyone last night, but she cuts me off by lifting onto her toes and pulling my head down to hers.

I let myself get lost in the kiss for a few seconds, knowing I need to tell her the truth, knowing that kissing another man's fiancée is wrong. It's only for a few seconds after a very emotional moment.

No one can blame us.

Not for needing this moment.

Not for needing to let all the truths come out.

Not for needing to close our eyes and wish none of this ever had to happen.

When she doesn't stop kissing me, I find it hard to be the strong one, the voice of reason. I've been playing that role for years. Now ... I just want to kiss my wife and not feel guilty.

When her hands slide down my chest, lifting my shirt to tease her fingertips along my abs, I find it hard to be the strong one.

When my hands frame her face, I tell myself to push her away, to end the kiss before we cross a line that will not be forgivable. But ... six years.

When she tugs at the button to my pants, making it perfectly clear where she intends on taking this, I do break the kiss. And we stare at each other, sharing labored breaths. For a second, I think something in her gaze changes, like her brain is catching up to the rest of her body. But then ... her fingers slide down the zipper to my jeans. My pulse becomes a runaway train speeding through my veins.

If only ...

If only I would have stopped thinking of her as my wife after the divorce, it would be easier to be the voice of reason as she lifts my shirt.

If only we didn't have a lifetime of memories begging to be embraced and resumed, it would be easier to be the voice of reason as my shirt lands on the floor and she backs me into the bedroom—our bedroom.

If only one of us would break the silence, waking our minds from this deep trance and seemingly unstoppable course of action, we'd have less to regret.

If only ...

But here's the problem, I hate that voice of reason, and I love my wife. And I do feel sorry for Josh. He tried to steal the wrong man's girl. He *knew* what had recently happened between us, yet he continued onward like he could erase me from her mind, like he could erase my touch from her body.

I pull off her shirt, and her bra quickly follows. We kiss and my hands cup her breasts like they're mine to caress. She slides her hand down the front of my exposed briefs like *that* is hers to touch, to stroke, to decide where it belongs. Her hand disappears to shimmy her pants and panties down her legs, quickly toeing off her shoes and freeing her legs—those sexy dancer's legs.

"Tatum ..." my conscience completely malfunctions and makes a weak effort to do the right thing. It's such a buzz kill. "Josh ..." I say his name with the knowledge that it will bring her back to reality.

She kisses her way down my chest and slides down my jeans and briefs together. "He's not here, Emmett. He's not welcome in our bedroom."

She has no fucking clue what that means to me.

I'm not just a weakness, a slip, a mistake. I'm her intention.

We kiss like we are only for each other. She pushes against my chest until I sit on the bed. Then she straddles my lap, and I find my place in her world again. I don't kiss her right away, and she doesn't kiss me. Our lips brush together, mixing our breaths that come harder and faster as I guide her hips down inch by inch. It feels familiar yet brand-new at the same time. We move together in this position for a while. Not kissing, just getting drunk from the feeling, the connection. I cup her breast, and she sucks in a sharp breath while curling her fingers into my back.

We rediscover each other and every inch of the bed, every position like it must be reclaimed.

I love hovering above her while she writhes beneath me, moaning my name.

I love when she rolls on top of me, her hair cascading down her back and over her breasts while she moves at her own pace.

And I love when she traps her lip between her teeth and crawls up my body, holding my gaze to hers until she's straddling my face. And while I don't want to think about Josh or him having sex with my wife, I know in my gut that she never did this with him.

It's Tatum at her most uninhibited, at her most vulnerable. It's something she only does with me because we have spent years in this bed feeding each other's fantasies and building what I now know, without a doubt, is a truly unbreakable trust—an unbreakable bond.

"Emmett ..." She grips the headboard and watches me, her mouth agape, her eyelids heavy.

"I love you," I say with my lips pressed to her inner

thigh on one side. Then I angle my face against her other leg and kiss along that thigh. "I've always loved you."

With a new round of unshed tears pooling in her eyes, she nods. "I love you too. Always …"

When my tongue slides against her, she arches her back and she grips the headboard tighter. I'm sure there's a special place in hell for us, but I'll deal with that when I'm dead. Right now, I'm alive … so very much alive.

By the time we're nothing but two limp bodies tangled in the sheets and with each other, I start to see the blinding light of reality cutting through our dark little bubble. She's supposed to marry Josh in two weeks. Lucy could come home any minute. Is this cheating? Can this kind of intimacy with my wife be wrong?

"If you don't tell Josh, I'm telling him," I murmur in her ear from our weird, legs-tangled version of spooning.

"I'll tell him," she whispers.

"Tell. Not confess. Right?"

"What's the difference?" she asks.

"You confessed the s'mores in the garage, and apparently you confessed to a little bit of what happened the day of the Royals game. But then you agreed to marry him. So … I don't like your version of confession. I'd rather you just tell him very matter-of-factly."

"You want me to tell him we had sex? Are you going to tell your new *friend* that we had sex?"

"Sure. She's imaginary, so I can basically tell her now. 'Hey, random woman, we can't have sex anymore. Okay? Great. Good talk.'"

Tatum elbows her way out of my hold and jackknives to sitting. "Are you kidding me? You'd better be kidding. And it's not funny. Not one bit. You had Lucy lie to me?"

I reach for her waist, and she bats my hand away. "No. I

didn't have Lucy lie for me. She did it on her own. I just found out about it."

"Bullshit." Tatum untangles herself from the sheets and jumps out of bed, but before she can take one single step, I swing my legs over the edge and hook her waist with my arm.

"It's not bullshit."

"Let go of me!"

"I will not." I lift her off her feet and carry her to the kitchen.

"Emmett! Goddammit, let go of me."

Retrieving my phone from the table next to my dinner, I turn and haul her back to the bedroom, shutting the door behind me and tossing her onto the bed. She skitters to sitting and pulls the covers over her chest like my confession has banned me from seeing her naked body.

"Before I show you this, I need you to tell me why this woman, imaginary or not, means anything beyond being a catalyst that brought you to your senses?"

With her signature pouty face and hair an absolute fucked-up mess, she glares at me. "I won't be lied to."

"I didn't lie to you. Lucy did. I may have played it a little bit because I had to know why you were so enraged at the idea of me being with another woman when your wedding is in two weeks. And I knew it wasn't because of the idea of Lucy being in the house."

"Emmett ..." My name is a warning.

"I'll show you the messages after you tell me that you love me."

"Emmett ..." She tightens her grip on the sheets she's holding over her breasts.

I sit on the end of the bed with my back to her. "My love for you has never wavered. Not for a second. And I wasn't going to stop you from marrying Josh *because* I love you. *Because* I care more about your happiness than my own. I know I promised to love our children more, but my love for you has always been so tightly interwoven with my love for them that loving them more just simply means loving you more."

Her arms encircle my neck as her bare chest presses to my back, her lips ghosting along my ear. "I love you," she whispers. "Always."

I hold up my phone as she rests her chin on my shoulder. It takes her a minute to read through my conversation with Lucy.

"Our daughter is evil," she says.

"Strong-willed like her mom."

"Relentless like her dad." Tatum kisses my neck.

"Had Lucy not lied ... would you have married Josh?"

"I ... I don't know. I know he's been concerned this past month about my well-being. He's been concerned about the canceled dates and my reluctance to commit to moving to Chicago. It's hard because I do care for him. I did fall in love with him. But the one thing that's harder than loving him and moving closer to our marriage is loving you more."

I kiss her hand. "It's nice to be loved a little more."

"Exponentially more." She bites my earlobe, and I twist my body to grab her waist and bring her to straddle my lap.

"I've missed my wife."

Her eyes redden behind a few captive tears. "I've been a terrible wife."

I shake my head. "A terrible fiancée, but not a terrible wife."

She laughs and it chases away those tears. Her hands press to my cheeks as she kisses me, and I decide I need to be inside of her again. It still doesn't feel real.

"Dad? Mom?"

Tatum jumps off my lap and scurries around, looking for her clothes. "Shit, shit, shit ..." she whispers.

I step into my underwear and jeans, but at a casual pace.

"Hurry up!" she whisper-yells at me.

"She's going to—"

Tatum leaps toward me, covering my mouth when I don't whisper. "Shh!"

I peel her hand away and lower my voice to appease her. "She's going to find out because the bedroom door is shut. Your car is in my driveway, and my shirt is in the hallway."

Tatum's eyes widen. "I don't want her to know I've cheated on Josh. It's a terrible example."

"Oh my god ... are you guys having sex?" Lucy yells.

Tatum's head drops, her chin nearly touching her chest as she zips her jeans at a much slower, defeated pace.

"No. Luce." I open the bedroom door and slip out into the hallway, closing it behind me.

Her jaw unhinges when she sees my naked chest as I bend down and pluck my shirt from the floor.

"You had sex," she says slowly and softly like she's surprised that her plan worked.

"I don't know what you're talking about. Your mom showed up angry as hell from the lie you told. We fought. She stormed out, but then she noticed she locked her keys in the car, so she started running toward home and I couldn't catch her. So ... feeling completely rejected, I had one of my friends from work hook me up with someone to physically ease the ache of rejection."

Lucy's brows knit together. "Oh my god ..." her head whips backward. "You have some random woman in your bedroom?" Disappointment bleeds along her cheeks and down her neck. That might be more than disappointment; it might be anger. She's one hundred percent her mom.

With a tight smile, I shrug.

Her hand goes to her mouth like she might get sick just as the bedroom door opens behind me.

"Enough with the random woman scenarios, you two." Tatum brushes past me, bringing life and hope back to Lucy.

I smirk as Tatum hugs her, and Lucy mouths to me, "Oh my god," before squeezing her eyes shut like all of her dreams just came true.

"Now ..." Tatum releases her. "I'm starving. What's for dinner?" She saunters into the kitchen, and Lucy and I follow.

Lucy grabs a glass of water while I sit in my chair to resume eating my now cold dinner. Before I even pick up my fork, Tatum plants her ass on my lap and steals my fork, then she starts eating my dinner.

This display brings so much joy to Lucy's face as she sits in the chair next to us.

"So, how was your date with Racer?" Tatum asks. "Did you have dinner with him?"

It takes Lucy a few seconds, like she still can't believe what's transpired tonight. Then she nods. "Yeah. His mom made us dinner."

CHAPTER TWENTY-EIGHT

TATUM CANCELS THE WEDDING.

We haven't talked in over two weeks. She asked me for time ... time to mourn the loss of what she had with Josh and his family, time to reconcile the part of her heart that knows she cheated on him no matter how hard we tried to justify our love being greater—destined from the day we met. I miss her, and it's hard to deal with the reality that she gave part of her heart, no matter how big or small, to another man.

"You should love her even more *because* she's the kind of woman who feels love and pain, who recognizes guilt and her imperfections and deals with them." Mom tries to cheer me up while Lucy and Racer ride the four-wheelers around my parents' property like she never lost use of her legs.

"I know. It doesn't make me miss her any less."

"Has Lucy seen her?"

"Yes."

"And? How does she feel Tatum is doing?"

"Fine." I stare out the window at the four-wheelers. "But Tatum would act fine around Lucy no matter what."

"Emmett, what are you afraid of? She's already chosen you."

"I'm afraid that she's been on this wave of emotions over the past eight months—the car accident, me forced back into her life, the engagement, the truth about Austin's death. Now she's dealing with the end of her relationship with Josh. Will she realize she's rushed into too many quick decisions? Maybe she doesn't want to marry Josh, but maybe she doesn't really want to be with me either. Am I the default? Is she doing this for me? For herself? For Lucy?"

"Oh dear, you are lovesick and delusional. Tatum loves you. Always has, always will. Maybe you should send her something. Just something to let her know you're thinking about her."

I nod slowly. "Maybe."

SEVERAL DAYS LATER, I head toward my truck after work. Guess who's sitting on my tailgate in a soft blue sundress, flip-flops on her feet, and red lips smiling at me? My heart does really weird things in my chest as my skin tingles from a rush of emotions—a rush of relief.

"Emmett the Thief, did you steal the shrubs from my front porch and replace them with a certain blue perennial?"

I toss my stuff into the back of my truck and make my way back to her. My hands casually slide into my back pockets. "Maybe." I shrug.

"Were you sending a message?" Her head cocks to the side.

"A message?"

She giggles. "They're Forget-Me-Nots."

Biting back my smile, I nod several times. "Huh. Interesting."

Tatum hooks her fingers into my front pockets and pulls me between her dangling legs. "Did you think I was going to forget you?"

"Maybe." I curl her hair behind her ears and slide my fingers down her neck. "I miss you. And Lucy's birthday is next week. And ... I miss you." I grin.

"I've been busy."

"Saying goodbye to Josh?"

"Packing. I think you should stop by my place on your way home and load up some of my stuff."

I smirk. "Oh? Where are you going?"

"Home." She wraps her arms around my neck, pulling me down to her as her legs latch to my waist.

"Lot of memories there." I narrow my eyes, reminding her of the reason she moved in the first place.

"Yes. I didn't know what to do with those memories. I felt alone with them. I don't have to be alone with them anymore. So I want them. All of them. With you and Lucy."

"We should stop on the way to your place and get some hot chocolate. I know a cafe not too far from here that has great hot chocolate with extra whipped cream."

"I think I know that cafe." She grins.

I peck her lips. Then I kiss her again because it's been too long to settle for a quick peck. All of a sudden, I don't want hot chocolate, just her. With the whipped cream.

She pulls back, and I convince myself that I can wait.

"Meet you there?" I help her off the tailgate.

"Better hurry. If some other redhead shows up before you ... well, I can't make any promises."

"Aw yes ..." I shake my head, opening the door to my truck. "That's right. You were never really mine."

She grabs my hand, squeezing it while gazing up at me with those eyes that fell in love with me so long ago. "Emmett ... I've always been yours."

EPILOGUE

One year later ...

Lucy graduates and moves downstate, two hours south of Redington to attend Missouri State University. She plans to major in psychology and rent an apartment with her boyfriend, Racer. I'm not happy about it, but I'm elated that our girl has made a full recovery. She has her whole, limitless life ahead of her. And if her walking means she's having sex with that Racer kid, I'll live with it.

Tatum still teaches dance, but she's also working on a book about our life. She wants every parent to know the facts.

Second only to congenital anomalies, drowning is the number one cause of death in children between the ages of one and four, and a majority of drownings happen at home.

Thirty seconds. That's all it takes.

Drowning is silent, and it's quick.

It is the responsibility of parents to keep our children safe. Children need to learn how to swim, and they need to learn survival skills.

But ...

It is the responsibility of parents to keep our children safe.

Austin had taken swimming lessons, but it wasn't enough. It didn't replace *adult* supervision. We didn't have a child safety pool cover. We had a locked fence that gave us a false sense of security. We didn't have a multi-layered plan to keep such a tragedy from happening because ... no one thinks it will happen to them.

Thirty seconds. That's all it takes.

"I'm meeting with another couple tonight after dinner. They invited me to their house. Do you want to come?" Tatum asks as she pours us coffee.

I butter our toast and slide eggs onto our plates. We've established a great morning routine since Lucy moved out.

Up at five.

Sex.

Jog.

Shower.

Coffee, eggs, toast.

Long kiss goodbye at seven.

The fact that we are empty nesters at this point in our life is incredibly bittersweet. We would trade all routines and free time to have Austin here to take to football practice or to teach him how to mow the lawn like a perfectionist— like all the Riley men.

"Yeah. I'd love to meet them." I set our plates on the table.

Tatum has met with so many families who have lost a child to drowning. She's including excerpts of their experiences in her book. I'm so proud of her. She now can talk to people about Austin without starting it with "Our son died." Now, like me, she tells Austin's real story. All the wonderful things about him, and then ... like a sad asterisk, she ends with the fact that he drowned in our swimming pool and we could have prevented it. And it's now our mission to prevent it from happening to other families.

"I was talking with Melanie yesterday. You remember her? Her son drowned two years ago." Tatum pushes up her blue framed glasses.

I nod before taking a sip of my coffee.

"We were discussing how insane it is that there's so much emphasis by doctors and other experts on things like proper safety restraints and seats for our children in cars. And my god ... if your child isn't up on all of their gazillion vaccinations, you get a long lecture. I'd live with the odds of surviving chicken pox over my child falling into a swimming pool. I bet chicken pox can't kill a child in thirty seconds. We were the 'good' parents. We always made sure our kids were safe in cars. We took them to the doctor. We did all the recommendations to keep them safe. I never ... *ever* recall the doctor talking to us about water safety. And maybe it's considered a no-brainer, but a child is fourteen times more likely to die from drowning than a car accident. Boys have a seventy-seven percent greater chance of drowning than girls. Why ... why is this not shoved into parents' faces in every parenting book? By every doctor? Why are we not hearing ads about this like the dangers of drunk driving?"

It's not funny, but I can't help but smile.

"What?" She takes a breath and gives me a sheepish grin.

"You're the woman I married ... twice. But I see the first version of you is back. I didn't recognize you for a few years. But here you are ... passionate, smart, motivated. Life is less about what we know and more about what we do. I think we always knew having a pool could be dangerous, but we didn't *do* the right things to really take the risks seriously. We should have had many layers of protection in place. You're *doing* it. You're making sure people know this isn't a sidebar to parenting. It's a real risk. It's as important as car seats, keeping guns locked in a safe, babyproofing outlets and cabinets."

After a few seconds, she nods and whispers, "Yes."

We eat the rest of our breakfast in silence. I'm going into work a few hours late because today we visit Austin's grave on the seventh anniversary of his drowning.

"Coming?" I call to Tatum, who's been in the bedroom for a while now.

When she doesn't respond, I check on her. She's kneeling on the floor in the closet, the secret door is open, and that birthday present with the blue and silver ribbon is in her hands.

A lump starts to form in my throat as she unwraps the box. I'm so incredibly proud of her. I think it every day. She's become the brave one in our family.

She slowly pulls out the Build a Bear wearing a neon vest and a hard hat. I can't breathe as she runs her hands over his face and slides her fingers to its paw. Tatum smiles, ignoring the tears on her cheeks. Leaving one hand on its paw, she lifts her other hand to me.

I take it and squeeze it as she squeezes the bear's paw to play the recording.

Our son's voice comes to life, like he's here in the closet. Like he never died. Like we're waking from a bad dream to his exuberant smile and boundless energy.

"Austin loves Daddy and dump trucks."

The End

ACKNOWLEDGMENTS

Thank you to my friend Shauna for planting this story's seed in my head. It took my heart a bit to feel brave enough to write it.

To my editing team, you are the best!

Jenn Beach, thanks for a stunning cover.

Nina and everyone at Valentine PR, thank you for helping me find an audience for this story.

To my wonderful reading community of bloggers, Instagrammers, ARC team, and Jewel's Jonesies, I owe so much to your enthusiasm, creativity, and generosity. Thank you!

Finally, to my mom, sister, husband, and three boys—thank you for listening to my crazy story ideas and enduring my insane level of excitement. I love you.

ALSO BY JEWEL E. ANN

Standalone Novels

Idle Bloom

Undeniably You

Naked Love

Only Trick

Perfectly Adequate

Look The Part

When Life Happened

A Place Without You

Jersey Six

Scarlet Stone

Not What I Expected

For Lucy

Jack & Jill Series

End of Day

Middle of Knight

Dawn of Forever

One (*standalone*)

Out of Love (*standalone*)

Holding You Series

Holding You

Releasing Me

Transcend Series

Transcend

Epoch

Fortuity (*standalone*)

The Life Series

The Life That Mattered

The Life You Stole

Receive a FREE book and stay informed of new releases, sales, and exclusive stories:

Mailing List

https://www.jeweleann.com/free-booksubscribe

ABOUT THE AUTHOR

Jewel is a free-spirited romance junkie with a quirky sense of humor.

With 10 years of flossing lectures under her belt, she took early retirement from her dental hygiene career to stay home with her three awesome boys and manage the family business.

After her best friend of nearly 30 years suggested a few books from the Contemporary Romance genre, Jewel was hooked. Devouring two and three books a week but still craving more, she decided to practice sustainable reading, AKA writing.

When she's not donning her cape and saving the planet one tree at a time, she enjoys yoga with friends, good food with family, rock climbing with her kids, watching How I Met Your Mother reruns, and of course...heart-wrenching, tear-jerking, panty-scorching novels.

www.jeweleann.com

Made in the USA
Columbia, SC
28 September 2022

68129334R10167